TRAPPED

Seneca Blue

CONNECT with the publisher:
ParisianPhoenix
parisbirdbooks
www.ParisianPhoenix.com

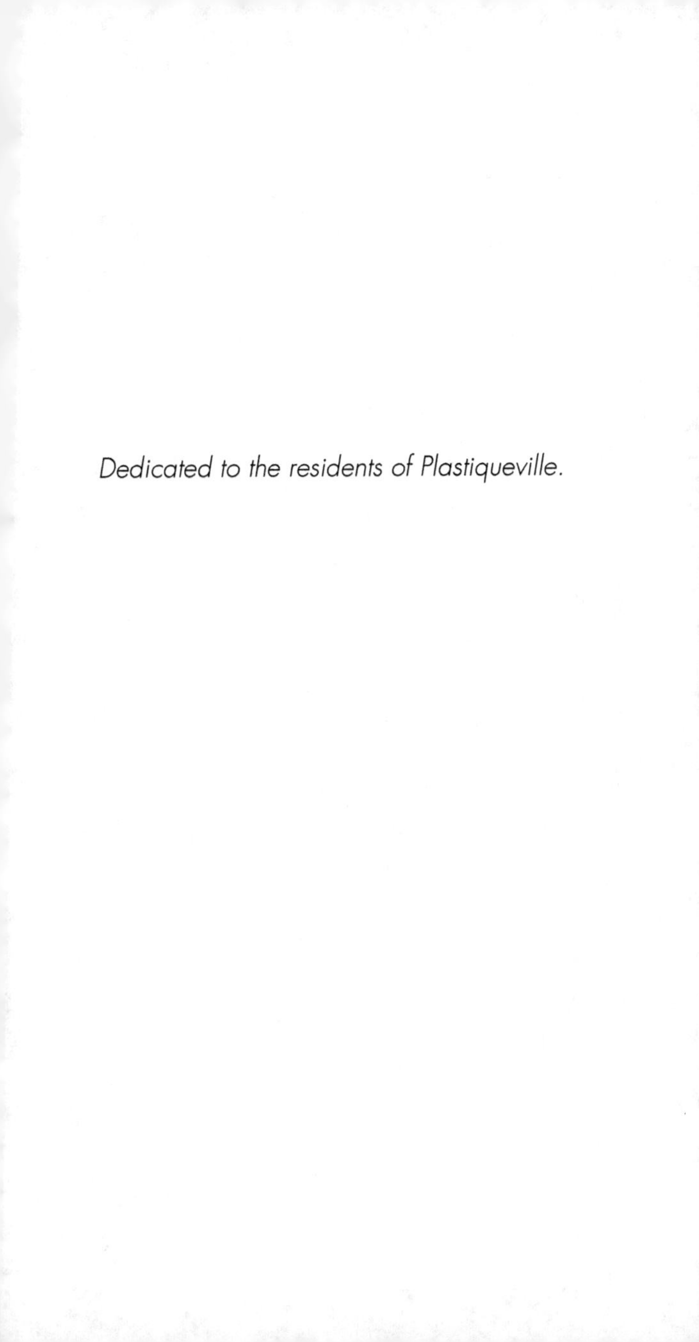

Dedicated to the residents of Plastiqueville.

ONE
2007

"Could this day get any worse?" Ed asked herself.

She slammed her cell phone closed, thrusting the electronic inconvenience into her pocket. With five part-time jobs and an old house constantly under renovation, Ed had no tolerance for stupidity.

Today, stupidity was everywhere.

"Of course I know where I live. Is it my fault you can't follow directions?" she mumbled.

Ed watched from the front window of her house as the idiot neighbor attempted to parallel park his enormous sport utility vehicle between Ed's new Ford and her other neighbor's beat-up mini van. The space obviously wouldn't fit the beastly truck, but he insisted on trying to do it. If he even breathed on Aretha (a great name for a car manufactured in Motown), she would rip him a new orifice.

Ed remained fixated as the idiot next-door once again backed toward the mini van in futile effort to squeeze the SUV into a compact car-sized space. This numb-nut couldn't park on the left side of the one-way street on a good day with ample space.

Meanwhile, the phone — her new leash, now everyone could keep tabs on her — vibrated spastically in her pocket. She pulled it out, and recognized the phone number of the directionally-challenged moron who couldn't find her house. Let it go to voice mail, she thought, as the SUV idiot backed into the mini van. At least it wasn't Aretha. She hadn't even made her first payment on Aretha yet.

She noticed a crumpled receipt in the crevice of the flip-phone. She tugged at it. She exhaled forcefully. It was the receipt for her new digital camera.

Three days ago, Ed had purchased a humdinger digital camera. It had every feature she had ever lusted for, in a camera, that is. She had partially treated herself since the hand-me-down camera she had previously wasn't making the grade for the newspaper.

In her most recent part-time job, she signed on as a freelance photographer (and reporter, though the editor hadn't realized yet that Ed couldn't write) at a start-up weekly newspaper. Ed reasoned the tax deduction would outweigh the expense. It was for business.

But that's not what this receipt was for. This receipt was for the second digital camera she had purchased this week. She found this one on sale at Best Buy, another freaking mega-chain raping the salivating American consumer eager to throw money away. It wasn't a humdinger, but it was an improvement over the hand-me-down.

The latest saga in Ed's boring yet dramatic life had started this morning. She had a light schedule: photo shoot at the library at ten, student projects to grade for her online graphic design course, a lunch date with a potential design client, and a pro bono project for the League of Women Voters.

It rained. It wasn't just rain, but a torrential downpour that transformed the steep grade of her street into a powerful waterfall. Ed, the graceful and (ahem) svelte (yeah, maybe one calf) creature, stepped onto the ramp outside her front door and slid. Ed had a reputation for clumsiness, and in the rain, her five-foot eleven, 230-pound body did not disappoint the neighbors who had to be watching. In her neighborhood, someone was always watching. Of course, usually, it was her drunken sister, Tootie.

Ed stepped out the front door, walked onto the ramp and crashed downward, her spine banging against the ground as her feet flew upwards and her heels landed on the sidewalk. Then, in slow-motion, she watched her brand new camera, right out of the box, never even plugged into a USB port on her computer, sail through the air, toward Aretha, and plunge drastically toward the gutter. The camera splashed into the torrent of water between the edge of the street and the curb.

If that weren't bad enough, before Ed could hoist her plump butt upright, the camera raced toward the storm water basin at the end of the block. Wet, rumpled and slightly limping, Ed ran after it, hoping to intercept. She dropped to her knees right before the inlet and jammed her hands between the garbage and the rotted flora. Rain bombarded her face, streaked her glasses, and drenched her outfit.

And the camera, despite her heroic efforts, dropped between her hands into the freshly-unclogged storm water basin. If she had left the basin alone, the debris would have stopped it.

That was when she changed clothes, grunted at her sister/annoying roommate, and headed to Best Buy. She still arrived at the library on time and photographed the toddlers and preschoolers at storytime with the "celebrity reader" from the local police department. She even got shots of kids eating green eggs and ham served by librarians in tall red- and white-striped hats.

The phone shook in her palm, indicating a voice-mail message. She didn't even need to listen to know what it said.

For weeks, Ed had spent every free moment reclaiming her overgrown garden, trading plants with friends and family and giving some away through Freecycle. Until today, she hadn't had a problem. But then again, today everything had gone wrong. Must be a full moon.

She had held some plants for a freecycler who was going out of town but "really wanted them." To exercise some kindness toward her fellow man, she said sure, she'd keep some. Being nice never pays off. You'd think, with her luck, she would have realized that by now. A good deed will always come back and bite you in the ass. Today, it resulted in a series of angry voice mail messages. She dialed into the system to retrieve the message. Beep. The automated voice greeted her. She often wished everyone else she came in contact with could emulate the voice's flat and emotionless tone.

"You have one new message."

Beep. "Message one." Beep.

"This is Floyd, from Freecycle. I wanted to get the monkey flower and partridge-berry this morning and can't find your damn house."

Nothing flat and emotionless here. Floyd was approaching irate.

"Turned right off of Main Street and your number doesn't freaking exist. Went up and down the block four times and there is a 516, and a 520 but no freaking 518. Then I went back, turned left and the numbers were going the wrong way."

Floyd screamed into the phone now.

"I went the heck home. Stuff you plants up your arse, I don't freaking want them anymore. Especially since I can't get a hold of you."

Beep. The knucklehead had gotten lost in the maze of one-way streets around the dead steel mill. Serves him right… That's why she told him to call first. She deleted the message, slammed the phone shut again, returned it to her pocket and smoothed the receipt so she could file it. Her hands trembled. It had not been a good day.

"I've got to calm down," she said, not that anybody was listening. No one would care anyway.

Horrible, horrible day. Her mind calculated just how behind she was on her "to do" list. In the hubbub, she hadn't even begun the project for the League of Women Voters. She should finish grading her on-line students, but she couldn't risk her bad mood rubbing off on her opinions of their work. Graphic design critiques and lousy moods didn't mix. When you didn't have face-to-face relationships, the slightest word choice misstep could crush, humiliate, or offend a student.

The phone vibrated in her pocket. Ed whipped it out and slapped it open without even looking at the caller ID.

"What?" Ed barked.

"What's your problem?" came the soft but firm reply.

It was her older sister, Martha.

"Sorry," Ed said, her temper simmering. "What did you want?"

"Just wanted to know if you could water the plants while we're on vacation."

"That's not until next week," Ed said, the edge returning to her voice even though she fought it. "Don't I always?"

"What's put you in a pissy mood?" Martha asked.

"It's just been a crappy day. Started the minute I got up. I whacked my foot on the couch trying to get to work on time," Ed said. "I think I broke my toe."

She headed up the stairs toward her office. She had moved her desk and computer into the guest bedroom. No one ever spent the night here. Everyone was afraid of Tootie. Ed had lost the spare bed under a pile of graphic design books and files from each of her ongoing projects.

As Ed began to tell Martha about her miserable day, including the story about her camera and how the potential client (the owner of the club basketball team) stood her up for a lunch meeting, bloodcurdling screams from the other end of the line interrupted. When they didn't stop promptly, Ed's sister had to intervene.

"The kids are trying to kill each other," Martha said.

From the commotion, Ed thought perhaps her niece and nephew really would murder one another.

"What's going on over there?" Ed asked.

"Jarrod is using his sister's pretty princess wand like a club and beating her with it," Martha said, exasperated. "They're both chasing the dog. He's nipping at Belinda… Belinda, Belinda! BEA! Leave the dog alone. Oh, no, I think Jarr just poked Bea in the eye."

Wails accompanied the play-by-play. The black lab yelped.

"Sorry, Sissy. I've got to go."

The line went dead. Once again, the phone returned to Ed's pocket. Ed dropped into her computer chair and pushed the power button on her trusty iMac—the only object in her life that she considered reliable. The computer boomed to life with that trademark chime.

Email, Ed thought. Maybe something in one of her eight email accounts would cheer her. She normally considered a silly picture or a dumb joke an annoyance, but today she needed a distraction desperately. Which account should she check first? Five of those eight accounts served as work addresses.

"Why," she said to herself, "couldn't I be normal and have one or maybe two jobs?"

She would wait to check her work accounts last. She didn't need more projects or problems. She opened her personal email, scanning the list of messages in her inbox for attachments that could be photographs.

"Maybe Islama sent pictures or video of the baby," she said as she scrolled.

Photos of a newborn would brighten an otherwise horrible day. Nevertheless, nothing came in her personal account, just fifteen messages from Celeste, her writer friend who always had questions of "What if this character did this? What if that character slept with her? What if so-and-so bought a new car?" Enough already!

Ed hadn't expected anything in her volunteer work account. She checked it just to be sure. That just left one, her planet-save account. She could depend on something fun or silly there. That's the account she gave to strangers—the freecycle group, newsletter subscriptions, and online shopping.

Thirty-seven messages, they all looked like spam. Surveying the list, Ed chuckled at the subject lines.

She pondered what it would take to enlarge her penis, get six-pack abs, and maintain longer lasting erections… So much for target marketing.

"Well," she said, "at least they're not weight loss ads."

Single, overweight, and on the cusp of forty, Ed considered Americans weight obsessed. If the people who spent billions on weight loss products and gym memberships (the kind where people went once and never visited again, even locked into a one-year contract) paid a tax that would funnel a fraction of that money to education, the world and her decaying neighborhood especially, would transform into a much better place.

Continuing to scan the subject lines, Ed noticed that the spammers had grown clever, jumbling the letters in their titles to trick the junk-mail filters. But Ed saw one familiar name. Against her better judgment, she leaned her fingers into the mouse and clicked open the e-mail. Now she could read a message from the knucklehead that left the angry voice mail. Maybe he's emailing to apologize. Men do sometimes realize when they act like jerks.

Ed started to read the email. No apologies here, just more incoherent, irrational musings. This was one angry man.

"Fuck him," she said, peeking over her shoulder to make sure her nosy sister wasn't spying.

Ed logged out of her email, still fuming about the Freecycle fiasco. They're free plants for Pete's sake! What does he want—them gift wrapped and delivered? Maybe with a nice ribbon and a card, or maybe a box of chocolates?

Riled up again, Ed couldn't think about grading. Why did she do this to herself? She stormed to the fridge for a cold A-Treat sarsaparilla. The local pop confectionery makes a good sarsaparilla. Not too sweet and not too bitter, it goes down as smooth as a fine brew or a perfectly blended margarita.

As she pulled open the fridge door, a jar of Pennsylvania Dutch pickled red beets crashed to the linoleum. The glass shattered, just about the same time Ed realized how much filth had layered on the floor. Now, red-stained vinegar laced across the fridge door, and liquid pooled in front of the refrigerator and oozed underneath. The smell of vinegar and eggs wafted through the kitchen.

"Shit!" Ed exclaimed. "Will this day ever end?"

She hated pickled eggs. She didn't even like to touch hard-boiled eggs. They reminded her of the peeled grapes people would make children feel at Halloween parties while they whispered menacingly, "Eyes."

"I should have stayed in bed today," she said.

Ed reached toward the kitchen sink for a rag. She expected the sky-high pile of dirty dishes. While she worked all day, most of her family treated her kitchen like a grocery store and helped themselves to everything without having the decency to clean up. She wasn't disappointed. She found the usual stack of dishes that she would wash later. She hadn't expected the extra surprise—the same surprise that explained why her evening had been so quiet on one front.

Five beer cans lined the counter. Obviously, her sister couldn't be bothered to rinse them and add them to the mound already in the recycling bucket. She flung the towel across the room, straight over the cluttered kitchen table. She left the refrigerator door open. She ignored the mess. Ed seized the soda from its spot on the door and marched to the deck.

Her eyes searched for the moon, wanting to see a

huge, white cratered orb. She saw something, all right.

In the silver beams of moonlight, she saw a feline shape, but too big and too fuzzy for a cat. A thick white stripe crossed its back as it showed her its hind end and curving tale. The soda bottle slipped from her fingers and fell to the deck. A skunk! Luckily, the plastic of the bottle bounced. It was enough to spook Pépé.

TWO

At six a.m., the fridge still stood wide open. The mess from last night had stained the floor a creepy shade of red. It looked like Ed finally killed Tootie… or Gertrude as the obituary would say. Ed didn't care about that right now. She rifled the contents of the refrigerator.

"There's got to be some in here somewhere," said Ed.

She pulled out butter, zucchinis, milk, eggs, and lots of beer. She had strewn everything on the floor.

"I kept a can for emergencies," she assured herself.

Ed sought the familiar red and white can. Her hands could feel the sleek, cool surface, even though she hadn't found it yet. She kept hearing the hiss of the pop-top, her longing intense.

She had needed a year to wean her from her twenty-year addiction to Coca Cola. She hit bottom at three two-liters bottles a day. That equaled something like twenty-four servings, 2,640 calories and 648 grams of sugar every day. She made herself calculate it one day as motivation to quit. Kicking her soda habit rendered her recycling bin nearly empty. She did well with it, except for the caffeine withdrawal headaches.

She couldn't blame any external force for her weight struggles. Her work schedule had her eating and drinking at drive-thru windows instead of at home or substituting Coke for meals. Rushed eating habits made her gain the kind of weight Michael Moore documents in movies. The thought of that much Coke made her queasy now, but man, how she drooled for that emergency can. Caffeine helped her think. The skunk attack made it impossible to concentrate. Skunks! That was the last thing she needed. The very last thing!

Ed found some comfort in the fact that she hadn't startled the skunk. When she dropped the bottle of sarsaparilla, the skunk had already noticed her neighbor, Doris, leaving for her night shift at the hospital. Poor Doris sustained the direct hit of sulfurous spray. Ed made a beeline into the house. She closed all the doors and slammed the windows to keep the odor outside. She didn't even offer to help Doris, though really, there wasn't anything she could have done.

Ed didn't sleep much last night. With the windows closed to prevent the spray from entering the house, her room turned suffocating. The fan just moved the air in circles. Her mind raced, recapping and replaying the day's events and the damn skunk in her yard.

Her room felt like a convection oven. Once she finally surrendered to the idea that she had insomnia, Ed sat on her bed and gazed out the window for hours. About 4 a.m., she finally saw it. She didn't like what she saw.

A parade of skunks progressed across her yard.

Not just one skunk, but one adult and numerous baby skunks. Ed thought she counted five. She immediately named them, because she named everything. She selected the moniker Pépé and the petite Le Pews, after the Looney Tunes cartoons. They came under the fence, sashayed across the lawn, and disappeared under the deck.

"Just what I need… more freeloaders…"

The discovery of a family of skunks, and considering what to do about them, sent her searching for that hidden can of Coke.

"Finally."

She popped the top and it crackled. She sighed, taking comfort in the familiar hiss. She poured some from the can and swished it around as if she tasted a fine wine, smelled it, then shot it down her throat in one gulp.

"Okay," she said, "this is not a job for a do-it-yourselfer. I've gone to enough Girl Scout wildlife workshops to know that this job takes a professional."

Ed hated to say it. The words tasted vile. She valued her independence and her self-sufficiency. Single-handedly, she had undertaken the remodeling of this house that she inherited from her father. She hired electricians to do rewiring, and plumbers to put in new pipes. Other than that, she did it. Sure, she thought the work backbreaking at times, but she found the rewards (and the financial savings) worth it.

But this wasn't a new sink or a peeling linoleum floor. This was a skunk and brood. Ed needed the yellow pages. She knew when to let her fingers do the walking. She hoisted the massive yellow pages from on top of the refrigerator. She considered the blue pages a good place to start. Logically, the city government should have an animal control officer listed.

Even if the ACO couldn't get the skunk, the official could tell her what to do. Or so she hoped.

At one of her former jobs, a rabid skunk meandered the property during the day and the police came and shot it. However, these skunks were nocturnal and appeared healthy. (Oh, good, she thought, at least she had normal skunks.)

Where would they list animal control? Not under Parks and Recreation or Forestry or Watershed or Sanitation or Recreation.

"I guess we don't have animal control," she told the empty kitchen.

She flipped into the *Yellow Pages'* yellow pages. She went first to the W's and checked for wildlife. No listing, not even a "please see 'whatever'" reference. Then, she tried animal removal. That yielded one listing, and it had an 800-number.

"An 800 number. Why would I need an 800-number for a local call?"

She knew the type of guy she wanted. He was the real guy who showed up at the wildlife workshops with the green Dickie pants, a faded Penn State t-shirt, steel-toed work boots, and a trucker hat. Of course, you cannot forget the buck teeth, with one tooth missing, and chewing a huge wad of bubble gum, or worse, tobacco. He took joy in talking about the animals, their habitats, their life cycles, and about trapping them humanely and leaving them loose in the forest.

She gulped more Coke.

"Well, when I used Terminex to kill the termites… Thanks, Dad. They were listed under pest control. I'll try there."

For that infestation, Ed had gotten five estimates, three from local companies. She did decide to go with the big corporation, only because of their money-back guarantee and termite-free certification process. It killed her, because of her instincts to shop locally. Ed preferred mom-and-pop type operations. She supported the little guy.

Under pest control, Ed discovered five pages of listings, some with huge ads, some in color. Ed scrutinized them all. As a graphic designer, she knew that the more money you spent the more results came from the ad. Only mega companies could afford large or color ads. She wasn't interested in supporting corporate America this time.

She needed the skunks removed promptly. Summer was quickly ending, too quickly, and she certainly did not want Le Pew family settling in for the winter, mating and delivering more petite Le Pews.

In a quest for the local companies, Ed ruled out the listings with 800-numbers and web sites. After ten minutes, she spotted the perfect ad.

It was small, almost invisible. It gave the pertinent information, everything Ed wanted to hear: "humanely removing skunks, raccoons, mice, rats and other wild animals," "third-generation, family-owned," "locally-operated," with "forty years experience." The address was conveniently on the outskirts of town.

Ed glanced at the clock, only 6:30 a.m. No civil, polite person called another that early. She'd do some work first.

She spent the next three hours grading her students' projects, the ones she avoided last night. Thankfully, the college's computer didn't send her a reminder email. That never looks good on a yearly review. Ed hoped the school would hire her full-time.

The grading became monotonous. The students repeated the same mistakes. Lack of what she called "type hierarchy" and mixing too many different serif and sans serif typefaces. Manipulating the point size of the text would do wonders for both problems. The boring projects had everything in eighteen-point type. The busy ones used every gaudy typeface their PCs had, and she would vomit if she saw Comic Sans one more time today.

Working on the computer makes it easy to lose all sense of time. It was nearly ten before Ed surfaced and placed the call.

"Hi," a recorded voice said from the answering machine.

Islama, as a Turk with a unique perspective on English, called an answering machine a tele-secretary. It was actually a good description. Ed had come to consider it more personal than an answering machine.

"You've reached Wildlife Wranglers. You've got 'em, we trap 'em. If you need to talk to a real person, call between six and seven a.m., or eight and nine p.m., otherwise we're out catching critters. If you like talking to machines, leave a message with your name, location and problem and we'll stop by."

"Shit," Ed said.

She could have called this morning. Ed hated machines. Though she had to admit, this tele-secretary's message had personality to spare.

"Hi, this is Ed Gardner, 518 Market Street. I have a family of skunks living under my deck and I'd like them evicted. I'll be working at home all day if you have a chance to stop by."

After leaving her number, she hung up and returned to her work. She still had plenty to keep her occupied. She hadn't finished The League of Women Voters project. She hadn't even started the YWCA project. Plus, she had to research her exposé on grease in the sewers for her newspaper job. How did her editor convince Ed that she could write, too? Ed knew the newspaper operated on a shoestring and a minimal staff, but a graphic designer as an investigative reporter? Okay, so it was the sewer, not gangs nor drugs nor a prostitution ring. But, hey, Ed couldn't say no to the extra income, even if it was a measly couple bucks. Of course, if she threw in some diagrams and charts, her editor would toss some additional money her way.

Ed poured herself some Cheerios. Then, she realized someone—damn Tootie—left a tablespoon of milk in the carton in the fridge. She set the cereal bowl on table. She grabbed the milk, dumping it down the drain and rinsed out the carton. She also dumped the remaining Coke. That made her proud of herself. She took her dry breakfast into her office and set to work.

Mid-afternoon, the phone rang.

"Hi, this is Clint from Wildlife Wranglers. Is this a good time to come check out your skunk problem?

"Umm, yeah, sure, Clint. Come on over. Do you know how to get here?"

She didn't want a repeat of the Freecycle asshole. She assumed a professional would be more…professional.

"Yeah," he answered. "You're squished between the university and the steel mill, right?"

"Make sure you turn left onto Market, the one-way side, or you'll never find the house."

"Got it. See you in twenty minutes."

At about four p.m., a black Ford F150 pulled in front of the house. Ed noticed it from her desk near the window of the front bedroom. What caught her eye was the lettering on the driver's door, Futura Extra Bold pronouncing, "Wildlife Wranglers, relocating animals since 1957," perfectly straight and kerned. Tasteful type, bold and clean. Wow, Ed thought, he cares about his business.

A dark head emerged from the truck. Ed headed for the door. She wanted these skunks gone. A man with lettering like that would get the job done. She hadn't seen him yet, but his truck spoke clearly.

Going downstairs and out the door, Ed didn't see him until she hit the porch. She lurked in the shadows under the awning. He appeared about her height, with black hair stretching toward his shoulders. It fell as if he forgot to get a haircut, because the style didn't look like one intended for long hair. His walk perplexed Ed. He walked with the long strides of confidence but kept his eyes on the sidewalk. He might be clumsy and afraid of tripping on something. She could certainly understand that.

It was humid, just like the rest of the month. Clint wore khaki shorts. This surprised her. She'd expected someone who worked with animals to protect himself with jeans. But she soon forgot about his lack of pants when she noticed his muscular calves. One item met her stereotype. He did have work boots. And big feet.

Clint reached the porch. Ed quickly looked into his face, meeting big brown eyes and a clean-shaven face hinting at five-o'clock shadow. He didn't have a hat or Dickies, or a Penn State t-shirt, but he would do. After all, Futura Extra Bold said everything she had needed to hear.

When Ed looked closer, she noticed a small emblem over the breast of Clint green tee-shirt. Was that? It was… She squinted and sure enough… It was a white recycling logo. He had a chasing arrow logo on his shirt. He had his shirt tucked into his shorts, and wore a woven brown belt. The shirt fit nicely, a tad loose around the chest and maybe a tad snug in the waist, but neat and clean. Their hands sprung out at the same time for a handshake.

"I'm Ed. You must be Clint," she said.

He accepted her extended hand.

"Clint Anderson."

He shook her hand. He had a nice grip. He had smooth hands, much smoother than she anticipated. She lingered for a moment. His face didn't change. He looked very serious, perhaps even confused.

"Show me where you saw the skunks," he directed her.

"This way," she said.

She escorted him between her house and Doris's. Ed brought him into her backyard. As his head turned, Ed suddenly realized how messy her yard must look. Dust, stones, patches of well-groomed bushes next to sections of weeds… She hadn't even put her tools away. Her rakes, spades and shovels leaned against the flaking paint of the garage. And Tootie had left an overflowing recycling can with her empty beers…

Would Clint assume Ed had a drinking problem? She should have cleaned the yard, but she didn't think of it. Clint's gaze fell like a hot ray of sunshine against her back. But unlike sunshine, it didn't comfort her. Ed wrung her hands together.

"The yard's a mess," she said apologetically.

Ed didn't know what else to say. She looked at him. Clint met her gaze for the first time, really meeting her eyes. Something soft and kind lingered in his irises… Her face grew warm. She hoped she wasn't blushing. She would shoot herself if she was blushing over something as stupid as the state of her yard. This man was a stranger, and someone who wanted to work for her. What he thought didn't matter.

"I've been working back here, but I do it alone so it's slow," Ed explained.

He stopped looking at her and turned his attention to the deck and the dilapidated porch.

"We used it for a staging area when we had to redo some floors," she continued.

"No problem," Clint said.

He knelt. He peaked under the deck. He nodded and leaned his hand against the wood.

"This is where I saw the skunk last night," Ed said, walking toward the fence. Clint nodded again, but seemed more interested in the ground.

"Then, he sprayed my neighbor, Doris," Ed said.

She pointed to Doris's house.

"Then, this is where they came through the fence," she said pointing to the exact location, "and walked across the lawn."

Clint rose to his feet.

"My initial fee is $125," Clint stated. "It has me or one of my daughters coming every day for a month to check the traps. Some companies make you check your own, then call them. That's illegal. So, if you go with someone else, keep that in mind."

Did $125 sound reasonable? Ed realized she had no idea.

"Okay," she said.

Without a word, Clint disappeared. His work boots pounded her sidewalk. Then, the sound faded completely. A tailgate slammed. Clint returned with two metal traps, one in each hand. He placed the first near the deck and the other about ten feet away from the spot where she spotted the skunks farther down chain link fence.

"But... I saw them over there," Ed protested.

"Doesn't matter," he said. "That's not how they are coming in. This is where it's dug under the fence. They need two inches. It's also dug under the deck."

Clint crouched to show her. She merely looked over his shoulder. Her knees wouldn't like it if she joined him.

"That's the main route," he said. "I bet you saw mama taking the kits out for a training run. That means soon they'll leave, mate, and make their own dens."

"But why my yard?" Ed asked. "The woods aren't far. Wouldn't they prefer the woods?"

"This neighborhood is an all-you-can-eat buffet, at least for a skunk," Clint explained as he set the traps. "This is a perfect ecosystem for skunks. Just look at garbage nights. To a skunk, that's take-out delivered to the door. It means easy food."

He got to his feet. Placing his hands on his hips, he shook his head slowly.

"Then, you've got mulberries," Clint said about Ed's neighbors' trees.

The way he said the word mulberry, she felt like she'd been diagnosed with an infectious disease.

"What's wrong with mulberries?" she replied.

"There's three I can see on the adjacent properties. Mulberries ferment in the sun. Skunks love them. That's how they get drunk. That's where the expression 'drunk as a skunk' comes from. Convince your neighbors to cut them down."

Ed scoffed.

"Easier said then done," she said. To herself, she added: I can't convince the neighbors to mow the lawn. Cut down a tree… You've got to be kidding.

"And your grubs don't help. This garden's organic, right?" Clint continued.

"Yes," she said quickly, almost as if he had struck a nerve.

"Skunks love grubs," he said. "If you don't use the chemical stuff, release beneficial nematodes, that'll solve that problem."

Nema-what? Ed thought. But she didn't have time

to ask. Clint mentioned more problems. He moved on to the next one, pointing to the deck.

"Nice and low. Plenty of room to hide," he said. "After we catch them you're going to have to skunk proof."

"Skunk-proof?" Ed repeated. How do I do that? she wondered.

He nodded and as if reading her mind, he offered instruction.

"Dig a trench around the deck, six inches deep by eighteen inches wide," he started. "Then, you get a roll of hardware cloth. Not chicken wire. Bend it in a 'L' shape. Screw the hardware cloth every eight inches. Don't staple. Never more than eight inches. Never. Less is okay. Six or seven. But never more. Make sure the screws are galvanized."

"Should I write this down?" Ed asked.

He shrugged.

"When we catch a skunk there's an additional charge," Clint warned. "Commonwealth law says we have to kill and dispose of them…"

"Kill them?" Ed interrupted, her hopes of a frolicking future for the Pépé family were dashed. She had preferred to believe they would have a better life elsewhere.

"Yep, threat of rabies," Clint said, heaviness in his voice. "Seems crazy to trap them humanely just to kill them, but it's for the best. If we catch anything else, we'll relocate it. But for the skunks, it's $70 per animal."

$70 per animal? She only had a couple skunks. It seemed reasonable to her, especially if it made Clint come back.

Where did that come from? Ed asked herself.

Clint continued talking.

"You don't ever want to see an animal in a snare trap. It's ugly," he said. "When my dad started this business he insisted on doing everything humanely. My girls have never even seen a snare trap."

"You have daughters?"

"Two in college. Geneva wants to take over the business. Olive wants to be a veterinarian. She's at Penn State. Genny's at U Delaware."

Two college-aged daughters. He should be older than her, but not by much. And Penn State—maybe he did have the t-shirt after all. She hadn't noticed any rings on his fingers and he looked about the right age…

Don't be ridiculous, Ed scolded herself. Nobody is interested in fat, old you.

"Anyway, my information, even my license number, is on the trap. I encourage you to contact the Fish and Game Commission."

"Can I get you a lemonade?" she asked.

"No, thanks. I have to get to another client. You think you got problems," Clint said with a chuckle. "He's got squirrels in the attic. They spend all night running through his bedroom walls. If that weren't bad enough, he's got a cat who scratches at the wall and meows at the squirrels."

He pulled a white handkerchief from his back pocket and wiped his hands.

"I've got some bottled tea leftover from the neighborhood block party if you'd like something to go," Ed said. "It's cold. I'd offer you water, but I don't use bottled water."

"Tea might be nice," he replied. "It sure is sticky out here today."

He patted the hanky against the back of his neck.

"I've got unsweetened blueberry and cherry," Ed

said. "It's funky stuff. I bought it at Wegmans."

"Either would be great," Clint said.

She went toward the house.

"Wegmans, eh? You don't seem the Wegmans type," Clint added.

Ed turned.

"Special occasions," she said.

Would he consider her stuck-up because she bought flavored, unsweetened iced teas from the upscale grocer?

"And they have the best take-out salads," Ed continued. "But mostly, I just like to roam the aisles. I'm not the hang-out-at-the-mall type."

"You hang out at a grocery store?" Clint replied.

Great, Ed thought, shaking her head. He would think she had serious food issues, if he didn't already.

"More like escape," Ed said. "As long as you don't impulse buy, Wegmans offers a nice place to relax especially if you're low on toilet paper and avoiding going home."

He said nothing. They had reached the deck.

"They have yummy hot chocolate. And you can't leave Wegmans in a bad mood. I think they drug the air," Ed finished.

He followed her onto the deck. When she opened the sliding glass door, he paused. She didn't invite him. He looked across the backyard and didn't acknowledge her disappearance into the pantry. He didn't attempt to enter the house. That was a relief.

Tootie's slovenly habits mortified her. Hell, Tootie mortified her. Ed slipped into the kitchen and opened the fridge, carefully walking around the sticky red stain on the floor. Ed grabbed a bottle, the first one she touched. She didn't even check the flavor. She returned to the deck, and suddenly wished she had curtains on the door. She offered him the tea.

He twisted the cap. It opened with a resonating pop. Clint drank half the bottle in several quick swallows. Walking almost as if afraid to turn his back to her, he hopped off the deck and kept glancing over his shoulder. He followed the sidewalk to the front of the house. She accompanied him.

"I'll check those traps tomorrow," he said.

He stepped from the curb and toward the driver's side of the truck. He got inside and started the engine.

"Oh!" Ed hollered, from the end of the ramp. "I didn't get you a check."

He shrugged.

"I'll get it tomorrow," Clint said. "So, I'll see you then."

The truck drove up the hill and turned left at the cemetery. Ed stared for a minute, at nothing. She caught herself, shook her head, and confined herself into the office. Something about the quiet and the unusual stillness of the house distracted her. Even the street outside her window seemed vaguely too empty. Well, Ed thought with a sigh, Tootie would be home soon with her twelve pack.

Maybe that would take her attention off the fluttering in her stomach… Ed gazed outside the window and daydreamed about Clint's broad shoulders as he succinctly explained the skunk habitat in her backyard. She dreamed of soft, brown eyes… She thought about his discussions about humanely trapping animals, which had offered a gentleness she didn't expect from a man. She could have sworn that she heard remorse in his voice when he explained the law's requirement that he kill any captured skunks. She felt bad about killing the skunks, too.

She also felt bad, and more than a little ridiculous,

that she wasted so much time dwelling on this guy. She didn't even know if he was single. And he certainly hadn't given her any reason to think he was prowling for women.

She couldn't deny her attraction to him. The butterflies in her stomach swirled again. That's what had her so distracted. She shook her head. Ed normally didn't experience such schoolgirl infatuations. She was older and supposedly wiser. Plus, she hadn't had a date since… a decade or so… It might have been during the Bush Sr. administration… or, there was a slim chance she had gone out during Clinton's term. Who was she kidding?

Clint was out of her league. The end.

THREE

The death toll rises. A dozen skunks have perished in the neighborhood since Ed first called Wildlife Wranglers, just over two weeks ago.

At daybreak, as was her daily habit, Ed rose early to take her "morning hike." She hated gyms (and exercise) but she needed to shed weight. The walking ritual accompanied her swearing-off of Coca Cola. It was part of Ed's plan to greet her middle age at least healthy, if not significantly thinner. She didn't want to look like a skinny bitch. She aimed for normal, as normal as could be for nearly forty. She liked curves. She knew she had inherited her mother's bombastic booty. But she could live without her thighs touching.

She liked her hilly neighborhood. The rigorous terrain challenged her thighs and her heart rate. This early in the morning, silence surrounded her. Amazing considering the population density of this formerly blue-collar neighborhood. The air smelled clean and fresh. Humidity lingered.

Since the sun had exposed only the minimum of light, Ed walked as delicately as she could. Walkers in this neighborhood and on the hills had to watch their steps. The sidewalks had heaved over time. The cement was quite irregular and tripping was a distinct possibility, one Ed had experienced in the past.

Another threat was falling over the daily newspaper. Van drivers threw them out the window. They landed everywhere. When Ed delivered the paper as a girl, she folded each copy and tucked it into her customers' doors. This was a case where progress wasn't really better.

Ed loved the taste of nature available in her urban neighborhood. At this hour in the morning, birds would chirp as they woke for the day. Crows observed her from perches amass the ironwork of the old railroad trestle. Bats rushed into chimneys and under the slates of the roofs, including Ed's. Ed didn't mind the bats. They ate the insects.

Ed's favorite part of her walk came when she reached the cemeteries on the edge of town. If she stood quietly between the Jewish cemetery and the public one, at just the right time, with the right amount of luck, Ed might see the red-tail hawk and his family. She had watched the hawk build that nest, watched the babies hatch, and now she wondered if the time had come for the babies to leave the nest. She hadn't seen them, and she hadn't heard their cries in quite some time.

As she waited, Ed noticed a turkey in the cemetery, but she did not see the herd of deer. Throughout the summer, Ed had tracked the growth of the fawns and counted the emerging points on young bucks' antlers. It constantly reminded Ed that while humans developed cities, nature never truly released her hold.

Ed had even heard rumors of turkey and deer building homes in the ruins of the decade-empty steel mill. She wondered if Clint had worked down there or knew how true the rumors were. She hadn't been on "The Steel" ground since her father retired, and that was twenty years ago.

Once the mammoth brick complex of the hospital appeared around the corner, Ed knew she was almost home. Luckily, it was downhill from here. The sun had risen fully, but the air retained its morning briskness. Sweat drenched Ed's clothing after the three-mile trek. She needed a shower.

But, she also needed to work in the yard. No point showering to get sweaty again, she reasoned. Her upcoming fall schedule wouldn't leave much room for gardening. The fifteen-hour days wouldn't leave much time for anything. She shouldn't complain. At least she had a job, or in this case, five. She needed the money.

Tootie didn't contribute to household expenses, not to mention the old house's tendency to create a money pit. But Ed loved the old house. She had lived in it for most of her life. She didn't plan to desert it in its hour of need for some cracker-box, McMansion in the suburbs. Besides, her house had passion, history and soul.

She headed to the backyard, avoiding the trap she had heard snap shut last night. When she looked from the bathroom this morning she saw something moving and it wasn't black. The animal she saw was thin with a ringed tail.

"Rats!" she yelled aloud. "Rats are worse than skunks!"

Fresh out of bed, dressed in the blue Habitat for Humanity t-shirt that she had slept in, Ed crashed down the stairs, into her Birkenstocks and out the front door. It took only a few minutes to remember that the opossum had a ringed tail. Those Girl Scout workshops were helping her deal with this situation.

Now that the sun had risen and Ed had a chance to clear her head with her morning walk, she could face whatever nocturnal beast waited in the trap. She still had no desire to get too close, not without Clint anyway.

When she entered the yard, Ed spotted a young, tanned woman with a long dark braid in a "Project Vote Smart" t-shirt and cut-off jean shorts. She carried two occupied traps as she moved toward the narrow space between the houses.

It took Ed a minute to register that she had not only expected, but anticipated, Clint's arrival to empty the traps. A disappointed Ed greeted Clint's daughter.

"Hi, I'm Ed. I live here."

"Hi, Ed. I'm Olive Anderson. My dad probably mentioned me," she said, resting one cage on her hip. "Ed, huh? And I thought Olive was a ridiculous name."

"Short for Edna, like my grandmother."

The girl nodded.

"We got a feral cat and a baby opossum," Olive said, changing the topic from their unusual nomenclature.

"I was worried I had a big, old rat," Ed admitted.

"This could be seen as a good sign," Olive said. "Opossums like to nest in abandoned skunk dens, so this shows you've had skunks for longer than you think. It could also mean the skunks have moved out."

She balanced the cages awkwardly.

"Let me set these guys down in the truck. Do you want to see him?" Olive asked, using her head to gesture toward the opossum's cage.

Ed pondered this. Did she need to get up close and personal with an opossum?

Olive arranged the cages in the back of a little black Nissan.

"Cute truck," Ed said.

"Grandpa has never forgiven me for buying a Nissan," Olive said 'Nissan' like a dirty word. "Our family has always bought Fords. I tried explaining that Nissan has American factories and American workers, and that Ford probably has more Mexican employees than American but… He doesn't get global economy."

She secured the cat's cage in the truck with a bungee cord. Olive jumped to the ground, slipping heavy gloves onto her hands. The opossum's cage waited on the tailgate. She reached into the cage and lifted the critter. She adeptly scruffed it by the neck.

"Okay, little guy," Olive turned to Ed.

Ed remained on the sidewalk. She did not share Olive's enthusiasm for nocturnal animals.

"Nope, girl," Olive corrected herself after a glance at the creature's underside.

"Meet Ed," Olive said.

Olive held the opossum in the air in front of Ed. Ed took one tentative step, curious but certainly not over-zealous. She adjusted her glasses to get a better look.

"Cute, in an ugly way," Ed decided.

But Olive wasn't really listening. She pried the opossum's toes apart.

"Did you know they have opposable thumbs?" Olive asked. "This one has a pouch, that's how I knew it was a girl. The opossum is the only American marsupial."

Olive stuffed the critter in the cage, jumped in the bed and secured the cage to the side.

"What happens to the cat?" Ed questioned.

"It's feral, so it can't be adopted," Olive said, hopping from the truck and slamming the tailgate closed. "Have you seen it before?"

Ed shook her head. She'd never seen the mangy

grey cat. It didn't belong to any of her neighbors.

"We work with the local TNR group. They trap ferals, neuter them and return them to their original locations. Theoretically, you might see this one again, though I doubt it. Ferals avoid people. Volunteers leave food for them. The cats can't reproduce. And leaving them in one place means new cats won't move in. A lot of people don't understand that about cats… That removing one batch just opens territory for more."

She peeled off her gloves and put them in her tool box.

"It always happens near colleges," Olive said. "The kids leave the cats when they go. If those cats have kittens, they become wild. They don't know people. They can't be pets without serious rehab."

Meeting Olive meant that Ed had now met the entire Anderson family. In addition to Clint and Olive, Ed had met Clint's dad, who went by C.A., and Geneva, Olive's sister. Olive and Genny looked so similar Ed had to look twice.

Often Ed either wasn't home or didn't notice when they came and took the animals. Drunken Gertrude never noticed the captives or the Andersons. Until now, Ed had thought Tootie never missed anything anybody did.

Maybe that vigilance only applied to Ed and the rest of the family. Exchanges regarding Martha demonstrated Tootie's tendency to snoop.

"Do you know what I saw Martha doing with that girl?" Tootie would snap.

"That's her wife," Ed would reply. "Mind your business."

Then, Gertrude would go off in a huff muttering that women didn't take wives.

So, neither Ed nor Tootie documented if Clint visited their house again. Every time Ed missed someone coming to check the traps, heaviness consumed her chest. She enjoyed talking to him. When Olive or Genny took his place, they were polite, even friendly, but Ed missed the unrealistic but still feasible possibility of having a friend her age and the opposite gender.

Three yards in the neighborhood had traps. Ed figured that might triple her chance of seeing Clint. She scolded herself heartily for even allowing the thought. Such things never worked out. You didn't catch a man with a trap. You certainly didn't catch one staring out the window waiting for him to empty your trap. Or your neighbor's. Or with skunks. Or with mini-marshmallows.

Ed had learned about the mini-marshmallows early on, when Genny rebaited the empty traps. That was when Doris noticed them, and how the neighborhood began its domino effect of hiring the trappers to remove the animals. Doris emerged from her dumpy half-double.

"Ed, is that skunk guy?"

"Today we have a skunk woman," Ed replied. "Doris, I'd like you to meet Genny Anderson."

"The skunk guy is my dad," Genny said, brushing off her knees as she rose.

Apparently, Doris, an independent single woman in her sixties, had never contemplated that the trapper would be a woman.

"A woman! Now I've seen everything." Doris leaned over the fence. "Can you get rid of my skunks, too? I was sprayed a couple weeks ago and I gotta tell you I can still smell it sometimes. Don't you get sprayed?"

"Sometimes," Genny said. "I just know how to get rid of the smell."

"Well, it sure isn't tomato juice," Doris said. "That just made me smell like tomatoes."

"Nope," Genny said. "Next time use a combination of hydrogen peroxide, baking soda and dish soap."

"I don't intend to have a 'next time.' Go get some traps," Doris commanded.

Genny went to her truck and reappeared on Doris' side of the fence. That's how Ed got Doris to chop her mulberry tree (which Ed would dry and cart to the city recycling/compost center) and skunk-proofing Doris' shed. Geneva waved as they discussed the details. She had more of a body count to tally.

With the entire Anderson family roaming the neighborhood, Ed felt like she couldn't escape the secret hope that she might have a chance to talk with Clint regarding something other than an animal. The days of trapping, watching and eagerly waiting for Clint continued, despite how many times Ed told herself not to do it.

Every time a trap slammed shut in the middle of the night, Ed woke up. In her head, she kept a score card for who's yard yielded what. Tonight it sounded like the Morgans' yard. The animal count, even if far from accurate, kept her mind occupied when she couldn't sleep. She stared out the window into the darkness, the pale orange glow of the streetlights brightening the horizon.

With a week to go, the Andersons had trapped at least thirty-five animals in the neighborhood: skunks, opossums, feral cats and a raccoon. Her yard had yielded four baby skunks, three normal-sized adults, and one elderly fat skunk. For the big one, C.A. didn't even squeeze him into the transport cage. C.A. took that huge skunk trap and all.

Ed thought about Clint lumbering from his truck

and flashing her a shy smile. In her half-asleep, insomniac vision Ed offered Clint lemonade. He joined her on the porch, in her rocking chairs, with the conversation turning to the best Middle Eastern food in the Valley… Ed fell asleep, with dreams of lamb kabobs shared with Clint.

Morning brought a fresh dose of reality. Ed's contract with the Andersons ended today. She, and especially the neighborhood children, would have to fight their disappointment and find new preoccupations for their time. Summer would fade into oblivion over the next few days as the school year approached. Ed thought the children would rather spend the final hours of summer vacation sleeping or swimming at the pool.

Instead, they congregated on the sidewalk, pacing from house to house as they waited for the Andersons to share the neighborhood menagerie with them. Apparently, one child—Jésus Cruz—started the vigil one day when he noticed Olive taking a kit to her truck and asked the questions pertinent to a nine-year-old.

"What do you have in the cage? Why is it covered with a cloth? Where are you taking it? Why were you in Miz Ed's yard?"

Olive answered every question, except the truth about where the skunk would go. A nine-year-old, even one who walked past drug dealers on his way to the bus stop, doesn't need that reality. Olive showed Jésus the skunk. Word spread. Four more neighbors hired the Andersons for skunk removal.

It took a long time before eight-year-old Alli Morgan got to see any animals, at least of the wild and unusual kind. When Frank Morgan hired Clint, he told his daughter never to go in the yard when something got caught in the trap. He also told the babysitter. The babysitter interpreted that as "don't go in the yard or off the porch." Poor Alli spent more than a week craning her neck for a view of the neighborhood goings-ons while the other kids got up close and personal.

Once Genny turned up at the Morgan yard when something had gotten caught in the trap, Alli finally got her chance. Alli, ever obedient, stood on the porch, but stretched as far as she could.

"Come with me," Genny said.

"I can't. Dad said so."

"That's a good rule," Genny said. "But I can handle the animals so you won't get hurt. Why don't you come with me, and I'll talk to your dad. Do you want to see a skunk?"

With Genny's expertise, and her feminine sweetness, Frank allowed Alli to join the other children curbside to watch the daily animal procession. Alli claimed her spot with the other children gathered around the truck. She usually ended up the closest to whatever Anderson had come to do the job. The babysitter glared from the porch.

On the first day her first day as an official part of the group, Alli spotted an injured barn owl Olive had in the truck.

"Just like Harry Potter!" Alli screamed.

Olive smiled.

"No, those are larger owls. Check out the snowy owl, the scops owl, and the Eurasian eagle owl," Olive suggested. "This is a common barn owl. It's endangered because houses are being built on farmland. They have nowhere to live. Someone shot this owl with an arrow. I'm going to take it to the wildlife rescue center."

She watched the crowd from the window, hoping—discreetly and perhaps pathetically—that Clint himself would come to collect the traps from her yard. She pulled on her dark blue walking shorts and her worn out Birkenstocks.

Ed headed out the door for her morning walk, losing herself in her thoughts. The weatherman said it would reach ninety-nine degrees with a heat index of one hundred five. Sweat poured from her body, despite the fact she had only gone a few blocks from home.

Ed kept thinking about school. She would teach two graphic design courses this fall, one on desktop publishing and another on images at the community college and two more classes online. Community college resumed Monday. That would mean a true test for her Coca Cola ban and new healthy eating plan. Nothing fried from the food court and nothing that she got from a vending machine—and that included the naughty red bottle.

Once school started, she hoped she would finally shake this juvenile feeling she had for Clint. She was too old to blame the problem on raging hormones.

Once home, Ed confirmed that she and Doris had nothing in their traps. If Ed didn't see Clint today, she'd probably never see him again.

The Andersons had solved her problem. She had no more skunks. With her Le Pew family evicted, she had undertaken the ultimate skunk-proofing mission in her backyard. Ed animal-proofed almost all the way around her deck, leaving an opening around the empty trap. Until the trap left, she didn't feel comfortable sealing the deck completely.

The job was grueling—hard work that the August heat wave made even more difficult. That heat had returned in full force today. Her attire post-walk demonstrated that. Her dark blue tee-shirt was completely soaked when she got home.

Even her pants were wet at the small of her back and where her large thighs rubbed together. She'd reach her goal weight when her legs no longer touched. She had no idea how many pounds that was. She didn't care what she weighed as long as her thighs no longer met.

Still, although she had sweat herself thoroughly, she decided to wait before she showered. She had a plan. Today, after the Andersons left, she'd seal the opening in the deck and finish the landscaping around it. Then, she'd water the plants, take a well-deserved shower (as long as her eco-mindedness would allow) and forget about Clint Anderson—once and for all.

She downed two huge glasses of water, made herself some toast with strawberry preserves, grabbed some orange juice and sat on the porch to read the paper. Hydrated and fed, she zoomed to her projects. She didn't want to get too cooled off and lose momentum. She had to seal that deck.

Weeding first. She started near the garage. She wanted to take advantage of the shade. What a sight she must have made with her hands deep in the soil and her large butt, still sticky with sweat, protruding in the air like lawn sculpture. The violent thunderstorm last night had moistened the ground, making it easier to pull those stubborn green invaders. She plodded forward on her hands and knees. Ed had almost reached the sidewalk when she heard a voice.

"Ed?"

Ed spun around on her knees. She clutched a handful of grass in her fingers. Oh dear God, it couldn't be, she thought. Not now. Not like this. She wanted to hide. Mortified, she choked out a greeting.

"Clint," she said, the name barely a whisper.

Painstakingly slowly, she hobbled to her feet. Those

fat thighs protested. Her knees wobbled. She didn't know if could walk.

"I must look frightful," Ed admitted.

"It's going to hit one hundred. Better get it done now."

Clint turned and suddenly became distracted by the nearly-completed skunk-proofing on her deck.

"You do this yourself?" he asked.

"Yes," she answered. "Digging the trench was brutal."

"Nice job," he replied.

Ed wanted to swoon. Her heart skipped a beat and she lost her breath. Clint had given her a compliment. She didn't know how to acknowledge it. She wanted to giggle. Except, she would never giggle. She just felt like she could giggle, a disorienting feeling at her age.

"You're taking no chances," Clint said, referring to her handiwork. "Worked right up to the trap."

"I don't want them to sneak back in."

"Once I put these traps in the truck, I'll help you finish it," Clint suggested.

He gathered the traps and disappeared in be-tween the houses. Glee swirled within Ed. Her chest swelled, with pride and pleasure.

"He wants to help me," she whispered.

She rushed around the yard gathering equipment and straightening. She didn't want any more random shovels and spades scattered about. Ed shook her head, appalled at her behavior.

I gave up men years ago, she remind herself. *I have resigned myself to living alone. I'm acting like a horny schoolgirl with a crush.* She hadn't forgotten what horny felt like, or how uncomfortable it could be. Clint returned. He immediately hopped in the trench and dropped to his knees.

"Thanks for your help," she said.

"Least I could do," Clint said. "You got me most of the houses in this neighborhood."

Ed deflated. This was just a way to thank her for word-of-mouth advertising?

"Plus, you listened to my advice," he added.

"Well, who wants skunks coming back?" she quipped.

"If they do, you know who to call," he said.

He paused.

"I'd be happy to come back."

Neither one of them spoke. He finally broke the silence.

"Did you get your screwdriver and the screws?" he asked.

"Yes, right here," she answered.

She knelt beside him. What did he mean when he said he'd be happy to come back? Her mind raced with the connotations. Ed could smell his sweat and the aroma of his aftershave. Clint smelled sweet, modern, not like an old man or Old Spice, more like citrus.

"You hold it. I'll screw," he directed.

Her hands held the cloth, but her mind wandered. In body, she quietly helped Clint. In her brain, obviously possessed by some primitive beast, she daydreamed about his screwing. If only this didn't involve a screwdriver and galvanized hardware. She wondered what it feel like to have a man hold her in his arms again, drop his mouth to her mouth, brush the hair from her eyes, their bodies meeting as their lips touched…

"Almost done. Hold on for one more," Clint said.

Then, he reached across her.

"Hold it. Right there. That's perfect," Clint went on.

Ed slipped into a daydream where his mouth kissed hers and perhaps his body touched her and the one more didn't refer to the turn of a screw in her deck.

While she lost herself in thought, Clint's arm—his real arm, the one in the trench, on this hot summer morning—vaguely brushed her breast. It grazed her and beyond, to place the last screw. Ed's nipples stiffened. She closed her eyes, embarrassed, fighting the warmth threatening to expose her in her cheeks.

"God, I hope my bra hid that," she thought.

While she focused on her own mortification, she noticed her warmth, and not the sweaty kind, spreading to other regions of her anatomy.

"That will do it," he said.

Then, he offered a hearty sigh as if pleased with himself. Clint got out of the trench. Ed stayed behind. Clint extended his hand. She took it. She stumbled to her feet trying not to look like a wounded elephant. Or worse, she would hate to knock him over.

"Thank you," she muttered.

"It was our pleasure helping you," he said, waving across the yard. "Are you putting in gates?"

She wanted to answer, but she couldn't right away. Ed nodded.

"Well," he answered. "Make sure you only leave an inch clearance, so any animals can't get in your yard."

"I'll do that," she said.

She nodded again. Slowly, she felt the thickness dissipate from her throat.

Her mind had a different answer: But if I do that, I'll never have an excuse to call you. Before she had a chance to make more conversation, Clint turned and walked to his truck. She focused her energies on filling in the trench. She scolded herself for her fantasies. She slung dirt like nobody's business.

At the same time, she still thought about him. Ed never even found out for sure if he was married. She really wanted to get to know him.

Who was she kidding? Hell, ten minutes ago she would have taken him, right in the trench.

The sun beat across Ed's back, making it impossible to continue. She kept thinking of Clint, dwelling. Thinking of soil-streaked limbs in the trench, imagining her skin screaming with intensity if he touched her... She decided that today she needed a cold shower, to wash this man out of her heart.

She stripped off her clothes as she walked up the stairs: a soggy tee-shirt near the landing, her shorts in the hall, her bra and panties as she stepped into her bedroom. Ed couldn't get the thought of Clint out of her mind. Her body burned. She feared she might implode. She needed to release the heat.

Ed closed her bedroom door. If any of her sisters let themselves in her house that would arouse suspicion. She never closed her bedroom door. She flung open her underwear drawer. She reached into the back, pushing aside all those Fruit of the Loom beige briefs.

It's got to be here somewhere, she screamed to herself. It's not the kind of thing you put on a yard sale or stick in the box for charity.

"Please," she said. "I've got to find it. I need it, and I need it now."

Finally, wedged deep into the corner, she wrapped her hand around the sleek surface. She pulled it free of its hiding spot, revealing her 'joystick.' Hannah—they'd been friends since elementary school, joined the same Girl Scout troops, and went to camp together every summer—gave it to her when she turned thirty. They'd gotten drunk that night, something neither of them usually did, and did a few experiments with the vibrator—clothed of course.

"Now you don't need a man, Ed," Hananh had said. "You have your own joystick."

Ed inhaled. She wasn't even sure what to do with it. She sat on the bed and switched it on. Nothing happened.

"Damn," she whined. "No, no, not now."

It took the same size batteries as her digital camera. She threw on a bathrobe and raced to her office and the battery charger. Ed grabbed the plastic bed where the AA batteries normally rested. Empty! Empty? She grimaced and starting searching for the actual camera.

"Talk about not being prepared."

She slapped herself in the forehead. She must have forgotten the camera at Martha's house. She brought it over there to take pictures of the kids in their new school clothes. She did not have any batteries for her vibrator since she left them at her lesbian sister's house. Ironic. She stomped to her room.

"Ed," she said to herself. "You can do this by yourself. Just relax."

She fluffed her pillow and sat on the bed. Ed closed her eyes as she reclined, thinking of Clint and the way her body surged when he accidentally touched her breasts. That was all it took to make her nipples stand erect. Her knees tumbled to the side. Ed imagined Clint's arms around her, his mouth against hers, their chests touching, their thighs bumping against each other as their lips tasted each other. The sensation between her legs had turned into searing lunacy. Slowly, she moved her hand down her body, working its way to the exact point of the fire inside her.

FOUR

Months passed with no more wild animals invading Ed's territory. With her semester packed with fifteen-hour days, whiny students, boring graphic design jobs that wouldn't challenge a college intern and alcoholic Tootie in the attic, Ed didn't have time for a fleeting memory of Clint Anderson. Her crush had faded.

The heat had gone. Actually, a cold front had replaced the passion of unrequited lust. Last night had produced the coldest temperatures of the mild winter season. The weather channel predicted a weekend of snow.

The prognostications of the local meteorologist did not chill Ed's spirits. She reveled in it. She had plans. This weekend was her annual winter camping trip with Hannah, and Ed had worried that the un-January-like conditions would spoil the fun. Who wants to hike in a barren forest when you can cross-country ski, build snowmen and ice skate?

Every January, Ed and Hannah had a girls weekend during Girl Scout Alumni camping at Hemlock Hill. Hannah married her college sweetheart, Charlie, and moved halfway across the state. While she and Ed spoke frequently, they rarely saw each other. As the reality of their everyday lives progressed, they had less and less time for travel and visits.

They registered for Lakeside Unit, a small cabin that had a covered porch. While the other campers spread sleeping bags on the cabin floors, Ed and Hannah would drag their gear outside, yes in January, and sleep on the porch. They would watch the sunrise over the lake, the chatter of girl talk having broken their night-time silence an hour earlier. They sipped hot chocolate as dawn colors broke the sky and reflected on the ice.

Ed needed this trip. Exhaustion plagued her, as did insomnia, and her hectic schedule had her working seven days a week more often than not. She needed the exercise. She needed the fresh air. In the chaos she called survival, Ed practically deserted her walking routine, but had maintained a fairly healthy eating plan. Yogurt, sunflower seeds and salads had made life bearable, even if she did have to scrutinize which items offered the most nutrition and satiating power for the calories. Ed had even continued her Coca-cola free lifestyle by stocking Aretha with a cooler of cold water. She could refill her mug with a trip to the parking lot (did that count as exercise?) when there was no water fountain nearby.

One especially stressful or long day, she succumbed to a Coke. She never allowed herself to finish the whole bottle. Ed preferred to satisfy her cravings, whether sweet, salty or crunchy, with trail mix consisting of nuts, seeds and dried fruit. She mixed a batch with chocolate chips for cross-country skiing. In another old-school trick of eco-consciousness, Ed filled the drawstring cloth bags she and Hannah would later stow in their pockets.

Camp preparations took most of the day: cooking and packing food and assembling gear. Then, Ed retrieved Hannah from the airport for the drive to Hemlock Hill. With people heading to the ski resorts and the outlets, Ed and Hannah faced an extra hour of travel time but they used it to share news. While they talked, they lamented the changes on Blue Mountain, how their childhood nature mecca had now transformed into a modern tourist destination, hardly recognizable.

Even their once-isolated Girl Scout camp now sat in the middle of a gated development of primarily multi-million dollar summer homes. Ed gave the Girl Scouts credit for not caving into the pressure of the developers to sell, especially with most of the camp's acreage on the lake. Developers had to offer the Girl Scout council millions.

The tranquility of the winter morning and the idyllic setting didn't last as long as Ed would have liked. Hannah asked the fateful question. She managed to do it before they finished unpacking Aretha.

"What ever happened with Clint?" she asked as she lugged groceries onto the cabin's porch. "It's been ages since you've been interested in someone."

"Nothing to tell," Ed replied. "I hired his family's services to eradicate my skunk problem, and only saw him twice. I don't know what made me go starry-eyed. I never considered it more than infatuation."

"Infatuation? Even Charlie thought there was more to it, just based on your emails," Hannah said.

"You read my emails to Charlie!" Ed exclaimed.

"How could you read our private communications to your husband?"

"I always do," Hannah answered. "I'm just going to tell him later anyway, so he might as well hear it from the horse's mouth. The Tootie stories send him into hysterics. He loves your emails and he was happy you were finally interested in someone. And I was very excited to hear that you may have used your special birthday gift—"

Ed tossed up her hand. Her friend stopped speaking.

"We aren't going to talk about this," she told Hannah. "It was a crush. It's over. It never really started."

"Leaving you man-free as usual," Hannah remarked sourly.

"We can't all get the happily ever after," Ed said. "I'm just glad most of my friends did, even if I'll be growing old alone and fat. It's fine."

"At least you've got Tootie," Hannah snickered.

"I'm not talking about her either," Ed snapped, even though she smiled slightly at the humor.

Hannah let the matter drop once again proving that she was a respectful friend and knew how far she could push Ed. The rest of the evening focused on Hannah's career and her children. It seemed like mindless prattle, until Ed went to brush her teeth. Hannah tucked her sleeping bag under her arm and headed for the porch. She returned for Ed's sleeping bag, which struck Ed as odd. When Hannah came left for her turn in the latrine, Ed slipped out to the porch. Hannah had arranged both sleeping bags with a book, the *Illustrated Kama Sutra*, between them.

"Hannah?" Ed called across the darkness.

"Don't worry," Hannah replied from the latrine. "It was a birthday present for Charlie and I thought you might like to see it."

"What do I need to see the *Kama Sutra*?" Ed asked when she returned. "Illustrated? Is that in case I forgot what sex looked like?"

"Don't be silly," Hannah said. "I just thought it might give us something to talk about."

It never failed. Every camping trip, Ed got snippets from Hannah's sex life as her bedtime story. Invariably, Ed felt like a teenager again.

"It's a long story," Hannah teased. "Are you sure you want to hear it?"

"Your stories are the closest thing I have to a sex life," Ed replied.

It started with a late night television interview, Hannah began. Charlie was working late. Curled on the couch, children in bed, and drinking a glass of chardonnay, she wore her standard evening uniform: boxer shorts, dilapidated Grateful Dead tee-shirt and fuzzy socks. The psychologist on the television remarked that "For emotional health and a balanced view of relationships, children had to witness love in order to learn how to love."

Apparently, according to this so-called expert, a healthy sex life between parents provided a critical component in this.

"I wanted to give my kids the modern version of 'Leave it to Beaver' and what they needed was 'The Addams Family,'" Hannah explained. "Who would have thought?"

Like any concerned modern mother, Hannah examined her own marriage. With separate careers and children in soccer, scouts, music lessons, and karate, not to mention she and Charlie's volunteer obligations, she and Charlie barely spoke. How could they offer a positive example if they never seemed to stay in the same room long enough to touch?

Like most couples they knew, Hannah and Charlie tumbled into bed half-dead. A trip between the sheets meant much needed sleep, not sex. Days would pass, then weeks, and one of them might notice the unintentional dry spell and contradict it. The attempts often fell flat and ended in brief encounters where neither of them broke a sweat.

"And that was your complaint last year at camp," Ed remarked.

"Do you want to hear this or not?" Hannah said.

"Continue."

So, Hannah lit the heat in her marriage. Step one, she reached deep into her dresser and retrieved an old nightgown, nothing sleazy, but sleek and satin, some lace trim. Heck, Hannah said with a laugh, it might have even been a slip. Whatever it was, it was sexier than a t-shirt and boxers. Charlie noticed. And he paid more attention to everything underneath the nightgown.

Next, she threw out her cotton panties, the old Hanes bikinis she had worn for as long as she could remember.

"That was wasteful," Ed told her. "You could have waited until they needed to be replaced."

"Ed," Hannah said. "I hadn't bought myself new underwear since before the children were born."

"Okay, then," Ed said. "I hope you cut up the old ones for dust rags or quilt filler or something."

"You can't recycle everything," Hannah replied.

"You can try," Ed responded.

After work one day, she went to Target. She bought racy bras, thong panties, even a pair of low-rise jeans. Charlie would hang around the bedroom in the morning, instead of rushing off to his coffee and his sports section. He enjoyed the glimpses of what went under her clothes these days.

Then, Hannah discovered Charlie rooting through the dirty laundry. He had bras and panties over his arm reading the tags. That's when the gifts started. He would leave new undergarments or nightgowns in the bathroom while she showered. Different lotions and eventually perfume followed. Before long their sex life returned to its collegiate intensity.

"Hannah, I remember those days. If half of what you told me was true…"

"Edna! Stop interrupting."

Occasionally Charlie would hire a sitter and they'd date, or leave the kids with his parents and check into a local motel—occasionally perusing the adult toy store first. She'd suggest, but ultimately he chose. She loved the silicone penis rings. Apparently, 'the triple' drove her crazy.

"Oh, Ed," Hannah gasped. "You've got to try them. They're incredible."

Ed didn't ask for more detail, because she knew Hannah would provide if prompted.

"Perhaps someday… Hannah, remember," Ed said. "I'm missing a key component. Continue."

In the heat of their new relationship, Hannah did notice a change in the children. When she and Charlie touched, flirted and kissed in front of the children, they offered more affection. Maybe the television psychologist was right. Of course, with the sex suddenly gratifying on its own, Hannah no longer cared.

Charlie grew bold. One night he drove them to lover's lane, in his Mercedes CLS550. In college, Hannah feared such public displays. She thought the cops would shine a flashlight in the window of Charlie's '79 Civic when she had one leg on the back window and the other over the gear shift. Now, almost thirty years later, her panties still clung to the rear view mirror. She was still worried about getting caught, but more importantly, she was satisfied.

Another night, Charlie headed to the interstate after dinner. She asked where they were going. Charlie didn't answer. Instead, he pulled into a remote area of the deserted rest stop. After setting the emergency brake, he wrapped one arm around her back, kissed her, and took her hand. He kissed each finger before setting it against his groin. Gently, he guided her around the gear shift and brought her face to meet her hand in his lap.

She peered at him, smiled coyly, and unbuttoned his pants. And afterward they went home. He sent her upstairs while he paid the babysitter and waited for her to leave. When Charlie finally came upstairs, he checked on the children, turned out the hall light, and reciprocated, twice.

Jealousy filled Ed. In one way, she wanted her to tell Hannah to shut up and go to sleep. But Ed still hadn't heard about the *Kama Sutra*.

"So, the book?"

"Soon, really soon," Hannah said. "Come on Ed, I can't tell anybody else these stories. My sisters would be mortified and call me a whore."

"You are a whore," Ed answered.

"Maybe," Hannah replied. "But a happily married whore. Whereas, my sisters think the missionary position every Friday night is a hot sex life."

Hannah continued her tale. One night, after an especially intense lovemaking session at a really shady motel that charged by the hour, Charlie mentioned to the guys at the weekly poker game talking about the *Kama Sutra*. One of Charlie's buddies had heard about the *Kama Sutra* on television. As she mounted him for the third time, she told him they didn't need it. As she caressed his chest and pulled him into her wetness, she decided to buy a copy for his birthday. She even wrote notes in the margins.

"You didn't!" Ed exclaimed, bolting upright in her sleeping bag.

She seized the book from the floor, flipping it open. "Oh, yes."

Hannah smirked. Even in the darkness, Ed could have sworn Hannah licked her lips. Ed thought she noticed the scribbles from a ball point pen in the book.

"Do you realize that this is the first night I have willingly not had sex since this all began?" Hannah said.

"You're kidding," Ed said.

"Well, Charlie had a couple of business trips."

"I feel honored that you would sacrifice such a robust sexual life for me."

"It was an easy decision," Hannah said. "Besides, it will give him a couple of days to think up new ways to please me."

Ed placed the book on the deck. She rolled over and immersed herself in the thick down of the sleeping bag. Ed didn't sleep. The discussions of sex and the *Kama Sutra* amplified her lack of love life and stirred restlessness in her. That primed her mind for visions of Clint. As Ed struggled between uneasy rest and dreams of her lost chance at a relationship, morning crept nearer. Dawn arrived quickly. Mother Nature did not disappoint with the sunrise. A fresh coating of about three inches of snow had coated the earth during the night.

After a hearty breakfast, Ed and Hannah retrieved cross country skis, boots, and maps. Hannah had just stepped out of the L.L. Bean catalog, with her blue Pearl

Izumi Whisper jacket, fitted, sleek and water resistant; SportHill XC pants, black and not only waterproof but windproof; Polartec shirt, the best in lightweight fleece; and Sugoi Speedster Hoodie, a glorified second skin. Ed wore a turtleneck, a sweatshirt, a flannel shirt, a down vest, and jeans, the worst choice for skiing because they wick up the water. Her frugality would not allow her to buy clothes specifically for skiing.

On the trail, the morning went quickly. They completed two-thirds of the route. They stopped at the beaver dam for lunch. The trees felled by camp beavers created natural chairs and picnic tables. Ed hoped to spot a beaver, since they don't hibernate. She even brought her camera, just in case. As they ate, voices approached from the opposite direction. Soon, two women rounded the corner.

"Wow," Ed said as she thought she recognized the newcomers. "Either I spend too much time here or Girl Scouts are all starting to look the same."

Under the ski clothes, Ed couldn't decipher with certainty who they were.

"Ed, is that you?" a voice called.

So she did know them, Ed thought.

"It's Olive," the voice identified herself as she and her partner reached the dam. "Olive Anderson."

"Clint's daughters?" Hannah asked.

Ed didn't like the mischief in Hannah's tone.

"Behave yourself," Ed replied tersely.

Ed put down her food.

"Hi, Olive," she called to their guests. "Is that you, Genny? I didn't know you were scouts."

"Yes," Genny said. "We attend alumni weekend every year. We love it here."

"I better have daughters," Olive added. "I can't imagine giving up Hemlock Hill."

"No one has to give up Hemlock Hill," Hannah interjected. "I'm living proof. I have sons."

Chilled silence followed. Hannah thrust out her hand.

"My friend here is rude," she said. "I'm Hannah Golden. Ed and I have been friends forever. Shared every camp."

Olive moved her ski poles into one hand and accepted Hannah's gloved fingers.

"Pleased to meet you," the girls said in unison.

"Is your mom here, too?" Hannah asked.

Ed cast daggers from her eyes to her friend, avoiding the girls.

"No, our mom's been out of the picture a long time," Genny said.

"Yeah," said Olive, "That's why we joined Girl Scouts. Dad thought we needed female mentors."

"No one can trap, fish, hunt, fix old cars, and build stuff like we can," Genny said.

"Of course, we did 4-H, too," Olive said.

"Dad didn't think dance or gymnastics practical," said Genny.

"I don't either," Ed muttered.

"Join us," Hannah offered.

"Not for long," Olive said as she selected a felled tree across from Ed and Hannah and rested her backpack against it. She pulled out her jacket and put it on. "Don't want to get too cooled off."

Olive glanced uneasily at Ed.

"I've been meaning to call you," Olive said. "I hate to ask for favors but I know you're a graphic designer. I plan to start a wildlife rehabilitation center if I can get the land. I'll go to vet school part-time. I need a logo designed, for fundraising and recruiting. I decided on The Olive Branch Ranch. Does that sound cheesy?"

Ed shook her head. Hannah pondered it.

"It's either you or Microsoft's word art," Genny said.

"Please don't," Ed remarked softly.

"Did you see Dad's truck?" Olive asked. "I really like the lettering. Beautiful and modern—"

"It's Futura extra bold style," Ed explained. "Paul Renner designed it in the thirties. It's the major typeface development from the Constructivist orientation of the German Bauhaus movement…"

Ed realized that she had slipped into type-geek speak and allowed her words to evaporate.

"That's cool," Olive said, obviously feigning interest. I want mine similar, but different."

"I'm getting cold," Genny said.

"Me, too," said Hannah. "Tell us what unit you're at and we'll bring by Ed's business card. This is her kind of project."

"We're in Harry's Hideaway," Genny answered.

Of course, Ed thought. Harry's Hideaway took its name from the camp's resident bear. Where else would a family of trappers stay?

"Dad has a tent pitched next to the cabin," Olive said. " He's crazy. He likes to sleep outside."

Clint was here at Girl Scout camp? Ed thought.

"Look!" Genny barked in a stage whisper.

Everyone turned. A beaver swam under the ice. Ed dropped to her knees in the snow and snapped photographs. She also captured the intense faces of Olive, Genny and Hannah. Once the beaver passed from view, the group gathered their trash, repacked their gear, and parted ways.

Once the girls were out of earshot, Hannah stopped. She peered right into Ed's face.

"Clint's here," Hannah said. "Make a move when we take the business card or I'll do it for you. This isn't just another job you'll never get paid for. You'll get paid, but not with cash. Next winter, you're telling me the sexy bedtime story."

FIVE

Ed almost felt sorry for Hannah. Hannah really thought her matchmaking ploy at camp would work. She had even briefed Ed on different lines she could use, what invitations might sound appealing… but in the end, it didn't matter.

Clint had gone to another site to teach a tracking workshop and wouldn't return until after dark. They never saw him. The rest of the weekend, they didn't see Olive or Genny either. It was amazing how large a small Girl Scout camp could become.

On the hike back to their campsite, Hannah pleaded with Ed regarding jump-starting her stalled social life and perhaps even have some casual, or not so casual, sex.

"Hannah, men are not interested in nearly 40-year-old, plain, fat people," Ed protested. "That ship sailed a long time ago."

"You're not a cow, Ed," Hannah replied. "With some effort, you could be attractive."

Ed didn't know why she had started thinking about this now. More than a month had passed. Ed faced her first day off since that camping trip. Of course, it she opened her email she could bid her free day adieu. Work constantly appeared in her email: proofs returned, pro bono requests, and copy changes.

Olive Anderson hadn't officially contacted her about the logo for the wildlife rescue center. School probably demanded her full attention. Graduation loomed in two months.

Ed's mind wandered. Hannah's next idea of how to draw suitors involved Internet dating services. Ed vetoed it, but Hannah had a persistence that made it easier to agree that to fight. To try and fail would be simpler in the long run.

"Try eHarmony or Match.com," Hannah suggested.

"For a married woman, you know a lot about this stuff," Ed remarked.

"I stay current," Hannah replied.

"It doesn't matter," Ed said. "Even if I struck up an interesting conversation, the minute they asked for a picture they'd know I was fat and plain. I'd be locked out of their inboxes in a New York minute."

That didn't deter Hannah. Hannah discovered bbpeoplemeet.com.

"What's that?" Ed asked.

"It's a dating website geared toward large women."

"Oh, no, Hannah."

"It looks good," Hannah said.

And now Ed had the pleasure of Internet dating… on a fat people service. Where on the home page everyone weighed in at size twelve. Ed was a twenty. She filled out her profile honestly: thirty-nine-year-old graphic designer, oops make that forty: when you're born on Leap Day, it's easy to forget a birthday.

She had no kids, non-smoker, environmentalist who loves the outdoors…"

A couple men replied. Some might have possibilities, but she really wasn't interested. No one had any spark.

Heck, nobody could spell or construct a complete sentence. She might not win any writer-of-the-year awards, and her sewer exposé for the local weekly wouldn't win any Pulitzers, but she could adeptly match subjects and verbs. The influence of text and instant messaging had destroyed people's ability to communicate intelligently.

That turned off Ed. She could blame Celeste. Celeste was a good friend and a published novelist who took the written word very seriously. Ed couldn't stand a poorly written, misspelled sentence.

Beyond the seemingly illiterate, Internet dating introduced Ed to a whole new type of reject: the pervert. Some of the messages got right to the point.

"Hi, baby. Saw your profile. How big are your tits?"

Ed resisted the temptation to reply 127 ZZ, but they might mistake the joke for some mammoth knockers.

The weirder ones would ask about her personal hygiene, or more specifically, if her "pussy was natural, groomed or mowed."

Ed hit the delete key.

Ed hated the prospect of sending her own "flirt." Why couldn't they leave people some dignity and call it a message? Hannah would say she didn't give it a fair chance if she didn't fully participate.

Ed picked three men, using her best anti-pervert radar and asked for a photo. One instant-messaged a picture of his erect penis. Block.

Another sent a picture of his torso and tidy whiteys. He had the most hair she had ever seen on a human.

Block. The third, while handsome, wanted to meet immediately. Block.

Ed surrendered. She hated dating and never mastered the skills required for it. She made peace with that reality a long time ago.

She wondered if she could enlist Celeste's help to write a few good dating stories to appease Hannah. A few emails, a couple months, and then a miserable break-up story to assure Hannah that Ed had tried. Would Hannah ever stop harassing Ed about her marital status?

She grabbed the morning paper and went outside to the patio to read the community calendar. The paper still had the rubber band on it from when the delivery person threw it from the car window. Today, it almost made it onto the porch. As she opened the paper she noticed the headline in the region section:

"Thorpe nonagenarian sells 250 acres for $9.83"

That stole Ed's attention.

In an unusual deal yesterday, Samuel Hooper, 92, of Thorpe, sold 250 acres of prime real estate to his neighbor Olive Anderson for $9.83—the amount of money she had in her pocket at the time of the transaction.

Olive! Ed thought. She got her rescue center!

In the last three years, Hooper has received several multi-million dollar bids for the property from prominent local developers, most recently Progress Development.

"What am I going to do with that kind of money?" Hooper said in a telephone interview yesterday. "At my age, there's only one place I'm going and I won't need money. The Andersons are good people and we think alike."

"There's no denying that," Ed said to no one in particular.

"We want to preserve open space and grow food. Now that will continue even after I'm gone," Hooper said.

With his own family dead and no surviving heirs, Hooper has known the Andersons for several generations.

"I've been neighbors with the members of Anderson family all my life," Hooper said. "I'm the sixth generation to farm this land."

Hooper said that with his declining health, he couldn't farm the land on his own. The Andersons had expressed interest in expanding their own family farm in addition to a wildlife rehabilitation center.

"I started thinking that with all the houses going up, it was a matter of time before the developers were darkening my doorstep," Hooper said. "So one day I asked little Clint to get me some information on agricultural conservatorships off that newfangled web thing."

"Little Clint," Ed said with a smile. She continued reading.

Hooper rents 200 acres land to a young farmer, who operates the farm stand on the property. The lease includes a house, barn and chicken coops. Anderson will honor the lease.

Anderson plans a non-profit wildlife rescue center on the other 50 acres, which include the main house, barn, some outbuildings and a small family cemetery. The entire 250 acres fall under the protection under the conservatorship.

Hooper will remain on the property until his death. But why $9.83?

"Well," Hooper said, "the lawyer said I couldn't give her the land. He suggested $1. That sounded low. So when Olive brought over some lasagna during a school break, I asked her how much she had in her pocket. Didn't tell her why. She was reared to respect her elders, so without question she dug around in her pockets and came up with $9.83. I put out my hand for the money, she gave it to me, and I said young lady, you just bought yourself a farm."

Ed laughed heartily. Damn, she hoped to meet Mr. Hooper. She predicted that old codger would live to 110. Ed returned to the house, trudged upstairs, and turned on the computer. She wanted to send Olive a congratulatory e-card. Her phone rang. She flipped it open. It was her editor.

"There goes my day off," Ed said.

Her boss didn't even waste time on a greeting.

"Ed, a family of bears built a den under a porch in the township and they have woken up from hibernation. After that skunk piece you did last summer… When the family saw a cub walking around, they called the Fish and Game Commission. Bears to be removed in an hour. I want pictures—cute bears, mean humans—and maybe a story."

"Sure," Ed said as she whipped out a pencil to record the details.

Within minutes, Ed, the ace reporter, headed to her big assignment. She couldn't even get lost, as every news agency within 100 miles had turned out to cover the family with the bears under their house. A large crowd had gathered on the suburban street. Among the onlookers, Ed spotted Clint Anderson.

"Ed," a little voice called to her. It was Hannah's voice, the devil on Ed's shoulder (or the monkey on her back). "Now's your chance. Go say hello."

Her knees started shaking as she stumbled her way over to him. She stopped and waited for the feeling to pass. She wouldn't approach him at all if her body

insisted on acting like a love struck teenager. After a minute, she seemed more like herself. Then, she finished walking toward Clint.

"Hi, Clint," she called. "Remember me?"

"Hey, Ed," he replied. "You are my current record holder for the most skunks removed in thirty days."

"There's an honor I can be proud of," she said.

"Yeah, it's a stinker," Clint responded.

He chuckled. He switched his refillable Stewarts mug to the other hand so he could shake hers.

"And I appreciate your offer to help Olive," he said.

"Happy to do it," she said as she released his hand.

"What are you doing here?" he asked. "Thought you had enough wildlife."

"I did," Ed replied. "I'm here today for the newspaper. I do some freelance work. I need to get photos. You working?"

"Not really," Clint answered. "The homeowner called me. I called fish and game. Jobs like this require tranquilizers and bear carriers. I'm not licensed to do that. Legally, I have to stick with small animals, birds, snakes, 'gators, that kind of thing. Of course, I could take a bear, no problem."

"No doubt," Ed said. "Do you know how many bears there are under there?"

"Is that an official question?" Clint asked. "There's at least one adult female and one cub, could be two or three. And there's a possibility of an older sibling."

Ed gawked at the scene with the other onlookers.

"Ed, head to the left if you want pictures," Clint directed her. "If I know the guys, they'll bring the bears that way and set the traps around back."

"How do you know that?" Ed asked. "Did you talk to them?"

"Nah, just logic," he said. "The left side is flat, and mostly grass. The right has plants, rocks and if my eyes don't deceive me a flat basketball."

Ed scurried in that direction. Then, she froze. Hannah would say she blew her chance if she didn't make a move. A real move. She turned back.

"Thanks, Clint," she called.

"Sure," he replied.

"Can I interview you about bears when this is over?" she asked.

"Sure, but don't you want fish and game?" Clint answered. "They're doing all the work."

"No, the big media will get them. What I need I can get from you," she replied.

Did I really say that? she thought to herself.

"How about coffee and an interview," Clint suggested.

As she walked away, she turned back again. "Where? Stewarts?"

He nodded yes.

Damn, Ed thought. Wait 'til I tell Hannah.

SIX

As Clint predicted, the fish and game commission officers forced the bears to the left of the house. To Ed's surprise, it didn't take long. It happened so quickly; she only got half the pictures she thought she would.

Without Clint's guidance, she would have missed the whole affair. She snapped one photo as officers shot the mama with tranquilizers. She reared with the sting of the dart, revealing her cub and a one-year-old sibling that had lived under the stairs with her.

While the larger news media descended upon the officers, jockeying for position and footage, yelling questions and praying for sound bytes, Ed headed to Aretha. She had her interview with Clint for what she needed.

"Interview with Clint," Ed said out loud as she put the key in the ignition.

Dear Lord, she thought to herself, I've never done a real interview. I've asked a question here or there, like for the sewer article, but I've never conducted a full-fledged interview. This is what I get for listening to Hannah. This is what I get for following my hormones instead of my brain.

She whipped out her phone, ready to send out an SOS. Who could she call in the middle of the day, on a weekday, which would have experience interviewing people...

Wait, Ed thought. Celeste! Not only was Celeste a writer, who worked at home, but she began her career as a journalist. She talked Ed into this gig as a reporter. She scanned her address book: domestic diva, *maison couture*, psychobitch, and sk8er gurl. As she scrolled, Ed tapped against the button impatiently.

"Celeste, Celeste, where are you?" Finally, Ed reached 'bookbabe.'

When she worked at the paper, Ed called her Lois Lane, but the newspaper reference no longer fit. So, Ed switched it. She picked the landline.

She pressed the green send button and it rang and rang and rang. Finally, on the sixth ring, someone answered.

"Hello," said Celeste's husband, Darren.

Ed worried she might have interrupted something. Ed exhaled and shook her head. Thinking with those hormones again...

"Hey, Big D," she said. "I need to talk to Celeste right away."

"Then you'll have to call her cell phone," Darren said. "She's not here. She's in New York on book tour. Didn't you see her on *Good Morning America* today? She even read a bit."

"I forgot," Ed replied.

"You'll have another chance to see her," Darren continued. "She's going from talk show to talk show.

Regis and Kelly, *The View*, then *iVillage*… Siobhan and I are making a day out of watching them all."

"I thought Siobhan couldn't watch television?"

"It's her mama, Ed," Darren said. "Celeste has her principles but she's also got an ego. Besides, Siobhan only watches when Celeste comes on. Otherwise she's just playing and reading. She's turning into a bookworm like Celeste. I actually have to remind her to look at the screen to see her mama."

"Thanks, Big D. I'll try her cell."

Ed hung up and tried Celeste's mobile number. After two rings, Celeste's fiery voicemail greeting chimed on. Ed snapped the phone closed. Ed sighed. She decided to wing it.

How hard could it be? She could call Celeste later, and Celeste could help her salvage the story. Or worse, what if she mangled it so badly she had to call Clint later?

After buckling her seatbelt and defrosting her windows, Ed drove to Stewarts.

"I don't have my damn mug with me," she growled to herself. "I can't go there and use a foam cup. That will give him the wrong impression. Besides I don't even drink coffee!"

She couldn't stand him up, not could she keep him waiting much longer. Never leave a man waiting, her mother had once told her.

Ed drove downtown on auto-pilot and found an amazing non-metered parking space two blocks from the famous coffee shop. The morning crowd had dissipated, and the lunch crowd hadn't arrived yet for the special of the day— chicken salad.

Stewarts only made chicken salad one day a week. Their recipe included honey, walnuts and apples. They even got their meat from a local poultry farmer.

Clint had a chosen a spot in the window, sitting in a wrought iron chair and his mug resting against the checkerboard tabletop. Ed flashed a wave. She checked her outfit, no unexpected stains and her fly was closed. The bell on the door tinkered as she opened it. She went directly to Clint.

"Sorry to keep you waiting," she said.

Ed placed her purse on the table and pulled out her chair.

"No problem," Clint said. "I haven't been here long. Can I get you some coffee?"

Ed half-smiled.

"I have to confess I don't drink coffee," she said. "Plus, I don't have my mug, and they use foam here. Guess I'll go to the cooler and get a Honest Tea."

She turned toward the cooler. Clint's voice stopped her.

"If it makes a difference…The local kids put a lot of pressure on the owners about the foam cups, so they switched to paper. Olive and Genny practically lived here during high school. For cold stuff, they have Greenware plastic cups and plates and flatware that biodegrades."

"I didn't know that," Ed said.

"You strike me as the hot chocolate type," Clint observed. "Want some?"

"How did you guess?" Ed replied. "That would be great."

"Extra marshmallows?"

"For the calories, I'd rather have the whipped cream."

"Me, too," Clint said emphatically.

He rose from his chair and practically sprinted for the counter. Ed realized she didn't give him any money.

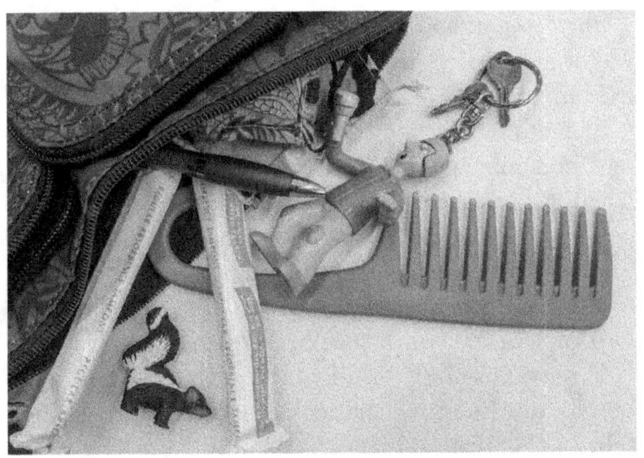

"Clint," she called after him.

He slowly turned. "Yes, Ed?"

"I forgot to give you money," she replied.

She groped through her bag for her wallet. As her hand circled it, the purse tumbled to the floor. It fell open side down, contents cascading from its interior and coating Ed's feet. She tried to act nonchalant. She even chuckled. She unfastened her wallet to give Clint some cash when a tampon rolled across the floor toward him.

Shit, she thought to herself, I hope he doesn't notice. Oh, please let me get to it before anyone notices.

"Really, it's no problem," he said. "Unless the paper gives you an expense account."

He winked at her. Ed froze for a minute, wide-eyed.

"Nope," she finally managed to say.

He smiled and walked to the counter. Ed dove under the table and gathered the contents of her purse. She shoved everything inside, not even remotely nicely. She wouldn't find anything in there for a week.

She thought about Clint's wink. Was he flirting? Or was it acknowledgment of his little joke? Did he see the tampon?

She almost forgot the tampon. She leapt to her feet and clocked her head against the table. Red-faced, rubbing the back of her skull, she surveyed the people around her. Tears started to stream her face. She seized the tampon from the floor and staggered to the table. She sat in her seat as Clint returned with two cups heaped with whipped cream.

"Are you crying?" he asked, puzzled.

"No, not literally," she replied. "I just bumped myself. No big deal."

He passed her one of the chocolates. It smelled of nutmeg and cinnamon. They had sprinkled spices on top and provided a cinnamon stick with chocolate on the end.

"Now what do you need to know about bears?" Clint asked, stirring his drink with the cinnamon stick.

He pulled it free of the white cream and licked the stick clean. Ed shivered.

"Why would bears be in the township? Although I think I know the answer."

"So tell me," he said.

He dipped the cinnamon stick in the whipped cream again. This time, when he rested it in his mouth a dollop of whipped cream stuck to his lip. His tongue pressed past his lips and removed it. Ed stared.

Damn it, Ed. You're working, she screamed to herself. You're working. Stop looking at the man's lips!

"Loss of habitat," she said.

She paused and took a hearty swig of her own chocolate. It was rich, and dark, and luscious, but also very hot, and it burned her throat all the way to her stomach.

"The developments on what used to be farmland," she said as soon as her throat cooled. "With clear-cutting the forest and wooded areas for more elaborate estates."

"Bingo," Clint confirmed.

Her confidence returned.

"Tell me about bears," Ed said.

"They mate in early summer. Female black bears, the sows, become sexually mature during their fourth summer. They leave a scent trail for the male, which are called boars," Clint said.

Now, he simply sipped his chocolate.

"More than one boar may pick up her sent, which occasionally leads to fights between suitors," he added.

"Sounds like people," Ed interrupted. "Some people anyway."

He nodded.

"Are they monogamous, Clint?"

"No," he said.

His hand tightened around the cup. Or did she imagine that?

"She may mate with one boar or many during her season," he answered.

"So, that's why no male bears were under the porch," Ed reasoned.

"Yes," he said.

He seemed to perk up when she connected some of the dots. Maybe it proved her genuine interest.

"And, the sows reject the boar after they copulate," he said.

"I think I know some girls like that," Ed quipped.

"They do spend a few days getting to know each other, before," Clint explained. "She's very careful. She doesn't want to be overpowered."

Ed watched his eyes as he spoke. He loved talking

about the bears. His face softened and his eyes sparkled.

"Each day he gets a little closer, and they start to nuzzle," Clint continued.

"Like us kissing," Ed commented.

She closed her eyes. Shit! she thought. I said that out loud! Time to back pedal...

"Not us... As in you and I but the general us... males and females, humans," she said.

He nodded.

"That's how their dates work," Clint said.

How do your dates work, Clint?

Ed had to bite her tongue to keep from saying it. She guzzled some chocolate.

"With the dating, so to speak, out of the way, mating begins usually for only a few minutes at first," Clint explained. "They repeatedly mate over the next several days, with some copulations lasting over an hour."

"An hour!" Ed exclaimed. "I can't imagine having sex for an hour..."

Ed threw her hand over her mouth. When she lowered it, she faked a smile.

"I can't believe I just said that."

"No problem," Clint said, a distinct blush in his cheeks. "After mating, the female may become pregnant but not bear any cubs. It's a process called delayed implantation. Only if the sow is in peak condition will the embryo implant itself in the uterus and begin development."

"Wow," Ed said as she finished her drink.

"You don't have to humor me. It's okay if you don't care."

"I do care," Ed said. "It's interesting that another species could be so like us and so different."

"We all know bears hibernate," Clint said, "but did you know a sow gives birth while hibernating? The sow can go months without food or water, during the coldest time of the year, and that's when she gives birth."

"Wait," Ed said. "A bear gets laid, perhaps by multiple partners, becomes pregnant and then gets to sleep through pregnancy? My friend Hannah will love that. She had the worse pregnancies. Shoot, I did it again. Sorry, you must think I'm an idiot."

"No, I think you're a woman. I had forgotten how a woman thinks," Clint responded. "It's been a long time. I bet the girls' mom would have said the same thing."

Mom. Not wife? Ed thought. Olive and Genny had mentioned growing up without a mother.

What happened to her? I wonder what the story is. Do I ask? Hannah would. Celeste would ask subtle questions until she could invent something.

Suddenly, Ed no longer cared about the mating rituals of bears. By the time she worked up the courage to broach the topic of the girls' mom, Clint had renewed his tale. She had lost her window.

"In January or February, the sow will wake up and give birth," Clint said.

"So she doesn't get to sleep through it?" Ed interrupted.

"No," Clint said, "though she'd probably prefer if she did. Anyway, she'll nurse the cubs for several months using fat stores from the fall. They stay awake long enough to eat the placenta, lick off the cubs and return to hibernation. When the cubs get hungry, they cry and the mother will change her body position so that they can nurse."

"What a life!" Ed said. "Give birth and go back to

sleep for a few months… Who watches the cubs?”

“Nobody,” Clint replied. He leaned back in his chair. “They’re awake. Occasionally one wonders away after some warm days, and an event like today happens. They’ll stay with mom until their second summer, then go off on their own. Shouldn’t you be writing this down?”

Ed had stopped writing a long time ago. She looked at the page in her notebook. It had at most ten words on it.

“You didn’t take many notes.”

“I got so engrossed. I forgot I was working. I’ll remember. Who can forget that?”

“Glad you enjoyed it.”

Ed remembered Olive and her purchase of the land next door. She hadn’t mentioned it to Clint.

“Clint, can I ask you a favor?”

“Sure, Ed. What is it?”

“Please let Olive know how happy I am that she got the land for the ranch.”

“You saw it in the paper?” Clint asked.

“I sure did,” Ed admitted. “And Mr. Hooper sounds like a hoot. But, really, Clint, you must be really proud.”

“I am,” he said. “Of both my girls.”

“Of course.”

Ed wiped her mouth with her napkin and put her notebook in her purse.

“Is Olive excited?”

“Beyond excited,” Clint said. “She can hardly focus on school. Genny said she’d help. They even plan to move to the Hooper house after graduation. I don’t think they realize how much work it will be… certifications, licenses, fund-raising, recruiting volunteers, working on the old buildings. And Olive still has vet school…”

"It's her dream, Clint," Ed said. "She's young. Don't spoil it."

"I won't," he promised. "I had dreams once."

"And so you're letting them move into a house with a 92-year old man that still calls you Little Clint."

"The Hoopers were always part of our family," Clint said. "They fit right it with my brothers and everyone. Mrs. Hooper watched the girls afterschool and summers. They never had their own grandkids. Their sons died in Vietnam."

Okay, now's your chance, Ed said to herself. Ask about the wife. But the question got stuck. Ed couldn't do it.

"Why does he call you Little Clint?"

"My great granddad was Clinton, my granddad is Clint, my dad, CA, and me, well, I became Little Clint like John-boy on *The Waltons*."

Ed never did gather the courage to ask about any Mrs. Anderson. The pair talked for hours: about Olive, Genny, The Hoopers, alternative energy, farming in America today… What stopped the conversation wasn't a lack of topics. It was Bing Crosby singing the Cole Porter song "Don't Fence Me In".

"I'm sorry," Clint said as he gazed at his iPhone. "I've got to take this. I'm surprised it hasn't rung sooner. It's my dad."

Ed could hear CA's boisterous voice.

"Son, where the Hell are you?"

"I'm still with the reporter."

"It takes four hours to tell her about bears mating? I could do it in ten minutes. Boy, do you have mating on the mind?"

Ed hid her eyes. She wondered if she should go to the restroom to give them privacy.

"No, Dad. We just got talking…"

Ed toned out the rest of Clint's exchange with his father as best she could. When he finally hung up, Ed lifted her purse.

"Sounded important. I should go."

"I hope he didn't bother you…" Clint said.

"No, he's right. I should apologize for eating up your whole day."

"No, Ed," Clint said. "Don't. I enjoyed it."

With that, he was out the door and in the truck. Ed lost herself in a daydream, a perfect moment between her, her hopes and her hot chocolate. Diana Krall interrupted her reverie with "I've Got You Under My Skin." This time, it was Ed's phone.

She flipped it open and greeted her friend, Celeste, with an exuberant "You're never going to believe what I did today."

SEVEN

Ed enjoyed her leisurely day talking with a man. She hadn't spent that much time with a member of the opposite sex in ages, and to think she might have spent it with an eligible bachelor gave her an unexpected thrill.

Maybe she should listen ton her friends. Maybe she needed to get out more and… Dare she say it? Date.

That sounds great in theory, Ed said to herself, but when?

Ed worked constantly. Between her teaching, volunteering, freelancing with the paper, and her pro bono designing, Ed would be hard pressed to squeeze in two hours for a movie. And her taste in movies wouldn't attract the most exciting men.

Matter of fact, the last movie she saw required a bus trip to New York City—the only place cosmopolitan enough to offer the documentary on the typeface *Helvetica*. Not exactly a Tom Cruise, *Mission Impossible*-type ride.

For fun in the Millville area, she enjoyed the local art museum. It didn't contain much when compared to the major collections in New York and Philadelphia, but for a small museum in her area, it consistently impressed Ed with its efforts to hold its own. Next on the roster, the museum had a Tiffany glass exhibit with Art Nouveau posters and prints. Ed greatly anticipated it.

Art Nouveau offered a distinct and contemporary style of type, especially for its era. But there you go... even in her leisure, Ed continued working.

She had at least two hours of grading to finish before her next class. This new crop of students, mostly seventeen- and eighteen-year-olds, presented mediocre design at best. They wanted A's, and for them they pleaded, conjoled, even had their parents send email. Yet, not a single one put in the required time and significant work. They complained when they got marks lower than what they desired, but no one took advantage of what she called her "second chance policy." Everyone could redo one project in the course, once they read and considered the comments from the critique.

Each year, the level of commitment and ability from the students dwindled even lower. She labeled it "the entitlement problem." Everyone who had children within the last twenty years kept calling everything the children did "awesome," whether they urinated in the potty or drew a straight line.

God, how Ed hated the word 'awesome' and removed it from her lexicon. For every simple, expected behavior a child could attain, many parents over-emphasized the achievement of it and created a generation of children who believed themselves perfect and invincible, or perhaps irritatingly infallible.

One student last semester demonstrated this phenomenon to a T.

It started with the standard "Introduce yourself to the class" exercise, very typical of the class environment. Each student completed a brief written statement. In it, he/she mentioned educational background, work experience, previous design, and generic items of interest.

Something like: "Hi, I'm Julie from Thorpe. I majored in design at the tech high school, and eventually I'm going to Kutztown for my bachelors. I work at the Staples in the mall in the copy shop."

From the beginning, Fannie had a boast for everything. Her opening statement read like a celebrity speech from the Oscars.

"Hi, I'm Frances. I am fabulous. I am a working designer. I have my own mega-successful design firm, Diva Designs. I'm an actress and a model. Soon, I will parlay my success from this one-horse town into a exciting design career working for a major motion picture studio in Hollywood. I will be very rich, and hang out with Paris Hilton. You may address me as Fannie."

Ed had never heard of Diva Designs. So, she did what any resourceful teacher would do. She googled it. When she didn't find it, she checked the on-line phone book. It had no listing. Interesting for a mega-successful design firm.

She finally discovered a lead—on myspace.com. The page presented a horrible jumble of bad design on a table of twenty five categories. The categories on the table had no sense of connection whatsoever, jumping from professional (with the Diva Design link under construction) to personal and to religious. Ed didn't want to click. She did brave a peek at the book Fannie wrote, designed, and apparently self-published, misspellings, harsh color and all.

As Ed tried to focus on the atrocious text of Fannie's story, *The Story of A Mall Girl*, Fannie committed Ed's biggest web peeve, the concurrent running of animation, video and audio. She had e-commerce links to sell her book (those worked) and its related merchandise (coffee mugs and mouse pads, primarily).

The reality of Fannie's success disappointed Ed, but didn't surprise her. After an introduction like that, Ed expected a protégé or a design whiz, perhaps the next Milton Glaser, David Carson, Gail Anderson, or Paula Scher. She should have known Fannie was another victim of the entitlement generation.

Ed feared Fannie's bubble might pop during the first student critique. Fannie stood in the classroom regal as a queen, shoulders back, head high and breasts jutting toward the males in the room as if her too-tight, too-low tee-shirts didn't advertise enough of the goods. Those had to be fake, Ed thought. Further evidence of a poorly thought out "I want…" from Daddy's pocketbook. The girl stood five-foot-ten and if she weighed 120 pounds, even with the tits, Ed would eat a hat.

She had the glossy blond hair, the vapid smile and the tendency to pose like a model but she showed more of her midriff and cleavage than appropriate for the classroom. Fannie could barely cover her fanny with the strap of fabric she often wore as a skirt. Ed had to remind herself not to shake her head disapprovingly when she stumbled around on her ridiculously-tall red patent leather platform stiletto pumps while balancing a portfolio of her so-called art.

The imaginary restaurant menu on the overhead projector lived up to the poor expectations Ed had developed for the girl. Ed kept rehearsing her standard "I know you're disappointed, but think of this as a building block" speech.

When the class really got a look at Fannie's project, a heavy gasp flooded the room. Fannie puffed with pride, interpreting the reaction as took it as confirmation of her fabulousness.

While her peers struggled to list politely the multitude of design sins, the criticism slid off her like fried egg against Teflon. While the other students grew stronger, Fannie somehow grew weaker. The girl existed in a parallel universe.

No matter how much Ed goaded, critiqued, coddled, or blatantly told Fannie the answer, Fannie had a nice solid "F" and must have believed it stood for "Fabulous." Ed worried about the ramifications of failing Fannie. The course was required for all design majors.

If Fannie failed, Ed had to teach her again next year. So, Ed designed a newspaper project. She told the class it was their capstone project. She presented them with a detailed list of what exactly to do, to facilitate the production of a newspaper according to industry standards. Ed acted like a helicopter teacher. She watched Fannie's every move to make sure she hit every possible item needed to pass. By the time Fannie finished, it looked bland and boring, which was a huge improvement over gaudy. Fannie passed.

If all students, or even half of them, behaved like Fannie, Ed would have to give up teaching before she scarred someone—emotionally or physically. What made the down-to-earth, polite girls like Olive, Genny, and those in her Girl Scout troop the anomaly instead of the norm?

Maybe because they didn't have what psychological and educational experts now termed "Helicopter parents." Some parents micro-managed every aspect of their children's lives. These children didn't have to learn through experience (good or bad) or even fight their own battles. The parenting strategy here balanced on listening to the child and catering to every single "I want…" It didn't matter whether that demand revolved around a toy, a meal, a certain college or a job.

Add this to the other major defect of the current crop of students. This group had grown up with computers, technology and other electronic advances that could spark their minds into limitless possibilities. Instead, those modern conveniences had obliterated their attention spans, destroyed their verbal skills, and, like Ed's experience with Internet dating, reduced their written communication to the lingo and vowel-less construction of a text message.

With spell-check a mere click away, few of them attempted to spell correctly. Then, they never remembered to spell-check. When they did remember, they selected homophones for the words they wanted or even words that had similar spellings, like "aria" for "area."

Barely literate students, three-hour design labs where students surfed the 'net instead of working, watching YouTube videos instead of listening to lectures…

Why did they even bother to come to school if they didn't want to learn? Ed had paid for and earned each of her degrees, in a variety of traditional and non-traditional programs, so she had a respect for education that these children didn't understand, let alone value.

Tonight proved no exception to the mediocrity of the student body, though Ed supposed she might be grumpy and venting inappropriately. She doubted it. As Ed lectured and demonstrated that lesson's Adobe Illustrator capability, they scanned MySpace and Facebook, checked email and some even played free online video games.

She almost locked the computers, even if just to prove a point, but then she'd never get them to work. It troubled her enough to explain why they got D's now, let alone if she limited their time on the computer. Another day, another critique, another creative and polite way to tell a kid a project stinks…

A teacher must remain constructive in their comments and fair in grading. Even negative comments must convey something the student would find positive, like "I can see you tried really hard and put in the time necessary, but you must master the concept of a single prominent element, even in a collage." Of course, in that example, you had to hope the kid did design a collage and not just made a mess of his project.

Oh, how Ed yearned lay it out directly. She could be the Simon Cowell of graphic design. Except teachers who caused controversy were fired, whereas Simon got a TV show and a cult following.

As her semi-attentive class at least pretended to work on the mini-exercises from their textbook, Ed's computer pinged. An email alert, she thought to herself. With the kids working, and judging from the movement of each mouse that they might really be using Photoshop and not Firefox, she could sneak into her email for a minute.

She ignored five messages from Celeste. None were important. The subject lines revealed as much: "Oreos," "What if he walks in on them," "They're not listening to me," "How do you spell atenolol," and "Nicolas Sarkozy is dating Carla Bruni." Celeste really needed to disconnect from her laptop more often during the day.

She scanned the list until she saw a familiar name that sparked her interest: Genny Anderson. Subject: "I need your help!"

Ed wondered if she should be concerned. Exclamation points rarely meant good news. That's a lie. The announcement, via email of course, of Celeste's last book deal had about eight thousand of them. Ed opened the email from Genny.

"Hi, Ed. I really need help. I'm at school and I've been working with the 4-H group on campus," the email began.

Ed snickered with the naturalness of Genny leading 4-H and relaxed as she read the rest of the email.

"Well, my 4-Hers work with the kids from Newark…those of us in animal science work with the animal club. The kids have done extraordinarily well taking care of the animals and they are flourishing, mating away, and now we've had a population explosion of bunnies, hamsters, and Guinea pigs, even some reptiles.

The kids decided to have an adoption fair. But the campus doesn't have a graphic design club, so I was wondering if you could help. I know you're really busy, so I thought maybe you could give it to your students for a design project. Let me know, what you think. I can email you the details, or you can call my dorm."

Gen might have solved one of Ed's classic problems—how to motivate her students. Maybe Genny's project would interest them and teach them to think less selfishly.

"In class now," she replied. "Send details quickly and I can pull the global warming poster for your project. If you have pictures of the 4-H'ers with the animals that would be great. Highest resolution if you can, so mail me a CD."

Ed had the specifics in twenty minutes and a compact disc arrived in the mail within two days. Genny must have anticipated Ed's response, and known it would be affirmative.

Genny may have been prepared for the project, but Ed wasn't. As soon as her students started worked, Ed couldn't believe the enthusiasm and the professionalism they displayed. Ed rubbed her eyes to verify she wasn't imagining this or that she hadn't walked into the wrong classroom.

Ed couldn't say what did it, maybe the cute animals, the inner-city kids, or maybe the theme. Her slacker students really rose to the occasion...most of them anyway. Everyone participated in the critique. One student even brought animal crackers as a snack. The projects soared above their previous works.

Ed sent five PDFs to Genny, the five strongest from the class. Genny chose Ed's favorite—the creation of Jessica, Ed's best student who had needed to break out of her shell and steal some of Fannie's self-confidence in order to turn innate talent into design gold.

Jessica had modeled her poster after the cover of a comic book, with animals and teenagers playing together, not always in the most realistic of circumstances. Ever see a leopard gecko with a baseball mitt? A kitten and a little girl baking chocolate chip cookies?

It would reach the target audience. Any small child who wanted a pet—and many who probably never thought about it—would push, pull and/or drag their parents to the 4-H Adoption Fair and "Be A Hero" as the poster proclaimed.

Once Ed called in a few professional favors, she had a pile of professionally printed posters shipped to Genny at University of Delaware. Ed kept one for her home office, one for the department head at the community college for the local advertising awards (student division) and one for Jessica. Hanging on her wall, the sunlight from the bay window lighting it, the poster in full CMYK popped with brilliant primary colors reminiscent of an old Superman cover in red, yellow and blue.

Apparently, the posters stirred quite the buzz in the community. Ed saw 60-second previews on the Philadelphia evening news. Genny forwarded Internet links to articles in the *Newark Post*, *The News Journal* in Wilmington and the region's Spanish language paper *El Latino*. Genny sent more daily.

Then, Ed did something less than rational; she promised Genny she'd drive to Newark for the actual event. Since the Brandywine Valley area of Delaware has a reputation for spectacular gardens, Ed would combine the trip with a visit to Winterthur, one of the best.

Besides, Aretha loved a road trip and the turnpike ranked as her favorite highway. Aretha loved tunnels.

The day arrived and Ed had Aretha gassed and ready to go. The first hour passed uneventfully, but as she reached the suburbs of Philadelphia an electronic road side announced a change in her luck. "Traffic warning." Ed switched from compact disc to AM station 1620.

"Figures, happens every time," Ed muttered. She intoned her best game show host voice. "Now it's time to play another exciting game of highway roulette. Which road today—the Blue Route? the Sure-kill? or I-95?"

She increased the volume.

"My money's on I-95," she said.

"Now for your traffic update," the generic male voice said. "Interstate 95 is backed up south bound from the Schuylkill Expressway to the 495 bypass in Wilmington."

"BINGO!" Ed yelled at the radio.

She plotted her alternate route in her head: Route 1, to 202, then to 95. She entertained the thought of stopping at Longwood Gardens and Chadd's Ford Winery. Briefly, she considered using the traffic as an excuse and exiting route 1 at 52 and going straight to Winterthur.

Ed didn't. She couldn't disappoint Genny like that. She went right to the Christiana Mall, the site of the Newark area 4H adoption fair in front of JCPenney.

"Ed, you came!" Genny exclaimed as Ed crossed the mall concourse. "I thought you'd bet stuck in traffic and go home."

"Despite visions of Longwood Gardens dancing in my head, I made it. My mother raised me wrong. When you make a commitment, you keep that commitment."

"Sounds like Dad. He's here, you know," she said off-handedly. "Come meet the kids."

Clint? here? Ed followed Genny toward the tables, nicely arranged in a U. Why didn't Genny tell me Clint would be here? Thank goodness I took the time to put my hair in a French braid. Is this a set-up? Genny wouldn't set me up. But Hannah would… Did Hannah get Genny's email? Oh, God, what did I wear?

She looked down to her A-line chino skirt. That set her mind at ease. At least she had on a nice V-neck sweater and her knee length skirt. She had even worn her good Berkinstocks, the ones with the floral on the leather strap.

"This is Harvey," Genny said, pointing to a tow-headed boy. "He has a way with rabbits."

Ed nearly tripped over an elaborate cage with

multi-colored plastic tubing jutting from it. A hamster ran in a wheel inside. Outside, a guinea pig darted across the floor in a red plastic sphere the size of a volleyball.

"Be careful," Genny said. "The hamster is Midge. Short for Midget. The guinea pig is Momma."

The kids wore blue University of Delaware polo shirts with the 4H clover logo embroidered on the left side and jeans. Several gathered behind the table, clutching pamphlets and offering passersby vivid smiles. They accosted every individual and made sure each received some literature. Other 4H kids worked the crowd. The college volunteers worked just as hard. Everyone who wanted to had a chance to hold the animal of their choice.

Even after an hour amidst the commotion, Ed hadn't noticed Clint. She relaxed. Somehow, she

gained a station at the reptile tanks, but she refused to touch any snakes. She gave out lots of brochures about pet care, but always reneged to a more experienced 4Her if someone wanted to hold the snake.

Then, for some inexplicable reason, Ed witnessed a run on hamsters. Children and parents mobbed the area, each family clamoring for a rodent. The club had done an impressive job not only promoting the event, but also securing supplies from merchants at cost so the profits would support 4H in the future. Reasonable prices on equipment coupled with the free animals meant when the creatures did find a home, at least the new owners have the right tools for responsible pet ownership. Each hamster's starter kit came with business cards promoting the stores that participated.

Ed didn't have time to read what businesses, because she earned a spot on the starter kit assembly line. They packed the kits by the dozen, everything but the hamster: cage, wheel, bedding, water bottle, care pamphlets, food dish, and food. In the midst of the second set, a voice interrupted her production.

"Ed? Ed, is that you?"

Ed pivoted, dropping a water bottle into the cage. For plastic on plastic, it made an incredible clang. There stood Clint, hair nicely trimmed in a fresh haircut, close-shaven and crisp in his green 4H tee-shirt and jeans, iPhone peeking from his pocket in its leather case. Faded work gloves dangled from his back pocket. He carried an ancient canvas tote, straight out of LL Bean, except for the patches holding it together.

"When did you enroll at Delaware?" Clint said.

Ed chuckled. "I didn't. Genny invited me. I couldn't say no."

"Wow," Clint said with a smile. "And I thought I

was the only one susceptible to her charms… Either of my girls can manipulate me with a simple 'but Daddy, I need you.' And I'm there. Especially if they use the quiet despondent voice."

"I've seen it in my family," Ed said.

"It's payback," Clint said. "Mom puts in nine months and one horrendous day, and dad spends a lifetime at their beck and call."

He paused.

"But what happens when one day they don't need me anymore?"

"Never happen," Ed said. "A little girl always needs her daddy. Especially at the age of your girls. The world gets pretty scary then."

"Don't let me keep you from your hamsters," Clint said.

Ed gazed at the table. The other workers had stacked up five cages behind the one she had her hand in. She had caused a bottleneck in the line.

"Will you be here all day?" Ed asked.

"I'm doing workshops every hour on not leaving your pets loose into the wild. What will happen to them if they aren't fed and cared for. What happens to them when a garbage truck rolls them over. What happens when you let them swim in the bathtub."

"Hey, guys," Genny said with an odd smirk.

"Geneva," Clint said.

"Ed, I need another favor," Genny said as the smirk progressed into a full smile.

"Geneva Anna Anderson, you made Ed drive a long way—"

Uh-oh, Ed thought, he used her full name. Had Ed's presence caused trouble in the Anderson family? Genny, in a bold move, interrupted her father.

"My dad has his last workshop at one," she said. "I'll

be busy here until three. Do you think you could take him out for a late lunch?"

Genny pulled a crumpled twenty out of her pocket.

"You both deserve a little something for your time and trouble."

So it was a set-up, Ed realized.

"You should have thought of Ed's time and trouble before you made her come here," Clint snapped.

"I did," Genny replied. "You're interested in Ed. Ed's interested in you. I figured this far away from home, you wouldn't have a choice."

She pressed the twenty into Ed's palm.

"Enjoy your lunch," Genny said as she turned toward the fish tank.

"Geneva!" Clint exclaimed.

She looked back at them.

"Olive and I decided this would be the perfect opportunity to get you together."

Before Clint had time to reply, Genny's phone rang.

"Matchmaker, matchmaker make me a match, find me a find, catch me a…"

Clint turned beet red. Ed didn't know him well enough to label it as anger or embarrassment.

"Dad," Genny said, covering the mouthpiece of her phone with her hand. "Olive wants to talk to you."

"And I'd like to talk to Olive," he said, snatching the phone. "I don't think I like what's going on here."

He looked to Ed before he answered the call.

"I'm sorry about this," he said.

"No reason to apologize," she said.

She returned to her work on the hamster cages, smiling and humming show tunes.

EIGHT

As soon as Clint took Genny deep into JCPenney, Ed recognized that the well-meaning young woman would get a stern lecture for her efforts at match-making. At least Clint had the manners not to chastise her in front of the 4H members and other college kids.

In her head, Ed imagined the whole conversation and she added some melodramatic music for emphasis.

Maybe Clint would start with a predictable line.

"Genny, I don't need you interfering in my personal life."

And she would reply with another classic.

"But Daddy," as she batted her eyelashes, "I don't want you to be alone."

Cue: "Someone to watch over me."

Meanwhile, Ed had to admit she hated that the plan backfired. Okay, hated might be harsh, but she couldn't hide her disappointment. She had day-dreamed about a date with Clint, a real date, and an impromptu lunch might break the ice enough for her to ask.

A girl her age should be able to muster the guts to invite an eligible man to a movie or a dinner. A girl her age, who had witnessed Martha's bra-burnings and unorthodox relationships, should not sit around waiting for a man to ask her.

Mama must be rolling in her grave at the thought.

Ed sighed. She'd never have the courage to do it.

As she waited for Genny to emerge from the white tile path through women's apparel in the department store, Ed took some photos. Heck, if her editor had one of those slow news weeks, she might run one as a local-girl-done-good-at-college stand-alone.

Of course, Genny wasn't in the photo, so maybe not. It provided a good distraction and a potential purpose, regardless. She wanted to leave. But, once again, Mama's good breeding stood in the way. She couldn't leave without saying goodbye.

When she tired with photography, Ed helped the 4H kids pack some of the remaining pamphlets into boxes. Still no Genny. Fifteen minutes passed, each few seconds lasting an eternity. Genny or no, Ed had to leave. She reached into her pocket for her keys and found nothing but the twenty-dollar bill from Genny. Her shoulders fell. Now, she really couldn't leave. She couldn't keep the girl's money.

How could she amuse herself? Ed's eyes lit up as a smirk crossed her face.

The Apple Store.

She could always kill time in the Apple Store. What respectable graphic artist couldn't? They had just opened one in the mall, and Hannah and Celeste nicknamed it Mecca. With Celeste's previous experience in newspapers and Hannah's expertise in marketing with her addiction to using iMovie to edit home footage of her sons, they had both caught the Mac bug. Mac people took their computers seriously... PC people couldn't understand.

Sure, some PC people took their computers apart, some networked, some built mega-computers with multiple hard drives and triple back-ups... But Mac people just enjoyed using their computers. PC people who liked their computers always seemed to be forcing the machine to do something it didn't want to do.

Yeah, heading to the Apple Store meant a religious experience, even if Ed didn't have money to spend.

Ed turned toward the corridor that would lead to her destination when she heard her name. She pivoted. Clint and Genny had returned.

"Where are you going?" he asked.

"Apple."

"Are you coming back?"

Ed paused.

"Yeah, I need to return this money."

She reached her hand in her pocket and pulled out the twenty.

"Actually, here," Ed said as she thrust her arm toward him. "You can return it."

He didn't accept the money. Clint left her hand dangling there. He shifted his weight.

"I kind of made a deal with Genny," he said.

He didn't look at her.

"A deal?" Ed repeated.

"A compromise," he said, slowly raising his head. "That's what life is all about, right?"

"Does it involve me?" Ed asked.

"It does," Clint said. "We'll have lunch and my lovely daughters will not set me up on dates. Ever."

"Sounds like I'm a consolation prize."

"It's not you. It's the principle. What do you say?"

Ed pondered. Clint must have seen the discomfort in her face.

"Honestly, I would have been happy to have lunch with you anyway. I just don't approve of their tactics."

"You're just saying that."

"Look, I have my talk in a few minutes. I can meet you about 1:45, in front of Sbarro."

"I don't know," Ed replied.

Are you nuts? Ed screamed at herself. You'll take lunch, dinner, sex... whatever he's offering.

"It's your call."

He started to walk away, but stopped. He turned and looked at her rather sheepishly.

"I hope you'll stay."

Her heart fluttered. She was pretty sure she blushed. Good grief, she said to herself, she was such a mess.

He began walking again, and, again, he froze.

"And Ed..."

"Yes?"

She hoped she didn't sound half as eager as she feared she did.

"Gen's twenty. May I have it?"

"Sure."

She approached him and gave him the bill. As the paper exchanged hands, she wondered why a grown man would take his daughter's twenty dollars. He laughed, a quiet, subdued chuckle that really didn't qualify as a laugh.

"I will not have my daughter paying for my lunch date."

Clint finally left. Ed headed for a nearby bench. She furrowed her brow. She sat. Did he want to spend time with her or didn't he? What would Martha say? Ed knew the answer to that: No man was worth it. Whatever it was,

Martha would say no man was worth it. Celeste would invent some tale of woe to explain why he gave Ed such mixed signals. And Hannah—Hannah would say that at her age, Ed couldn't be too choosy. Ed retrieved her cell phone and considered dialing one of the three. She didn't. She resumed her path to the Apple Store.

MacBook Air... enough said.

Even the eerily thin laptop didn't settle Ed's mind. Ed couldn't believe that a thirty-inch flat panel cinema display did not distract her. As she stared, eyes brimming with lust, at the iPhones, she kept thinking of her impending lunch date. Surrounded by software, iPods, peripherals and hardware, Ed couldn't move past the boredom.

She tried the bookstore. She walked through the cookbooks. She was fat; a new cookbook would only get her into trouble. She flipped through some pages of a quilt book, finding the same old, same old. She perused the titles in the craft section, sought out Celeste's latest novel, and even checked the new age heading. Nothing helped.

She ducked back into the inside of the mall. She walked laps, letting her mind drift completely out of focus and into the zone where only the paces mattered. She could use the exercise. The weaving in and out of people gave her direction, and prevented monotony from seeping into it.

When she arrived at the Sbarro at 1:46, after three laps of the mega-mall, she couldn't spot Clint. She stood with her hands on her hips outside the mock fence. She scanned the crowd, and seeing no sign of Clint, Ed planned to bolt.

"Oh, Ed," a relieved masculine voice said as he cut through a group of teen girls in identical baby-tees and low-rise jeans. "I'm sorry I'm late."

Wow, did she suddenly feel light, Ed thought. He didn't stand her up.

"Only a minute or two," she said.

He set his hand against her back, a reassuring gesture that implied both closeness and distance. Clint's eyes jumped from person-to-person in the mall.

"I'd hate to lose you in this crowd," he joked.

Lose me? Hello? Amid these skeletal teenyboppers I stick out like a sore thumb, Ed thought.

"Anyway," Clint said, lowering his hand to his side. "The last batch of kids had tons of questions. I finally had to tell them it was time to go."

The food court, behind another cheesy fence, had the typical arrangement of small tables that leaned unstably and a few cocktail style tables with high stools. Only a few of the sea of napkin-strewn table-tops had occupants.

"Do we need to see the maitre d' for the best table?" Ed asked.

Clint smiled. Ed patted herself on the back. She could never think of anything witty. Yet, she just had.

"Maybe if I slip him Gen's twenty, he'll find us a clean one," Clint replied.

Despite the successful humor, emptiness replaced their conversation. Ed pushed her Birkenstock across the dirty floor.

"What are you hungry for? We got the usual food-court cast of characters: Starbuck's, pizza, Subway, Chinese, Arby's —"

"Oh, God, no!" Ed interrupted.

"Not a Arby's fan?" Clint snickered. "Okay that's one point in your favor."

"I don't like my meat pink and cold." Ed replied. "There's a salad place over there".

"You dieting?"

He said it with distaste. It was almost as if he tried not to, but failed. Subtle, it was definitely distaste.

"Does that cancel out the Arby's point?" Ed asked.

"I just… You didn't seem…"

"I'm trying to eat better. My blood pressure's a mess and I don't need to get fatter."

"You're not fat," Clint commented.

"It's a relative term," Ed said. "You don't have to be polite. The doctor says it. I can say it. I'm overweight. I walk three miles a day but that's not enough."

"So, can I buy you a salad?" he said apologetically.

She tapped the side of her purse.

"I don't need your daughter to buy my lunch, either," she answered.

"I'd like to," he insisted. "Maybe I'll join you at… Saladworks? Saladworks, it is."

Ed looked at the booth and the sign extended from the wall with the triple carrot logo in a black square, their heads poking up as if planted in soil, with the word "saladworks" in white stylized type Ed didn't recognize.

"Cute design," Ed said, pointing. "I don't know that typeface."

"You can't even look at a sign without analyzing the design?" Clint remarked.

"No, or movie and TV titles. Signs are the worst. Sometimes I won't go into a store because their signs are so bad."

"Do they have a 12-step program for that?"

"Maybe. People who really like me don't care. They think it's an eccentric quirk. Celeste is just as bad."

"Celeste dissects signs?"

"No. She dissects the words while I dissect the design. Road trips with us are a gas. Especially if we find backwards apostrophes. Then we both go nuts."

He didn't answer. She stood closer to the glass covered display of signature salads, each complete with goofy names that conveyed nothing. Like the Bently, it looked like a chef's salad to her, but apparently adding provolone to it gave it the need for a strange nomenclature. As for fire-roasted fiesta, she didn't want a salad that sounded like a party. The ingredients list included tri-color tortilla strips, fire-roasted corn, and black beans that offered "the exciting colors of Mexico." Ed preferred to keep life, especially food, simple.

"The panini sandwiches look good," Clint said. "What are you looking at? Any of those lettuce piles turn you on?"

"I'm not sure. They have a build your own, but I'm always afraid I'll make an expensive mistake," Ed said. "Then I feel bad when I throw it way."

"So your mother gave you the starving children in Africa line, too."

"India."

"Ah," he said.

"If you want a sandwich, we can go to Subway. They have salad, too."

"I'm thinking a little less bread," he replied. "And there's a one thousand calorie bacon-laden artery-clogger calling my name, right there."

He shot his arm triumphantly toward the "Smokey T," an overpriced turkey sandwich with bacon, cheddar and a mustard Saladworks referred to as "zingy."

"That's one thousand calories?" she said with a gasp.

"And twenty grams of saturated fat," he added proudly.

"Clint! That will kill you."

"You never struck me as the food police," he countered.

She exhaled.

"I'm not," Ed replied. "I didn't get this fat eating

carrots and celery. It's just that's a lot of calories for one sandwich."

"It's the bacon and the cheese," Clint explained. "But I never eat bacon at home, I swear. Besides, I'm very active. I chase and ferry animals all day long. I've never even seen a desk. Moreover, when I'm not working, I'm helping tend the farm. Really, farmers don't die of high cholesterol."

"I hope you're right," Ed said.

"I'm glad you'd like to keep me around," he responded. "What about you?"

"As good as that looks, I have seen a desk," Ed said. "And sometimes I sit at it for fifteen hours a day. No thousand calorie sandwiches for me."

"So you're going for the 700 calorie salad."

"I hate that they're putting nutrition labels on fast food," Ed quipped. "It used to be a guilty pleasure. You knew that it was bad for you. Now they put the facts in your face in black and white."

"I believe they call it making a informed choice," Clint said.

"If I want to be informed, I'll go to the library," she remarked.

The woman behind the counter skirted her way toward them. Clint did indeed order the Smokey T, while Ed carefully selected the Newport, with tuna, tomatoes, shrimp, hard-boiled eggs and black olives. She opted for the honey mustard dressing and requested all romaine lettuce instead of any iceberg.

"The salad puts me at 190, the dressing an additional 45, that's shy of 250," Ed said as she calculated. "I'd love to have the blue cheese, but that's almost as much as the salad itself. The oriental sesame might do, but that's a whole 90. Nope, honey mustard will be fine."

"Do you always talk calories?"

"Never," she admitted.

The server collected their meals and placed them on the red tray textured to resemble a weave.

"Then why today?"

"I'm nervous," Ed said. "When I'm nervous I chatter. Sorry. I'll shut up now."

"Why are you nervous?" Clint asked as he accepted the tray. "Shoot! I almost forgot drinks."

He put the tray on the counter and pulled more money from his wallet. Ed set her hand on his wrist to stop him.

"I'll pay for the drinks."

Clint nodded.

"Coke or diet?" he asked, motioning to the girl who stood at the ready with the lined paper cups tipped toward the soda fountain.

"Neither," Ed responded.

The word just popped out. Ed smiled. Had she licked her Coca Cola habit? This was a moment of stress and she had not accepted use of her crutch. She turned to the girl.

"Anything non-carbonated is fine."

The girl poured her lemonade. Ed paid her and took the drinks. Clint carried the tray. They stepped from the raised walkway into the sunken seating area.

"So, why are you nervous?" Clint asked again.

"This is a pseudo-date," she said. "You were forced into it and I want you to have a good time."

"Don't mention any more calories and lunch will be fine."

"Deal."

Ed walked ahead, set the beverages down, and cleared the extra napkins from the table after she used one to wipe the crumbs and the stickiness from the surface. She hung her handbag over the chair.

"Where are your bags? Did you take them to the car?" Clint inquired.

"Bags?" Ed repeated.

"Shopping bags."

"Oh, don't have any," she answered. "Didn't buy anything."

"Not even at the Apple Store? But you're a graphic designer."

"I don't have money to waste," she said as she lifted her plastic fork. "And I'm not much of a shopper."

"My girls are," he replied.

He picked up one-half of the panini and nibbled a corner before continuing.

"I was so happy when the girls were old enough to drive and could go shopping themselves."

Ed nodded as she pushed her greens around her salad bowl. She couldn't eat. She didn't feel hungry, just jittery, the kind of jittery where she fought nausea. Which was silly and she knew it. She ate the shrimp, because you could not waste shrimp. If she went to the bathroom, she probably would vomit.

Wouldn't that make an impression? Excuse me, Clint, I need to throw up. No, no, I don't have an eating disorder. I just haven't dated in a decade.

Meanwhile, this cute little food moan escaped from Clint's mouth every time he took a bite of his super sandwich. After each chomp, he licked his lips. It was just like the hot chocolate, but less sensual. The man had bacon hanging from his mouth.

"Good?" she finally said.

His eyes got big and he nodded.

"Even better than you can imagine," he said in what she could only classify as a bedroom voice.

She pulled a sliver of tuna toward her mouth, but the smell turned her stomach.

"Something wrong with your salad?" he asked.

"No. No, it's fine," she said. "It's good. It's... healthy."

"That bad?"

Ed laughed, so much that the butterflies in her stomach zoomed free. As soon as she consciously realized it, she held her hand over her mouth and stifled her commotion.

"Sorry."

"Happy to make you laugh."

Ed couldn't think of anything to say. She hoped to steer the conversation away from food.

"You're going to have a busy summer."

"How's that?" he asked. "You're not releasing skunks in the 'hood are you?"

She chuckled.

"No," she replied. "I was thinking two graduations and the fundraiser."

"That's nothing. We're headed straight into the busy season , so those events will be pleasant distractions," he answered. "I'm more afraid of being left short-handed."

"Why's that?"

"Ed, I really don't want to talk business."

And he went back to his sandwich.

She ate her salad and didn't speak. With the business off the table, what did they have to talk about? Nothing.

"Ed?"

"Yes?"

"Are you done? I'll take the trays."

She piled her garbage into the near-full plastic dish.

"I can take my own..." she hesitated.

Let the man take the tray. She handed it to him.

"Thank you."

They went home. Separately, of course.

NINE

Any idiot can throw his/her cans, bottles and news-paper into a bucket for weekly collection. Ed took recycling further. She stood in her garage, so full of recyclables that Aretha hadn't seen the inside of it in months.

It must mean the end of the semester. She'd finished her lectures, waited for the students' final projects, completed a month's worth of annual reports for her volunteer work, and designed a boat-load of invitations. That meant she finally had the time to tackle the garage. She had piles of news-papers, bags and bags of cans, discarded electronics and a drum of batteries. Ed used rechargeable batteries.

Like most of the items it her garage, they came from neighbors.

Every elderly person in the neighborhood saved recycling for Ed. Every family collected batteries from their children's toys. Outside the garage, brown bags of yard waste, from trimmings to the removed mulberry trees, leaned against the wall waiting for their trip to the compost center.

In Aretha, this would require at least four trips: one trip to the city's recycling center for paper, cardboard, and for plastic; then one to the composting center for the yard waste; another circuit to take Tootie's beer cans to the salvage yard (at least she'd get money for that one); and finally the municipal electronics collection at the pool.

Next week, she'd have this cleaned enough to take the miscellaneous items from dad's workshop to the county biannual hazmat collection.

To make it more manageable, Ed decided she'd start with the newspapers and other household recyclables. If that went well, she might even wait until tomorrow for the yard waste and continue the process daily until everything disappeared. As an added bonus, removing the newspapers, plastic and cardboard should open enough space for Aretha. She pulled Aretha into the alley, opened the garage door, and loaded.

As she piled paper into the car, Ed realized that since she took her classes "paperless" she had generated a lot more paper. She wondered how that was that possible. The election mail for the primaries didn't help either. If the candidates spent as much time and effort on the office once they won it, the world would be a better place. In the last few weeks, most of Ed's mail didn't even make it into the house. It ended up going from mailbox to recycle bin.

It took a mere twenty minutes to fill Aretha. Inside the cabin, there was only enough room for Ed. She'd tied the trunk closed with a bungee cord. She arrived at the recycling center as they opened and eased right into a prime parking spot, between the newspaper and mixed office paper sheds.

Still amazed by her lucky parking space, Ed set to work hauling the piles into the center and back again. That's why she didn't really pay any attention to the Ford pick-up beside her. She grabbed the next crate of paper. She partially lowered the trunk lid, using it to hide herself as she stared at the truck and its occupant.

"Is that Clint's truck?" she thought.

She breathed a sigh of relief that she had just emptied the backseat and didn't have her ass hanging out of the car. A man hopped out of the truck. Ed froze, waiting. The man went to the paper bins. Then, he turned. He walked toward her. There was no denying it.

It was Clint. Ed hoped he wouldn't notice her. She slammed Aretha's shut. Clint returned to his truck, on the driver's side, and Ed used the chance to slip between their cars into the building. She made it inside and dumped the crate into the paper container. When she had nearly finished and righted her crate, someone walked up behind her.

"Ed?"

So, Clint had spotted her. Ed turned.

"Hi," she said. "Recycling day at your house too?"

"Mr. Hooper's place. I don't think he's thrown anything away in seventy years," Clint answered.

"That must be quite the load," she remarked.

"Yeah, I'll be here awhile," he said. "I've got fifty years of newspapers alone."

"I could help," she offered.

"You've got your own work," Clint said, dumping several bundles of *The Globe Times* into the bin.

"I'm nearly finished," Ed insisted. Liar, Ed thought. Then she gave herself a mental pat on the back for closing the trunk.

"If you've got the time, I could use the help.

Someone needs to go to shredding shed. I've got bank records that I promised Mr. Hopper I'd have them shredded."

"Go ahead," Ed said, as they started to the cars. "I'll deal with the paper."

Clint headed toward the shredder and Ed grabbed her first box from the mountain of paper. Ed had made about fifteen trips by the time Clint returned, not a surprise since the shredder usually had a line and Clint had a serious shredding order. Her arms ached dully from the extra work, but it felt good. Ed never shied away from a laborious job. The challenge and the satisfaction of meeting it pleased her.

They took one load silently, side by side, approaching the bins. They dumped everything, and Ed led the way. She climbed into the truck and passed Clint a box. Then she pushed another to the end of the bed, hopped free, and carried it to the shed. The last cycle, Clint stopped her from taking the final box.

"I really appreciate this," Clint said. "I would have been here all day."

"No problem," Ed replied. "I can always use the exercise."

He took the box inside as Ed walked to her car. He followed her.

"Ed," he beckoned. "I'm relieved you're still willing to talk to me."

Ed stood with the car door open, her arms over the top, her body wedged toward the cabin.

"Why wouldn't I?" she asked.

"The stunt my daughters pulled at the mall," he said.

"Clint, you weren't too hard on the girls were you?" Ed asked. "They love you and want to see you happy."

"I thought their match-making days ended in high

school, but I guess I was wrong," he said. "Do you know how many times they begged me to meet a single mom they liked. It never worked. Women at that point of life are looking for doctors or businessmen or something that pays well, at least. I got nothing but some land, a drafty farmhouse, some stinky animals and a riveting career as a trapper."

"Not all of us want material things, Clint," she said. "When people want those things, it's usually to mask some other hurt. I don't know. You've got an incredible family and a job you like. And your girls are amazing."

"That reminds me, I told them not to bother you for free design work."

"I'm a big girl, Clint," Ed said, slightly defensive and pissed at herself for the pun. "I can tell them no if it's a problem. I want to help, and when the ranch opens, I want to be the first official volunteer."

"I think you already are," he said. "And I can't quite get why you do it."

His voice had fallen to a hush. You can't? Ed thought. Isn't it obvious? I do it because they're great girls. They're great girls because of you. And every time I see them, I'm reminded of you.

I've spent more than one night dreaming about you, waking up with insatiable desire, saturated between my legs, wishing I could mount you but knowing you're not there, so I quiet the heat when I can with cold showers. I'm embarrassed to say how many times I'm gone to bed with freshly-charged batteries on the nightstand because I can't make it through the night like that…

Ed noticed the familiar dampness in her panties. She adjusted her legs to embrace it.

"Well, then you better get brainstorming," Clint

said. "Because if I tell Olive we had this conversation, she'll be calling you tonight to ask for help with the black-tie gala she has planned this summer. Her first major fundraiser."

"The first of many," Ed remarked.

"Can you see me in a tux?" Clint questioned her.

"I think you'll look mighty fine."

She pictured him in a white tuxedo shirt and a black bow tie draped on top of the ribbed slats. She imagined removing it, and going on to unbutton the shirt...

"Ed, you sure are good for a man's ego," he said.

He glanced at his watch.

"I got to run," he said.

Clint waved and disappeared. Ed remembered as Clint drove away that she still needed to unload the rest of her recycling, alone. Trudging back and forth to the bins, she daydreamed about Clint in his imaginary tuxedo. Bow tie? Ascot? Cummerbund? Vest? Straight cut? Tails?

Finally, she got into Aretha, her job finished. By that point, she had developed the image completely. She reclined the seat to allow herself to rest before riding home, and caught a glance of the caretaker's shed.

If Clint were still here would he have taken the time to thank her with a kiss? Maybe he'd pull her into the shed. In her car, Ed leaned her head against the seat. She closed her eyes and wondered what it would feel like, what would happen if they did sneak away from everything, from the girls, from her crazy house... Yes, what could happen in a shed on municipal property?

She could imagine Clint's hands against her sides as he pushed her against the wall, greedily tossing her tee-shirt aside and ripping off her bra, releasing her breasts. With one in his hand and the one in his mouth, the anticipation flickered through her. His mouth moved against her with the hunger of a newborn. It rocked her, as his other hand explored the curves and folds of her torso. With each touch of finger or tongue against her body, the longing intensified and she wanted to drop her remaining clothes and offer herself to him. A layer of sweat glistened against her skin.

Finally, in her fantasy, he reached her shorts, opening them and dropping them to the floor. With his hand at her hips he went for her panties. He pulled the elastic low enough so he could reach inside, his fingers prodding her wetness. As his fingers teased and manipulated her, his mouth released from her breast, then leaned in again to consume the nipple, and he lapped across the flesh.

Ed moaned. She kept imagining. Her hips bucked against his hand. Clint kissed his way up the mound of her breast, across her chest to her clavicle, before delving into her mouth. His hands fell away from her. Her panties rolled back across her abdomen as emptiness and stillness fell between her legs. Then, his tongue penetrated her mouth. Her tongue responded, meeting it and coming alive in this taunting game that she hadn't played for a decade.

The movie in Ed's brain didn't stop there. Clint planted a hand against each hip so he could slide her panties down, cupping and stroking her ample bottom. She undid his belt and his zipper, so that his shorts dropped revealing his boxers. She didn't give him a chance to remove them, instead reaching inside the slat front to urge him out. With her spine still against the wall, Clint seized her hips and lifted her. Her legs opened, then wrapped around his waist. His girth filled her in a way she'd never known and she screamed in ecstasy.

And then a pounding… What the hell was that? That noise wasn't part of her fantasy.

A knock repeated on her car window.

Her car.

Alone.

Just her and Aretha.

"Hey lady, you okay? Is something wrong?" the caretaker asked. "I could hear you screaming from the shed."

"Sorry," Ed said, floundering for some explanation. "It was the end of a murder mystery. You know a book on CD. Someone just got killed. Wasn't expecting it. Good thing I wasn't driving."

"Maybe you shouldn't listen to murder mysteries in the car."

"You're probably right."

Ed rushed home, and it wasn't just because of the embarrassment. She couldn't shake Clint fever. So instead of reloading more recycling from the garage, she retreated to her bedroom to unload. With a trembling hand, she snapped the batteries into the vibrator and crumpled onto her bed. When that settled her nerves, she showered.

Her clothes, specifically her big white briefs, distressed her. She promised herself she'd go underwear shopping. With Celeste. Celeste should have stock in Victoria's Secret. Even little Siobhan said she couldn't wait to be old enough to have a bra like Mommy. Ed forced thoughts of sexy underwear aside, fairly convinced she'd never need anything but her granny briefs. But that didn't stop her from wanting to prepare herself for the possibility. She quickly dressed, big cotton undies and all.

With nothing left to distract her, Ed put the yard waste into Aretha and headed to the compost center. At the gate, the attendant told her to follow the left road and stay with the black pick up.

"The black pickup?" she said.

"Yeah, the only other car up there. Can't miss it."

Ed wondered if Clint might have turned his attention to yard debris once he returned to the Hooper place. Could it be possible, to meet randomly twice in one day. She spotted the pick-up, black Ford… with perfectly kerned letters on the door.

"I suppose it's possible," she said.

She inhaled, shifted Aretha into reverse and pulled along side the truck. Clint loomed from within the bed heaving dead tree branches. Thick and forked, they scraped against the bed as Clint lifted them and fell with the others on the pile with a raspy thud.

"We have to stop meeting like this," Ed said.

As soon as he recognized her voice, he jumped. He turned around, hand still tight on a branch.

"Ed? Again?"

"It must be fate," she said. "Maybe the girls are right. Maybe we should give a date another try."

It popped out. She hadn't meant to say that. By the end of today, she would probably reach a new record high for how many times she could embarrass herself.

"I'll tell you what. How about I help you unload this time?" Clint suggested.

A moment ago she thought of rainbows and song-birds, the reality of dead tree branches and rotting leaves replaced it.

"Thanks, but that's not necessary," Ed replied.

"Of course it's not necessary. But I'm hungry. We've both been working all morning. We'll unload. Then we'll head over to the Middle Eastern deli and have some killer falafel."

Falafel? Before she had time to ponder more, Clint leapt from his truck and pulled some of the brown bags from Aretha's trunk.

"Okay. Sure," she consented as she took a bag. "I'd love to."

"You know where it is?" he asked.

She nodded. Clint placed another bag onto the pile. Ed hurled hers.

"See you there," he said.

He climbed into his truck and drove off. Ed jumped into Aretha, dug through her purse for Celli and scrolled for Celeste. She skipped the house phone. This was an emergency. She chose Celeste's mobile. Celeste answered on the first ring.

"Celeste, thank God," Ed said, breathless. "Clint just invited me to lunch. I ran into him at the compost center and he said to meet him at the deli. I need your help."

"No, you don't," Celeste said.

"Yes I do," Ed insisted. "It's been a million years since I've been on a date. I don't know what to do. I don't know what to say."

Celeste offered a sigh.

"Ed," she said. "Step one, go to the deli. Why are you wasting time calling me? Are you driving?"

Ed reached into her purse and grabbed the hands-free device for her phone. She had never used the little earbud thing. She plugged it in, pushed it into her ear and set the phone in the console.

"I put the headset on," Ed replied.

Ed drove.

"Now, relax," Celeste said. "Last time I checked a date at a deli qualified as lunch, no strings attached.

Unless, of course, you're a character in my novel. So, go eat a sandwich, talk to the man, and as long as neither one of you does something mortifying, as you tend to do, get an invitation for dinner."

"Dinner?" Ed repeated.

"If he's serious or if you're ever going to get any, you'll have to go to dinner first. Unless it's my house. The rules don't work in this house."

Ed stopped at a red light in the intersection before the plaza she needed.

"Feel better?" Celeste asked.

"No," Ed admitted. "It's awfully quite at your house. Where's Siobhan?"

"With her grammy," Celeste answered. "I have some research I need to do this afternoon. Darren took the afternoon off for a special lunch meeting."

"You don't mean the kind of lunch meeting I'm having… right?"

Celeste laughed heartily. "Nope. This is one of those inspirational lunch meetings. I'm at that point and I need ideas."

"Oh, no," Ed said.

Celeste took the sex scenes in her novel very seriously. She worked hard on those paragraphs, wanting every word and sensation to seem perfect. As a consequence, she tended to recreate them in her own bedroom.

"Should I even ask?" Ed told her.

Another laugh followed.

"I'm wearing one of Darren's dress shirts, and that's all. I'm in the bedroom, completely clean shaven, if you can imagine, and I've got Nutella and apples. And champagne. So you tell me."

"You shaved? There?"

Celeste giggled. A honk emanated from the car

behind Ed since the light had turned green and she ignored it.

"Yes," Celeste said. "I never thought I'd do that. Too little girly. But I want to know Darren's reaction. This novel, a lot of the girls are fashion models, so they're bald. I just thought I'd test it."

"Does D know?"

"Not yet," Celeste said.

"Why can't I have normal friends?" Ed asked.

Ed turned into the parking lot.

"My call waiting is beeping. Speaking of the devil. D must be on his way. You okay? Can you do this?"

"I'm here, so here goes nothing."

"Call me later. Just wait at least two hours."

Ed shook her head, hung up the phone, and spotted Clint waving from in front of the deli.

TEN

Ed had arranged to meet Celeste for lunch and shopping at the mall after she dropped Siobhan off at preschool. They were to meet in front of Ed's least favorite store, Victoria's Secret. If there was ever a store to kill a fat woman's self-esteem, Vicki's was it. Ed was sitting on the bench outside the store, reading student papers on copyrights and ethics in graphic design as she waited.

Ed hated to shop. She was the retailer's worse nightmare—forty, tall, fat, she preferred tailored clothes and knew fabric a well as any designer. She wanted cotton and linen in the summer and wools in the winter. Her mother taught her to sew at an early age, and she spent a good portion of her youth, combing fabric stores for fabric and patterns. Perhaps she was spoiled, cursed by good taste. The constraints of all her jobs made it impossible for Ed to make clothes, so she had to shop. Mall stores had plus departments filled with ugly clothes, made from horrible fabrics, with silk-screened motifs, and featuring elastic waists. Her mom called it the fat people's uniform. Even stores that featured career clothes geared their merchandise to the 15-30 crowds.

However, a closet full of quickly disintegrating clothes, an invitation to the summer solstice black tire fundraiser for the Olive Branch Ranch, and a first date with Clint made the torture of the mall inevitable.

"Hey girlfriend," Celeste called from across the hall, waving the *New York Times*. "No reading while we're shopping, unless of course you're reading my book…look I'm number three!"

"Congratulations, Celeste!" Ed said as she hugged her friend and they both sat down. "Do we really have to go into Vicky's? This store is for skinny people with boobs, like you."

"They will be getting bigger, I'm pregnant!"

"What?"

"Pregnant. Didn't your parents tell you about the birds and the bees?"

"Yes, Celeste. What about all that talk about Siobhan being an only child so you could lavish her with your undivided attention?"

"One night the condom broke. I was planning on going to go to the doctor for the morning after pill, but in the morning Darrin convinced me not to. He loves Siobhan so much and wants another. He's even willing work from home, or quit his job, just to be with the kids. I turn into a marshmallow when I'm around that man you know that. I can't say no. So we rolled the dice, and here I am—knocked up."

"You're taking this well."

"Yeah, I'm actually excited. That's one reason we're at Vicki's, I need to get bras for my ever-expanding chest, and maybe new thongs. I go through a lot when

I'm pregnant. Darren keeps ripping them off. That is partially my fault, of course. I'm a horny toad when I'm pregnant."

"Why buy them at Vicki's, why not at K-mart, you'll save yourself a bundle of cash."

"Ed, you are way too practical for your own good. Men don't just respond to the garment. They respond to the package, the bag, and the label. I'm serious, if you ever get Clint Anderson in your pants, you'll realize what I'm saying is true."

"Celeste, I had one lunch, and one coffee non-date with the man. I won't be getting into his pants any time soon."

"You have a real-date Saturday night, so we need to get you ready. You'll need a whole outfit, starting with lingerie."

"He's not going to see my underwear on the first date."

"Not with that attitude he's not."

"Celeste!"

"Alright, save that for the big fundraising ball"

"He hasn't asked to escort me to the ball yet. He probably won't. I can't picture Clint in a tux anyway."

She lied. She had certainly imagined Clint in a tux.

"Are you kidding? That man will be hot in a tux, throw in a decent haircut, and you'll be doing the mattress tango until the wee hours of the morning," Celeste replied.

Ed inwardly sighed. "Can we not talk about this and go eat?"

"Sure, we can eat, but we'll continue this discussion in the restaurant."

They chose the Thai Escapes, because the food was excellent, inexpensive, nutritious, and quick. After the waiter brought the food, Celeste whipped out her notebook.

"I've made two lists, one for me and one for you."

"You and your dammed lists. Can you do anything without a list?"

Celeste ignored her and started to read. "For you we need to go to Lane Bryant for bras and panties, they had some nice stuff on line, but we need to find the correct size bra."

"48C."

"I said the correct size. We need to get the girls measured, supported, and put them back were they belong. You'll look like you lost 20 lbs with a good fitting bra. Then we will look at matching thongs."

"Thong, there is no way I'm wearing a thong. I like my Fruit of the Loom briefs. Heck you can get 6 pair on sale for $6.99 at Kmart and they last years."

"Ed, no granny panties."

"Hey Fruit of the Loom makes lots of styles, not just granny panties. Heck, they even make thongs! Not that I'd wear them."

Celeste said quietly "If you want something other than a joystick between your legs, you're going to have to compromise."

Nearby they heard a crash. It appeared that the waiter had returned with dessert, overheard Celeste and dropped the tray. Ed turned red.

The waiter apologized profusely and promised to get them another dessert.

"How about those boy shorts or a bikini brief to start, and work your way into a thong. I tell you it's like wearing nothing at all."

"If I say yes, will you change the conversation before the waiter comes back?"

"Okay."

The waiter returned with coconut ice cream, with shaved coconut on top, and a warm chocolate sauce on the side.

"Then we need to get you an outfit for the big date. That shouldn't be too hard."

"Excuse me? You don't shop for plus size clothes. You don't realize how hard it is."

"Ed, you're exaggerating. We'll find something in an hour, trust me. We'll go to Dress Barn. You like their stuff. I peeked in the closet the last time we were at your place. We'll also need to get shoes and accessories. Your selection is dreadful and nearly as worn out as your clothes. It will be harder finding something for the black tie. We'll try Macy's but we might have to take a road trip into the city to find something. Siobhan loves road trips."

True to her word, Celeste found the perfect date outfit at Dress Barn, a short brown tulip skirt with droopy skinny belt and a v-neck sweater. At Payless Shoe Source, Celeste found brown mules with a kitten heel that Ed could actually walk in without falling over.

At Macy's, Sarah, the expert bra fitter, measured her and found her perfect size, a 40D. After trying on a dozen bras, Sarah found the perfect style to accent Ed's assets. Ed hated to admit it by Celeste was right, she looked 15 pounds lighter in that bra. Celeste was delighted that it came in multiple colors with matching bikini panties, and before she knew it, Ed has spent $300 on lingerie, more than she had ever spent in her entire life.

Ed's debit card was smoking by the time they left. Maybe they should shop together more often. She might be having fun.

As Ed rushed to her late afternoon class, Celeste went to pick up Siobhan at preschool. It wasn't until later that night, when she was putting away her new clothing that Ed started feeling buyer's remorse.

It probably didn't help that Gertrude was up when Ed got home. Tootie went into one of her rants about shopping and how Ed had plenty of clothes. Ed's clothes were worn out, but nothing compared to Tootie's. Being a drunk, Gertrude wore the same clothes for days at a time and they were threadbare at best. Most had holes. When begged to buy new clothes, Tootie would say, these are perfectly fine. Some days she'd walk around in her shapeless bra and thin panties and never bother getting dressed at all. No wonder her husband threw her out.

It was shortly after their father's death that Gertrude showed up at her door with a paper shopping bag with her belongings, begging for a place to stay for a few weeks. Boris had thrown her out and at first, Tootie went to stay with Martha and Terri. That didn't work out. Martha finally asked her to leave the morning after she found her drunk, drooling, and naked in the living room.

When she arrived at Ed's place, she had been sober for a week. Ed thought she was cleaning up her act and said she could stay in the attic. Quickly, she fell off the wagon, and really hasn't gotten back on since.

A few weeks turned into years. Ed had resigned herself to the fact that Gertrude was now the drunk in the attic. Tootie didn't work; she barely ate, and bought her beer with her savings. Tootie even found a beer distributor that delivers five cases of the local lager right to Ed's house. Tootie had an account, just like the neighborhood bar. If Ed had the time, she'd write a blog about Tootie. Maybe someone would turn her stories into a television sitcom.

Ed wanted to tell Tootie that she was a freeloader, and not Ed's parent or spouse. Therefore, Tootie really didn't have the right to say how she spent her hard-earned money. Fighting with Tootie was pointless. When Tootie thinks she's right, she's like a pit-bull who grabs on and won't let go.

If Tootie got wind of Ed's date Saturday night, she can't imagine what will happen. Ed knew better than to mention her lunch with Clint last week.

Before she met Clint for lunch, she took money out of her wallet and put her purse in Aretha's trunk. She didn't want a repeat of their hot chocolate interview after the bear relocation.

They met at the Middle Eastern deli in a half-empty strip mall close to the composting center. Clint had the falafel pita, mashed spicy chickpeas formed like meatballs, then fried, rolled in pita slathered with garlic spread and topped with tabouli. He ate it in four bites. His Coke went down quicker than Tootie drinks a beer. Ed barely touched her roasted vegetable wrap. The whole idea of eating lunch with a man made her so nervous she wanted to vomit. They talked about the girls, graduation, and Clint's business.

Every time he tried to steer the conversation to her, she brought it back to him. What was she going to tell him? That her family puts the "fun" in dysfunctional? That her students drove her crazy and there were days this semester that she wanted to lock them all in a closet and throw away the key? As she sipped her lemon water, she really wanted a Coke. The caffeine would calm her down.

He had an appointment with a new customer relocating bats right after lunch so they couldn't linger. He offered to get her some foil to wrap her sandwich. As she cleaned the table, she thought, "He's so sweet, getting me foil for my sandwich."

Before she knew it, he had returned, wrapped the

sandwich, gathered and threw away the trash and recycled his Coke bottle. He walked her to Aretha, and as he unlocked and opened the door for her, he asked her on a date next Saturday night. She said yes.

"Oh my goodness," Ed yelled aloud. "I have a date Saturday night."

Tootie came running up the stairs. Ed had no intention of sharing any of that information with her.

ELEVEN

A car door thumped. Ed gazed from her window. Martha ushered her daughter, Belinda, from her Lexus hybrid SUV, across the street, and toward the house. The girl broke into a run as soon as they hit the sidewalk.

"Wait for me, Bea," Martha called.

Downstairs, the doorknob rattled.

"It won't open," the child whined.

"I have the key," Martha replied.

"Hurry, Mommy, I really have to use the bathroom bad," Belinda said.

"I'm coming as fast as I can, Bea," Martha said as she stuck the key into the lock.

As the door opened, Belinda ran into the house and upstairs. Martha's footsteps entered the hallway. The door closed.

"Martha?" Ed called from her office.

"Yup," Martha said, climbing the stairs. "It's just us. Bea needed the bathroom. She might be sick."

"So I gathered," Ed replied.

"Where are you?" Martha asked.

"In the office," Ed answered.

The toilet flushed.

"She had better not be contagious," Ed continued. "I have a date tonight."

"Date!" Martha exclaimed as she entered the office. "You have a date and didn't tell me? Start spilling, girl."

The water ran in the nearby bathroom and the soap dispenser clanged against the counter.

"There's nothing to tell," Ed replied.

"How about who, where, and did you pack an overnight bag?" Martha returned.

"Clint, dinner, and no," Ed said. "Why does everyone want me to get laid?"

"Mommy," a little voice said from the hall. "What does laid mean?"

Martha spun. Belinda stood in the doorway.

"How are you, baby?" Martha asked her daughter. "Did you have to throw up?"

"No, Mommy," Belinda answered as she twisted her small face into a fowl grimace. "But somebody did. Aunt Ed's bathroom is gross. Somebody threw up in the bathtub, and did number two on the floor!"

Martha and Ed locked eyes.

"GERTRUDE," they said in unison.

Not hitting the target was classic Tootie.

"Is Aunt Tootie sick?"

"Yes, Aunt Tootie has been sick for a long time," Ed said quietly. "I'm sorry she left the bathroom a mess, Bea. I'll go clean it up."

Ed and Martha exchanged knowing glances.

"If you need to use the toilet again, use the one off the kitchen," Ed said. "Aunt Tootie never goes in there. It's always clean."

"Feel better, baby?" Martha asked.

Belinda nodded and headed for Ed's desk, her hand reaching for the stuffed skunk next to the monitor.

"I had a big poo and I feel better," she said as her fingers closed on the skunk's tail. "My belly doesn't ache any more. What's this?"

"It's Pépé LePew. He's a character from *Looney Toones* like Bugs Bunny," Ed explained.

"I know that," Belinda said in her 'silly grown-ups' voice. "Why do you have him? Do you have Penelope, too?"

"No," Ed replied. "A friend gave him to me. Without any others."

"He'll get lonely," Belinda said.

"Clint?" Martha muttered.

"No, Celeste," Ed snapped. "She bought it for me at the mall."

"Baby," Martha said, her head moving as she made a scan of the surroundings. "You're right. Pépé will be lonely. Why don't you take him into Auntie Ed's room and play? I think I need to talk to Ed."

"Grown-up talk?" the little girl asked.

Martha nodded, and threw in sigh for emphasis.

"Okay," Belinda said with a shrug.

Martha followed Belinda to the door and watched as she turned the corner in Ed's room. With Belinda out of earshot, Martha turned to Ed and placed a hand on her upper arm.

"Yes," Martha said, too dramatically for Ed's liking, "it would be nice if you got laid tonight, but I don't expect that to happen."

Her sister smiled, perhaps even something along the lines of a smirk.

"Hell, even if you officially date this guy, you'll

make him wait months."

"What makes you think I'll make him wait months?" Ed replied.

"History," Martha quipped.

"Martha!"

"You string men along so long, they loose interest."

"That's not true, Martha."

"Yes, it is. Now, a girl should not go out un-prepared. Especially in your case. How many men have you had? One? Two?"

"Three," Ed replied.

"I've had more lovers in a week."

"I'm not you."

"You certainly aren't. How long has it been, a decade?" Martha asked.

"More or less," Ed responded.

"Really, how can anyone go that long without sex?"

"I was taking care of dad," Ed said. "I was busy with my career."

"And your interest in your career got you far."

"Martha," Ed answered. "This really isn't what I needed to hear. Regardless of the reasons, I didn't have any interest."

In the next few seconds, the world swirled just like in the movies, when a character realized some-thing that would impact everything and everyone around them. Ed's eyes must have swollen to the size of half-dollars as her mouth dropped and her hand covered it.

"Oh my God," Ed muttered.

"What?" Martha asked, one brow wrinkled in concern.

"Oh my God," Ed repeated, louder this time. She sunk her hands into her sister's arms. "My interest... Clint has reawakened my interest in sex."

"That's what happens. It's called 'lust.' Really, it's nothing to be afraid of—"

"No," Ed said, frantically shaking her head. "Belinda is in my bedroom. I don't remember if I put my… you know… my vibrator away."

"If she finds it," Martha said as she scurried into the hall, "you field the questions."

"I'm surprised she hasn't seen one before in your house…"

Martha shot Ed a dirty look. A hum filled the air.

"I put my toys away," she remarked.

The two women appeared in the door of Ed's room, Belinda sat cross-legged on the crazy quilt made by Ed's and Martha's grandmother, on the four-poster bed that once belonged to Ed's and Martha's parents. Belinda had the skunk in one hand, and the vibrator shaking quietly on her leg. Ed turned six shades of red.

"Mommy is it time to go?" Belinda said as she peered up. "I didn't know Aunt Ed has so many toys in her house."

Belinda lifted the vibrator and offered it to her mother.

"This one moves," she said nonchalantly. "Put it on your hand. It sure feels funny."

She set it against the back of her hand. Her giggles cascaded through the small room.

"Feel," Belinda directed.

"I'll take your word for it, honey," Martha said, taking Belinda's free hand. "Give your aunt her toys and let's go home. Jarr and Terri are waiting for us."

Belinda gave Ed the vibrator. She quickly turned the base so it stopped twitching. Thank God no one ever got her anything that looked realistic, or worse, obscene. Celeste kept talking about her life-like ten-inch. She swore it even felt like skin. Why someone with a willing husband would need something like that, Ed didn't know.

"That was close," Ed whispered.

Martha snickered. Ed escorted Belinda and Martha to their truck. Ed strapped her niece into her booster seat. Everyone waved as the car departed from the curb. Ed returned to the house, planning to clean the bathroom. One of these days, she would change the locks. That would be easier than collecting the keys. Each of her siblings had a key to her house. When Dad was alive, they needed the access. But now... now her family used her house like a public toilet, or leave packages in her living room, and some of them even raided the fridge, leaving behind a sink full of dirty dishes and empty milk cartons.

Ed trudged upstairs to tackle the bathroom. Stepping close to it, the combination smell of feces and vomit assailed her and challenged her gag reflex. Poor Bea! Having to use those facilities...

Grumbling about her sister, Ed entered the bathroom, gathered the cleaning supplies from the cupboard and thanked the Powers That Be for Lysol.

Putting the glitter into that room left her forty-five minutes behind schedule. Ed showered, shaved, washed her hair and headed for her room to don her clothes. She even attempted makeup, but only a little blush, lipstick and mascara. She didn't want to scare Clint by painting herself into a clown or worse, over-dressing for their first date.

She headed downstairs and started to pace. Gertrude had retreated upstairs. The downstairs was a clean as it was going to get. Clint wasn't due for another half-hour. The phone rang. Ed jumped.

"Shit," she thought.

Clint's calling to cancel. The phone rang again.

"Hello?" Ed answered.

"Hey, Ed," Hannah's familiar voice greeted her. "You back out of the date yet?"

"No, I haven't. He's due in about twenty-five minutes."

"What are you wearing?" Hannah asked.

"Well," Ed said, "A tulip skirt, brown. A v-neck cashmere sweater and kitten heels. Some vintage jewelry from Mom."

She reflexively touched the beaded necklace and twisted it around her neck.

Do you have your lucky panties on?" Hannah asked.

"Excuse me, Hannah?"

"Celeste told me about the shopping spree. This is a big night. You're not wearing those granny panties, are you?"

"No," Ed answered. "Celeste should have told you she came over one day and burned them. The cops saw the smoke from the front of the house and almost gave me a ticket for an open fire."

Hannah cackled. "Sometimes I wish I lived closer."

"And sometimes I'm glad you don't," Ed returned. "I'm getting used to these bikini things. I've stopped tugging at them at least. What does it matter? He won't see them anyway."

"Not with that attitude, he won't. Seriously, Ed. It's 2008. You're forty, but you act ten. Premarital sex is okay. Besides, if you don't start getting some soon you're going to miss the boat. You're not getting any younger, Ms. Leap Year."

"Then, I'll miss the boat. I'm sorry, Hannah. I'll never believe in casual sex. You need to build a relationship before you become intimate."

"Sometimes," Hannah said softly. "But sometimes

there's something about casual sex, as you say. I mean, if you're both attracted to each other and you both want it. You can't just do it because you want to please the man—"

"It's a first date, for Pete's sake," Ed interrupted.

"What am I going to do with you? Did you ever think maybe it's been a while for him, and he could use it as much as you?"

"Really, Hannah! Don't expect me to act like something I'm not."

"You don't have to be celibate."

"Hannah, drop it. If you want to talk sex, tell me if you're still on the everyday plan."

"You betcha," Hannah replied.

Then she told launched into another tale of sexual adventure. Apparently, Charlie had developed a taste for public sex. It started simply enough: in his office, the elevator, then public restrooms when they went out to eat. The most recent escapade brought them to the park near their house.

"We were mostly dressed, but it was obvious what was happening, based on what parts came together where," Hannah said.

"Good Lord, Hannah. That's something a teenager would do."

"No, what we did on the swings was something a teenager would do," Hannah replied. "Oh my, did my legs hurt for a couple days."

"But that's not all, is it?" Ed said.

"No," Hannah responded. "The body might be going. The eyes may not be twenty-twenty but the ears work just fine."

"Oh, no. Who found you?"

"Bicycle cop," she admitted. "But I heard him. Chain had a slight squeak. I flew off Charlie and started running, leaving him to get to his feet and zipped up. It was funny…later."

"You flew off… You were on top, then."

"Yeah, and good thing, because I couldn't have reassembled myself fast enough and that's the last thing some young bicycle cop needs. A clear view of my—"

"I got it," Ed said.

"So, Edna… Relax and enjoy yourself tonight. No pressure. But if he asks, say yes."

"He won't ask, and I won't say yes."

"I can hope. Call me in the morning. I want to be first. Before Celeste, with ALL of the details. Maybe you should call me tonight."

"Maybe I should do a conference call…you, Celeste and Martha. Then I only need to do it once."

"Fine by me. Ta-ta."

"Bye, Hannah."

By the time Clint arrived fifteen minutes later, Ed was practically staring out the window. Doris had just left for a seven-to-seven shift at the hospital so the spot in front of the house was available. The door of Clint's truck opened and Ed recognized one khaki leg. Poking from it came a Cordovan loafer, polished and brown.

As he circled the truck and approached the house, Ed took stock of the rest of his outfit: flat front trousers and a thin burgundy crew neck sweater. He had combed his hair back and shaved. The sight of that face so smooth and clean and Ed's hand reached out as if to stroke it.

She caught herself and rebalanced, so she wouldn't tumble on her soft knees. Ed leaned toward the door, not sure if she should open it or wait for him to ring the bell. She couldn't bear to wait. She swung the door wide in time to hear a voice billowing up the hill.

"Hey," the voice called. "You the neighborhood skunk guy?"

Clint turned. A middle-aged woman, with untamed hair, wearing a snapped house dress, ankle socks and slippers ran up the hill. Ed didn't know her. And from the look of her jiggling bosom, she had left the house without a bra.

"Can I help you?" Clint said, cautiously.

"They live under my shed. Skunks, that is," she said as she fought to reclaim her breath after her half-block marathon. "I have a big skunk problem. The kids went to fetch a tennis ball and disturbed the skunk. It was daytime, for Pete's sake. Took me days to get rid of the smell."

"And you are…"

"Millicent Roberts."

"Nice to meet you, Mrs. Roberts."

He extended his hand, but Millicent didn't reciprocate.

"I'm not dressed for work right now," Clint said apologetically. "Give me your address and I'll stop by first thing in the morning. We'll talk business then."

He reached into his pants' pocket and withdrew his wallet. Opening it, he extracted a business card and again held out his hand. She took the card.

"Isn't it possible for you to set a trap now? I see one in the truck," Millicent insisted. "I'd like to get rid of them before they attack my babies again."

"Ma'am, they didn't attack. As you yourself said the children disturbed them—"

Ed stepped closer and interrupted. "Go ahead, Clint. It's okay. It will only take a few minutes. I'll be here when you're done."

"Are you sure?"

I've waited this long, she thought to herself. A skunk guy seemed as prone to emergencies as a surgeon.

"Go."

He went to his truck, grabbed the trap and walked down the hill to the Roberts' residence. Ed returned to the house, cracking her knuckles. She sat in the armchair by the door and pretended to read Celeste's latest novel. She glossed over the first page five times, without even realizing she had gone over it before. Somehow, she progressed to page three. A knock on the door penetrated Celeste's normally captivating prose.

"Hi," Clint's voice carried into the room. "It's me."

"Come on in."

He crossed the threshold and smiled weakly.

"Sorry about that," he said. "May I use your bathroom to cleanup?"

"Of course."

She gestured toward the stairs.

"Right at the top," Ed added.

Well, she thought, at least all my cleaning wasn't for nothing. He mounted the staircase.

"Would you like a beer?" Ed said as he climbed. "I have a local microbrew that I've hidden in the coal cellar from Tootie or maybe wine? Josie's husband ferments a killer red."

"Josie?"

"Josephina, my younger sister," Ed said, failing to stop her nervous rambling. "Her husband, Geoff, is a fermenting devotée. He makes beer, wine, cheese, sauerkraut, sourdoughs... If you can ferment it, he makes it."

"Sounds like an interesting fellow," Clint said from the second to top step. "Surprise me."

He slipped into the bathroom and closed the door. Ed walked to the kitchen, praying Tootie wouldn't hear Clint rustling. The toilet seat banged. The echo of the noise across the house reminded Ed how long it had been since a man, of any kind, in any way, had a presence in her life. Ed, for half a second, pondered what Clint had in hand up there in that bathroom and sighed, wishing she could slap herself silly.

She arranged a tray with two mismatched wine glasses, one with a gold rim and the other with a rainbow stem. She filled the goblets with wine. She added a small platter of Geoff's cheese, uncertain what flavor by the smell, and added some Triscuits. Two dessert plates and cloth napkins finished the presentation. As footfalls returned down the stairs, Ed emerged with her bounty. She set it on the table in front of the couch.

"If you want to try the wine, you might like the cheese," Ed said. "It's quite tasty."

Clint sat on the sofa and lifted his wine. He sipped it, then placed some cheese on the cracker. He popped it into his mouth.

"You're right," he said. "Delicious."

She lingered in front of the table. He drank more. He dabbed his lips with the napkin.

"Millicent might steal your skunk record," he said.

"Really?" she said as she picked up her glass. She hoped her hands wouldn't shake.

"Yes, she had six tunnels under her shed and several under her fence," he said. "I'll need to bring more traps tomorrow. I might be wrong, but I think Millicent is a major source of the whole neighborhood's skunk prob-lem. You name it, she's got it. The yard is a mess, there's garbage everywhere, animal food out, mulberry trees—"

"You always talk shop?"

He chuckled, while nibbling more cheese. Clint nodded.

"I guess I haven't done this in a while," he said.

"Do we have reservations?" Ed asked.

"Yes," Clint replied. "But if we're a tad late, it won't be a problem."

Ed gazed at him quizzically. She replaced her glass on the tray.

"Anyway, no more shop talk," Clint said.

He took her hand, and it sent electricity through her fingertips as he guided her from the house. He opened her door and kept her hand as she got inside. They drove forever, about forty-five minutes on country roads, nothing but trees and the first bright stars of the silver evening light.

Finally, they pulled into the driveway of a stone farmhouse, on the top of a mountain, spreading before them an incredible view of the valley full of farmland, orchards and vineyards.

Only a few cars sat in the driveway—a Mercedes, a Jag, a Lexus and an Escalade.

"Clint, where are we?" Ed asked. "This doesn't look like a restaurant."

"It is," he said.

"From the look of those cars, we don't belong here."

"Sure, we do," he said. "A friend of mine owns it. She's one of the best-kept secrets in the area. She has never advertised, relies on word of mouth."

"Clint, you don't have to take me to some expensive restaurant. Really, a cheesesteak is fine for this girl."

"I told you, we're friends. She was shocked when I called for a reservation for dinner. It's been a long time since I came down here," Clint said. "Rebekkah offered to cater Olive's fundraiser this summer, so she needs to talk to me. She can't wait to meet you."

Ed surveyed what, until a few minutes ago, seemed like the perfect date outfit.

"Am I dressed okay?"

His hands rested on top of the steering wheel. He closed his eyes.

"I'm sorry, with the interruption…" he paused. "I forgot."

"Forgot? Forgot what?"

He turned to her. The pale image of the moon hung about his shoulder.

"You look beautiful," he said.

He hopped out of the truck and walked to her door. He opened it.

"Thanks," she said. He took her hand again. "I wasn't fishing for a compliment."

"You got one anyway," he said.

They trotted to the rustic front door, painted a burnt shade of barn red. When they crested the last step, a man in a dark suit and bow tie stepped out to greet them.

"Welcome to The Farmhouse, Mr. Anderson, Ms. Gardner," he said. "I have your table prepared."

The *maître-d'* ushered them toward the immaculate dining room. A staircase stretched before them with the bright glow of the kitchen tucked beyond it. Ed stared. She couldn't help it. The *maître-d'* stopped on the wide sill of the arched doorway. He gestured to Ed's shoulders.

"May I take your coat?" he asked.

"Of course," Ed slipped her arms free as he caught it.

She moved away, and nearly knocked a waitress with a cup of coffee and a creamer pitcher.

"Sorry," Ed murmured.

Clint inched closer, ducking under the short door jamb.

"People sure were tiny a couple hundred years ago," he remarked.

The *maître-d'* must have sensed that Ed was breathing in the scene. He lingered near the closet for a moment. Ed basked in the warm orange tones of the massive fireplace, framed with wrought iron cooking utensils. Inside, licked by flames, roasted a small pig, two ducks and a chicken.

Candles and globed lanterns lit the room atop wide-plank tables with chunky chairs. The homespun linen tablecloths had delicate lace trim that reminded Ed of something her grandmother would tat on a rainy day. The *maître-d'* accompanied them to a corner table set for two, immaculate, with redware and goblets and a metal pitcher of water. It rested against the window, an arrangement of local wildflowers on the wide sill, while the view faced the valley.

Ed took her seat, reeling from the ambiance. She kept picturing George Washington and the troops strategizing before the fire.

"Ed, you still here?" Clint joked.

She gazed at him, the flicker of the lantern reflecting in his eyes. He offered a relaxed smile as he unfolded his napkin and smoothed it across his lap.

"Yes…" she said absent-mindedly. "Sorry."

Ed reached for her napkin.

"I've never seen anything like this," she admitted. "It's… just… I don't know, fantastic."

"Glad you like it," a woman's voice replied.

A tall, willowy woman appeared at their table. Short wisps of red hair framed her oval face.

"You can see why I have to keep this place a secret," she whispered.

Her stiff white jacket crackled as her arms reached for Ed's shoulders.

"Rebekkah," Clint said quietly.

Her perfect face approached Ed's. Arched eyebrows,

high cheekbones, swooping eyelashes, and a tiny diamond adorning her pixie nose, her face brushed across Ed's with a faint kissing noise. Then, Rebekkah did the same to Clint.

"Really, could you see the Food Network swarming my quaint oasis?" Rebekkah said.

She patted Ed's hand.

"I'm Rebekkah Snowe," she said.

"Edna Gardner," Ed returned. "But I'm always Ed."

"In that case, Ed, perhaps you should know that Snowe is not my real name," Rebekkah said with a wink. "It's a *nom de plume*, or in my case, *nom de poêle*."

Rebekkah chuckled, and Ed didn't know if she should laugh. Clint didn't, so apparently Ed wasn't alone in missing the humor.

"Any allergies, Ed? Foods you don't like?" she asked.

"No," Ed replied, wrinkling her nose with the questions.

"Clinton," Rebekkah said with playful formality. "It's about time you came back, and I'm so glad it's not to celebrate a milestone of the twins. Not that I don't adore the twins…"

"Olive thanks you for helping with the fundraiser. She's very excited," Clint said.

"How could I say no?" she said. "Those two ladies are exquisite. I don't know how a boorish man like you did it."

She peered over her shoulder toward the kitchen.

"My work calls," Rebekkah said. "I will have dinner out shortly. Especially now that I've gotten a good look at her."

She kissed Clint again and nodded toward Ed. Rebekkah headed for the kitchen, feet nearly silent in perforated leather clogs.

"We didn't order dinner," Ed observed. "How can it be ready shortly?"

"There's no menu. Rebekkah makes food and you eat it."

"Hence, the questions," Ed replied.

Clint nodded.

"How long have you known her? She's obviously a close friend," Ed remarked, wondering how close the friendship was.

"I've known her for years," Clint answered. "Since before my girls were born. She was Emma's best friend, and when Emma left, she left Rebekkah behind, too. We commiserated. It's a long story."

Emma. The girls' mom. She has a name. And apparently a best friend.

"You've never mentioned your ex-wife—"

"We never married."

The word fell between them spawning silence and tension. Ed could feel it, practically see it, but she had no idea how to diffuse it. Clint... never married... with two grown daughters? Ed swallowed. Maybe he would expect some after dinner exercise...

"I asked her," Clint said. "But she wasn't interested. We were born too late, I guess, because she should have been a hippie."

"So, why'd she leave?" Ed asked, the words awkward and sticking in her throat.

She hated to pry. He lifted the bulky flatware into his hand and she stared. Neither of them spoke.

"Clint," she said. "If you are serious about me, then I should know. It's fine if you're not... serious."

"I asked you to dinner," he said. "Why ruin that?"

"If that's the way you feel. I don't want to push you."

He sighed. "I must sound like a prick."

"No," Ed said. "You sound like a man who's been hurt."

"True," he said.

"How about Twenty Questions?" she said lightheartedly.

"Compromise. Five easy ones and I'll do it," he said.

"Where did you meet?"

"Number one," he said, leaning in his chair and refilling his goblet from the water pitcher. "Penn State. She was pre-law. I was animal science. She was out of my league: wealthy, connected, beautiful, elite. I asked her to the football game, expecting her to turn me down flat. She didn't."

In his eyes, behind the heaviness of his expression as he frowned, there glimmered something bright. As he talked of Emma, it brightened and spread across his face. It mesmerized Ed more than the painstakingly accurate historical setting, the scent of roasting meat, or the precision of the staff.

"Something changes when you talk about her like that," Ed said. "It's like a glow."

"Ed, I never loved anyone like I loved her. As much as I love my girls… It was different."

"So what happened next? To the young college kids."

"By senior year, we had an apartment, then after graduation we moved to the farm. I built a cabin for us on a wooded end of the property. We locked ourselves away, lost in each other."

"What happened next? Her family threatened to cut her off without a penny?"

"No," Clint answered, "despite their distress that she did not attend Harvard Law like her father. They never gave us a dime, and we didn't want their money. No, it wasn't that."

"Then why did she leave?"

He shrugged. "I'd have to say it was post-partum depression, based on the changes in her after the children were born. She had a tough time, adjusting to life with two babies and one day she packed her things and left. I didn't hear from her for ten years. The girls don't even remember her."

"So, what happened to her?"

"She went to Harvard Law, met a young lawyer, married and had more children," Clint said. "At least, that's what Rebekkah has heard. They talk, but not like they did."

He offered an odd grunt.

"She named the babies Olive and Geneva because she thought she'd found her peace," Clint said. "Guess she was wrong."

"We all make mistakes," Ed said. "Thanks."

"For what?"

"You didn't have to share that story."

"What story?" Rebekkah said as she reappeared at the table, a waiter at her heels with their food.

"Our sordid pasts, my love." Clint replied with a smirk.

"That took three seconds," Rebekkah said, scoffing. "After all, you string me along, Clint Anderson."

"I'd like to know what's on that tray," Ed interjected.

"Of course," Rebekkah said with a smile.

The waiter set the tray on a stand and paused. Rebekkah pointed to the platters. "How about spring salad with dried cranberries, pecans, and goat cheese and my house berry vinaigrette? I grow the blueberries myself. Followed by roasted spring lamb with mint chutney, tri-colored roasted potatoes with rosemary, and a 2005 Merlot."

She bowed and returned to her kitchen. The waiter

served. He uncorked the wine while they tasted their salads. The waiter also departed and Ed didn't even think about Clint for the next thirty minutes. The lamb melted against her tongue, saturated with its own juice yet alive with the mint. She had one lonely potato left on her plate when the waiter came bearing chocolate.

The potato, like Clint earlier, was forgotten. The waiter gave Ed a chocolate brownie so rich and gooey it was practically fudge. Served warm, the brownie became a bed for alternating layers of chocolate mousse, chocolate sauce and homemade chocolate ice cream. Ed savored every sliver, and when she finished, the waiter brought her a portion of raspberry brandy to cleanse the palate.

While she sipped her brandy, Clint excused himself and went into the kitchen. Upon his return, he escorted Ed to the truck, heaviness consuming her muscles (and not from the food and drink). They would disembark this paradise and she would end up in the world of drunken sisters, too many deadlines, and other real world disappointments. Because whatever happened next had to end in disappointment.

Ed didn't want the evening to end. She wanted to remain, fixed in time, on this mountaintop, forever. Maybe not forever, but certainly for now. And maybe she could listen to Hannah's advice. If he asked, she'd say yes.

But would he be disappointed? Look at her... forty, fat, stuffed with way too many delectable calories...

And if he didn't ask... She would be disappointed.

Because a man didn't put that much effort into an evening without the hope of...

Something.

Her purse suddenly shook and something rang. It

was muffled, as if buried in something.

"Clint, did you hear that?" she asked.

"Sounded like a phone ringing. It wasn't mine. I turned it off."

"I thought I turned mine off," she replied, "besides it plays Cole Porter. It doesn't ring."

She reached inside her handbag. Her phone flashed red. The display read "one new text message."

"It has a message," she said. "I didn't know I could text."

"What does it say?"

"How do I find out?" she asked.

"Do what it tells you," Clint said.

She opened the phone and 'clicked' her way to her in-box.

"Oh my God," Ed said. "It's my sister. It just says 9-1-1."

TWELVE

After listening to the cacophony of her friends' voices for a half-hour, Ed had finally exhausted her tale of the date that surpassed every gastronomical expectation, lead to the heart-rending story of love that did not conquer all, and ended with another classic Tootie episode. As promised, Ed dialed each of her friends, and her sister Martha, into a conference call. It began with a barrage of questions and ended with a chorus of goodbyes that would rival the closing of *The Waltons*.

"Good night, John-boy," Ed said to no one after they hung up. "Good night, Mary Ellen."

She told them the details that were hers to tell, but she would not reveal the intimacies of Clint's relationship with Emma or why she left. Instead, she filled everyone in on her trip to the emergency room to watch the doctor's staple Tootie's head.

While Ed dined on the finest lamb ever, Josie and Geoff had stopped Ed's house with more cheese, sourdough bread and wine. When no one answered, they let themselves in. Everyone always did.

What they didn't count on was what they found: Tootie, laying at the bottom of the stairs in a ratty tee-shirt and heavily soiled panties surrounded by blood. The blood came from a gaping head wound. In tandem, Geoff called the paramedics while Josie called Ed.

Ed heard all of this when she called her sister from Clint's truck. Clint routed them to the hospital where a few moments before the doctor had finished stapling Tootie's head back together after surveying the x-ray of Tootie's thick skull. Really, the doctor said she had a thick skull. Hospital staff settled Tootie into a semi-private room, while the doctor pulled Josie and Ed aside.

"Does Gertrude have a problem with alcoholism?" he asked.

"Is the sky blue?" Ed answered.

"That answer's obvious, doc," Josie added.

"I'd like to admit her to the detox unit," he said.

Josie laughed.

"She won't agree to that," she said.

"After tonight, she won't have much choice," the doctor said. "If a patient appears a danger to themselves or their family I can commit them, whether or not she agrees. She could have broken her neck tonight."

On that somber note, Clint drove Ed home to her now-empty residence. He pulled to the curb, cut the engine, and faced her without releasing the steering wheel. Fatigue had drooped some of the polished look he had earlier, but he still looked handsome, even in the awkward light from the streetlamps.

"I had a wonderful evening," Clint said.

His tone did nothing to reveal his earnestness.

"Do all your dates end at the emergency room?" Ed replied.

"No," he said. "Only the interesting ones."

A pregnant pause weighed across the cabin of the truck and for the first time Ed understood the root of the idiom. Something hung between them. That pause was indeed pregnant. The birth of the next sentence came as no surprise.

"Your sister Tootie… Gertrude… She has a real problem, doesn't she?"

"Alcoholism runs in my family. It ruined her marriage and her career," Ed said. "I fear she's pickled herself and might be immortal. That would drive me to drink."

"I hope not," Clint responded.

More silence followed.

"Come on," he said as he opened his door. "I'll walk you to the porch."

Clint hopped to the street and reached for the handle on her side of the truck.

"You don't need to do that," she replied. "It's ten feet."

"You may be an independent woman, but my mama raised me to be a gentleman," he said offering her his hand. They stepped onto the sidewalk. A few more paces and they'd reached the porch, despite their exaggerated slowness. Ed retrieved her keys, slipping them onto her finger.

"Thank you for an incredible evening," she said.

At her door, Clint gently eased her keys from her finger, found the only one that looked like a house key, and stuck it into the doorknob. He turned it, and as the door swung wide, he held her gently by the arms. Her hands flopped to her sides, unsure what was happening.

His lips found hers and brushed them softly, once then twice. Ed willed her mouth to respond, and it did, but painstakingly slowly, as if it had forgotten, or maybe just couldn't focus as the heat caused by his physical contact rocketed through her. Clint pulled away, squeezed her hand, and met her eyes.

"Good night, Ed," he said.

In the morning, Ed had refrained from sharing the details about the kiss with her gang of Nosy Nellies. And she tried not to be disappointed that he hadn't… asked. She appreciated him more because he didn't.

So, would there be a next time?

She couldn't ponder that now.

She had dried blood on the stairs to clean. The only respite Ed received from her labors was an irate phone call from Tootie in her hospital bed when she caught wind of the doctor's plans. Tootie swore she'd never talk to Josie or Geoff again—lucky them. Meanwhile, Ed bore the brunt of Tootie's hostility.

But today was too nice a day to worry about Tootie in her captivity. Ed planned to drag out and clean the patio furniture. Then she had to grade her online students' final projects. And she should get to her walk.

This date, even before it happened, had spurred her interest in her health. She didn't like to diet, and not many exercises appealed to her. She didn't want to loose her Reubenesque curves, just refine them, maybe even accentuate them with some muscle tone. More importantly, she liked the prospect of spending time with an outdoorsy-type like Clint. She didn't want to worry about whether or not she could keep up—whatever the activity might entail.

"Sorry, baby, I'm out of breath," would never pass her lips.

As she trekked across the yard, she considered the types of exercise she might enjoy with Clint. Her insides tingled and burned with an intensity she had never felt before. In the light of the morning after, Ed wrung her hands as her thoughts drifted to past suitors, not a single one of which lived up to any expectation of decency, let alone romance.

But Clint wouldn't do that, would he?

Ed went into the house and retrieved her black MacBook, still shiny and hardly used. It had cost her a small fortune. She struggled with buyer's remorse. She had a perfectly functional iMac in her office. But, with so many commitments and part-time jobs, portability won over practicality.

She set the laptop on the freshly washed table on the deck and noticed the pungent odor of skunk on the breeze. It wasn't there earlier. She sniffed again. Definitely skunk, she determined, her face twisting, and definitely daytime.

To err on the safe side, Ed retreated to the kitchen. She fired the MacBook to life. The familiar chime echoed. The computer booted. Ed turned on her airport and as soon as the waves of signal strength registered and her hand moved the cursor to the Firefox icon, her doorbell rang.

She sighed.

"Now what," she muttered.

She snapped the lid closed on the computer, as she pushed her chair out and clamored to the door. There stood Clint, in khaki shorts and the same recycling tee-shirt he had worn the day she met him. She paused to check her reflection in the face of the television and proceeded out to answer the door.

"Clint," she said. "What a surprise. I wasn't expecting you."

"Hi," he said.

His foot pushed against the porch and his lips

pressed together in an unnatural expression. He had one hand deep in a pocket. Then, he exhaled.

"Everything alright? You seem… agitated," she said.

"Can I come in?" he asked.

"Sure," she said.

She moved aside and he entered. Ed surveyed the street. She couldn't find his truck.

"Did your car break down?" she asked.

"No," he answered. "Truck's fine. It's in the alley down by Water Street. I just can't believe what I saw."

"What happened?"

"The Roberts place. I went to check the traps. There was a couple of teenagers pegging the cages with pebbles. With a skunk inside! The skunk raised tail, so I didn't get out of the truck. Damn kids figured it out too. Ran just in time."

"Oh my! Those Roberts! I know those kids. Monsters."

"Yeah, well. After I calmed down, I gave Mrs. Roberts a piece of my mind, in a professional manner, of course."

"Of course," Ed said.

"I have to come back later for the skunks," he said. "But I hoped you might brighten my mood."

"I don't know how much brightening I can do," she said, "but I could make a cup of coffee. Would that help?"

"Yeah, it would," he replied. "Especially if you'd join me. You're the type of person I can relate to."

"I am?" she said.

"Yeah," he continued. "People always seem so stupid or so superficial. You're real, Ed. And I appreciate that."

He talked about the girls' upcoming graduation. Clint stirred sugar into his coffee, his tension melting with each mention of "Genny…" or "Olive…" Not to mention the pride in his smile. Ed rested her arms on the table and hung on every word. She liked to hear about the twins. She liked that he was so active in their lives. She could have listened for hours. Unfortunately, he excused himself after about thirty minutes.

"I feel better," he said. "I guess I'm ready to head back down to the Roberts' house to get my truck."

She stepped toward the door, his empty coffee mug in hand. She hoped he might invite her to walk down the hill, but he didn't. She almost asked him about the fund-raiser. But she didn't. She didn't want to ruin the warmth she felt because he had stopped to see her in his duress.

Did that mean she had a shot? Could she win this man?

WWMS.

What would Mama say?

Mama encouraged her siblings to date, but not Ed. As the gang of them married, many in less than ideal situations, Mama would smile and work on wedding plans and dresses and flowers. But when Ed came of age, Mama declared that no one would want dowdy Ed. And back then she wasn't even fat!

"You got no personality, Ed," Mama said. "There's the easy girls, the boys like them for obvious reasons. But nobody marries an easy girl. The nice girls… they're milder. You're too bold, Ed. Too loud and too dowdy."

Ed could imagine Mama kneading bread as she talked.

"A successful man," she'd say, "the suit-and-tie type, he wants a girl who has a sparkling personality, the outgoing kind who can throw parties and make an impression. Nice shape helps. You look like a bean-pole. No man wants that. You might break."

During these mortifying conversations, Ed often

wanted to mention Twiggy, but she knew that would really get her mother going. She kept her mouth shut and conformed to her mother's perception. In her mother's eye, Ed would accept the role as nursemaid to her elderly parents and live at home with only a cat for company.

And so it happened with Dad.

Without the cat, since Ed was allergic.

Ed slapped on her Birkinstocks and stocked a backpack with the necessities: her MacBook, a reusable water bottle, an apple and an orange. She headed for the reservoir, where she hiked for an hour before settling to work under a mammoth tree. The rest of the week followed the same pattern: work, hike, clean, try not to dwell on Clint. It worked fairly well until Thursday.

Olive graduated. She emailed Ed a link to her online photos. When Ed got a look at the photos, she burst out laughing. Apparently, Penn State gave Mr. Hooper an honorary doctorate in animal science for his contributions to Pennsylvania agriculture and wildlife. The two of them—Olive and Hooper—stood side-by-side in black gowns.

Ed researched Hooper's degree and discovered that the Anderson girls rescued Hooper's collection of papers, maps and journals that chronicled the county's farming heritage for the last two centuries. The city didn't want them, so Olive approached the university about the 'collection' and the university sent a team of agriculture professors and an archivist to transport everything to State College.

A few days later, Genny's graduation photos arrived via email. Still no word from Clint. Logically, Ed knew he had to travel for the two graduations. He still had the farm and he still had the traps. That didn't leave much time for dating.

She told the machine to shut down. As the windows flashed closed, she heard the quiet, lusty tones of "I've Got You Under My Skin." Her heart throbbed as she dug for the phone. Caller ID confirmed the source of the call. It could be one of the twins, she thought.

"Ed here."

"Hi," Clint replied.

"I've been wondering when you'd call."

"It's been tough this week. I'm exhausted," he answered. "Dad's covered my business calls. I drove all over for those graduations."

"I figured as much. I'm glad your back."

"Listen," he said. "I'm having a picnic tomorrow, after we move the girls' worldly possessions to the Hooper house. Would you join us?"

"Sure. Can I bring anything?"

"No," he responded. "I'd just really like to see you."

Ed spent the rest of the evening designing custom type illustrations for each girl. Ed arranged a dove with an olive branch, using text from Thoreau's *Walden*. For Genny, she couldn't resist using a rabbit and a gerbil, reminiscent of the 4-H pet fair. That featured the key scenes from *The Velveteen Rabbit*. She constructed mats for each and inserted them into frames. Then she tucked a modest check into the corner of each frame. To wrap the gifts, she used old and imperfect posters.

The next afternoon, after a shower and thoroughly agonizing over what clothes best suited her figure, Ed selected a sleeveless polo shirt in navy blue (good since she had a tendency to spill) and madras capris. She followed Clint's directions and arrived at the property a few minutes before four. She easily found Olive and Genny, lounging on a red and white blanket surrounded by a gaggle of girls their own age. They leapt to their feet as soon as they recognized Ed's silhouette, screeching and cooing as their arms grabbed her, one twin kissing each cheek.

"Ed!" Olive yelled.

"We're so glad you could come!" Genny added.

"Not as glad as I am," a masculine voice said from behind her.

"Clint," Ed said as she pivoted.

Wet hair, clean-shaven face, a slight smile, and khaki shorts again, but her glimpse of him ended too soon. The girls tore into their presents, causing Ed to redirect her attention elsewhere. Clint lingered behind her, the scent of aftershave carrying across her shoulder. She had only seen him for a second, but his proximity heightened her senses.

"I moved furniture all day and I didn't get a single present," Clint joked.

Even though the girls had parted the wrapping and were about to reveal their gifts, Ed turned to Clint. She leaned into him and placed her lips with a feather-light touch against his.

"Will that work?" she asked.

"For now," he answered.

The banter hit her below the stomach, sucking the air from her temporarily and setting her thighs on fire. The twins showed the framed designs to everyone in the circle.

"Ed, it's beautiful," Olive exclaimed.

"Oh, Ed, this is incredible," Genny gushed. "No one has ever done anything this original for us. Thank you."

"Yes, thank you," Olive repeated.

Another rounded of kisses followed.

"I moved furniture all day and I didn't get a single 'thank you,'" Clint said.

The twins kissed their father and laughed.

"Thanks, Dad," they said in unison.

"Well," Clint said as the girls dropped back onto the blanket, passing the artwork to their friends. "I'm not needed here. Would you like a tour of the farm?"

Olive's head turned, throwing her hair over her shoulder.

"Dad," she said. "Look at her shoes."

Ed gazed at her brown huaraches. At least she hadn't worn heels.

"If she tumbles, I'll catch her," Clint said.

"After you stop laughing," Genny added.

"That's only when you fall," Clint teased.

"Despite my reputation as a klutz," Ed said, "I do unthinkable feats in impractical shoes."

Ed stepped away from the small grove of trees shading the party-goers. To her right, a classic white Victorian complete with gingerbread trim and wrap-around porch matched Clint's description of the home where he raised the girls, after abandoning the cabin. Following Emma's departure, it held too many memories.

The Anderson farm spanned the acreage across the two-lane country highway, with Hooper's farmland beyond the Victorian, again, meeting Clint's tales. Corn, already more than ankle high and mighty green, sprouted behind wooden fences. In the distance, she could see the outline of the farmhouse Hooper rented to his farming tenants. Ed returned her attention to the girls and their friends.

"Once at Hemlock Hills I forgot to change my shoes," Ed told. "I hiked through three inches of snow in penny loafers and hose. Cheap loafers, too, not even real leather. So my feet were quite wet and cold by the end of it."

Everyone laughed. Clint seemed the most amused.

"These," she said, pointing to her feet. "A farm? Piece of cake."

They started with an outbuilding Clint called his work shed, which probably rivaled the size of her half-a-double in town. It held traps and other supplies, like the biggest pile of gloves she'd ever seen. In one corner, there stood a desk, an old wooden roller chair, a wooden filing cabinet, and next to them, an over-sized capacity Maytag washer and dryer and a metal shower stall.

"That looks out of place," Ed remarked.

"Not really," Clint replied. "Think of all the mud

and stink I bring home. Would you want that in your house?"

"Good point," she said.

Clint directed her across the yard and into the street, the only street in the area, the scenic route that connected Millville to Clint's farming community before the interstate went in. Clint reached for the mailbox, and pulled out some flyers, stuffed them in his back pocket as they meandered into the dirt lane that served as the driveway to Hidden Hills Farm.

A vegetable patch—green bean vines climbing lattice and early tomato plants already filling out, pepper plants with their tiny flowers—sat between the road and a huge red barn (a few moos escaping toward them). Marigolds edged the entire vegetable garden, in shades of orange and yellow. A breeze washed across them, carrying with them a wonderful sweetness. Along the road, there was an herb row straight down the property line. Ed recognized lavender at every other fence post, with oregano, chives, basil, parsley, thyme, even rosemary, and at the alternating posts, clumps of spearmint.

The lane looped between barn and farmhouse. A flagpole displaying Old Glory. Ed knew that Clint had grown up on this farm, and that his brother Rick now lived in the farmhouse with his family.

She also remembered that Don and his wife lived in an apartment in the barn, a small living space added when the family stopped growing their own hay. CA lived in a modular atop a knoll that gave him view of the cornfields and the irrigation pond.

Clint brought her into the barn to meet Bessy, Missy and Claude, the three Guernseys who remained on the farm. Of course, Bessy, Missy and Claude had left the barn to enjoy the sunshine in their pasture.

Clint escorted her to them, Bessy the first to raise

a bobbing brown head to her. Claude expressed no interest, merely swatting his tail and making two bold paces away from them.

"Bessy and Missy seem like good cow names," Ed said. "But Claude?"

"He started as George," Clint remarked, patting the cow's brown back. "But as you can see, he's a bit of a snob. The girls changed his name to Claude, thinking he got too much of his European ancestry showing."

Clint must have read the blank look on her face.

"Geurnseys originated on an island in the English Channel, close to France."

"So, Claude," Ed replied.

Clint nodded. She smiled.

"*Bonjour*, Claude," she added.

Clint nudged the cow's head toward her.

"*Bonjour, mam'selle*," he said in the silliest of French accents. "Now, go. Leave me be. I am here with my girls."

Ed laughed. Claude lowered his mouth to the field grass and chewed. Clint leaned across the cow's neck, pressing his lips to Ed's. They brushed hers as if uttering a secret greeting, Clint's way of saying 'I'm glad you're here.' She returned the gesture. Their lips danced across each other, as his tongue hinted at meeting hers. The cow lifted his neck and knocked them apart.

"I think we've offended him," Clint said.

Ed smiled again as Clint's eyes met hers with a lingering stare.

"Then we better go," Ed said. "I don't know much about cows, but he's got a few pounds on me…"

The two of them walked the edge of the fields—not the entire 200 acres—but almost to the wooded corner of the property.

Clint didn't have to say anything. She could tell by the way he abruptly turned that they had s tumbled too close to the cabin where he and Emma had lived.

They returned to the picnic, while Mr. Hooper pitched quoits with Clint's brothers, and some of the cousins and friends played checkers at the table while Mrs. Anderson poured from the glistening glass pitcher of lemonade, adorning each glass with a few leaves of spearmint.

Ed eagerly accepted a glass. Clint introduced her to Rick's wife, and then apologized as he said he needed to tend to the venison on the grill.

"Clint," she whispered. "I've never had venison."

"Then start with the sausage," he said. "You'll love it."

"Start with the sausage?" Ed replied.

Clint motioned to the grill, platters stacked with sausage, hamburgers and steaks.

"We could get you some elk or maybe bear…"

"Elk and bear!" she exclaimed, interrupting him.

"Welcome to a hunting and farming family. My girls never saw the inside of a supermarket until college," Clint replied. "We butcher everything and eat it."

While hesitant regarding deer meat, Ed sampled the sausage. Mrs. Anderson served it to Ed on a steak roll with the first peppers and onions of the season, fried on a cast iron skillet on a cooking fire. She accented the flavor of the meat with her family gravy, as she called the tomato sauce. Ed hadn't expected a farm wife in this neck of the woods to have some Italian heritage. One taste confirmed it. The herb garden wasn't just for pretty and Mrs. Anderson had a way with red sauce.

The meat wasn't too bad either. Gamier than Ed was accustomed to, a flavor she'd have learn to like.

She turned down Clint's offer of seconds, partially because she wasn't sure she could handle it and partly because she didn't want to be a glutton.

The day passed too quickly, the experience capped by Clint giving Ed quoits lessons, his arm over hers and his hand on hers as they pitched. She and Clint played against Don and Rick. She couldn't even tell you her score or if she threw respectively.

As the sun descended the horizon, the girls gave Ed hugs and Clint walked her to Aretha. He kissed her as she stood inside Aretha's driver side door. This time, it knocked the strength from her ankles, as there was nothing meek about it. Matter of fact, Ed felt the aftershocks in her entire body. She might have clung to his body and pulled him closer if the girls hadn't hooted in the background.

The next time Clint was in the neighborhood, he stopped by Ed's house. Before long, Clint's definition of 'in the neighborhood' expanded to anywhere within the boundaries of Millville.

On average, he stopped by every other day, usually once he checked his traps in the evening. As long as he didn't have critters to dispose of or relocate, he swung by Ed's house for a leisurely stroll. Tootie had been sprung from detox, and the lack of alcohol in her system made her increasingly miserable and nosy. So, Ed sneaked around like a teenager avoiding Mom.

Most of the evenings started with Clint holding her hand. By the time they reached the park that Ed used as her two-mile marker, he'd pull her to the park beach furthest from the street and they'd kiss, also like a couple of adolescents, not like Ed had ever attracted that kind of attention.

The shyness that seemed to surround Clint faded more with each of these visits, but he never progressed beyond his mouth on hers or his lips on her neck. This continued for close to a month. It electrified Ed's senses and her body in ways she had never experienced before, and the slowness at which everything progressed increased the anticipation. Ed could live with the stalled physical contact. What bothered her was the fact that Clint hadn't asked her to the formal. The fundraiser was three weeks away.

It took Celeste and her natural straightforwardness to puncture Ed's wait-and-see attitude.

"Ed," Celeste said one afternoon on the phone, "honey, you have to take that bull by the horn and lead him where you want to go. He's a man, Ed. He won't say no."

Celeste had a knack for boiling things to the simplest solution.

So, she did what Celeste would do. Ed invited Clint to her place on the night of her last class, to celebrate. It would end before the official 9 p.m. 'bell' and Ed told Clint to get there about 9:15. That gave her time to get home and prepare refreshments. Tootie had resumed her volunteer position with the city historical society and wouldn't be home until at least ten. The other women liked to stop at Perkins after their shift. Tootie hated Perkins (didn't she hate everything) but she didn't have any other ride home, especially with Ed still teaching.

She dressed in her most feminine lace bra, yellow with a front closure, and matching panties. She wore a button-down blouse with faux pearl buttons and an A-line Georgette black skirt. The summer season made it easy to skip the hose and slip on black sandals. But one part of her plan failed, when she got home, he was on the porch, long legs crossed as he relaxed in the rocking chair.

"You're early," she remarked. "Been waiting long?"

"Nope," he said. "This is the most I got to sit all day."

"Then, enjoy it, and let me get you a drink. Beer or wine?"

"Wine, but only if you'll join me."

"Of course," she said, pulling her keys from her purse.

He leapt to his feet and took the keychain from her hand. Clint opened the door and surveyed the stairs and the living room.

"Coast is clear," he said. "No bodies in the hall or on the couch."

She laughed.

"Tootie's not home," Ed said.

"Lucky us," Clint replied.

"I'll go get the wine," she said, hoping he wouldn't notice the tremors of her nervousness. She prepared two glasses of wine, dropping some fresh cherries into the bottom of each. When she carried them into the living room, he had plopped onto one end of the couch. She snuggled against him. He clinked his glass against hers.

They each tasted a sip and within seconds, their lips fell together. Their glasses got propped on the coffee table as their mouths had other pursuits.

Celeste's voice popped into Ed's head: "Take that bull by the horns."

She broke the kiss, taking a hearty gulp of her wine. Clint finished his. When she leaned into the couch cushions, Clint placed his arm across her lap to kiss her again. She intercepted his hand. As he pushed into his own side of the couch, she placed his hand against her breast.

He paled as his fingertips tightened against her clothed body. His chest rose and fell while those slow-motion seconds passed. She opened a button at her collar and then another. The hand against her chest squeezed. Her nipples grew erect and her skin tingled with that preliminary yet innocent touch. Her hand froze at the third pearl button, an inch from his hand as it toyed with her. She couldn't stifle the quiet moan that crossed her closed lips. His mouth grazed her knuckles. His tongue moved across her fingers as he pulled one into his mouth tugging her hand away from her torso.

Ed's face flushed, which was nothing compared to the heat below her skirt. He pulled her finger from between his lips and dropped her hand to her side. Then he undid the next button and pushed his hand inside. His hand quivered as it rested against the flesh above her heart, his palm brushing the center of her bra.

Ed's heart raced. Her body screamed with an intensity that wouldn't be satiated with the toy upstairs in her underwear drawer. A tear gathered in her eye as his body pressed further against hers on the couch. Clint's hand wandered across her bra, and stroked the ridge of flesh along the cup. His fingers paused at the metal of the closure. They dipped below it, exploring, twisting to each side and then back to the clasp as Ed fought not to writhe, her body desperate for him.

Clint withdrew his hand. He slowly unbuttoned the rest of her shirt, opening it and unclipping the closure. The fabric of the bra dropped into her armpits, her breasts spilling free. Clint stared.

"Oh, Ed," he gasped.

His mouth lowered to her chest. He covered her flesh with kisses, his tongue circling the nipple and causing the delicate flesh to prickle. The pressure of his mouth rose, to the point where Ed no longer knew if it were pleasure or pain.

His body, in his own urgency, knocked her across the couch. She laughed as her back struck the cushions and her head, luckily, hit a throw pillow. Her skirt gathered at the base of her thighs as his leg pushed against her. The scratch of the denim against her only tormented her more. Then, as his mouth sucked and his body bucked, she noticed the thickness under his jeans. It ground against the softness of her skirt pooled in her groin.

She wanted to find his zipper and plunge into it, but that's not what a nice girl would do, Mama's voice warned in her head.

Meanwhile, the image of Celeste, like a devil on her other shoulder, joined with Hannah's, rooting her on.

He had one hand wrapped around her back, keeping her chest tight against him. The other lingered in the crease under her other breast, his fingers tickling it from the underside.

Ed grabbed it. She moved it to her thigh, pausing before she hit her bunched skirt. His mouth still poised against her breast, his hand slipped toward the Georgette. His fingertips grazed the leg of her panties, dipping below.

As his fingers spread and almost pierced her wetness, trembling broke across his leg to hers followed with a booming chorus of "Cause my heart belongs to Daddy."

His head snapped away from her breast. His hand whipped from her panties and sunk into his pocket.

"This better be goddamned important," he muttered.

He brought the phone to his ear.

Ed jumped upright, slammed her legs closed,

adjusted her skirt, and overlapped the unbuttoned flaps of her shirt.

"Hello," Clint said gruffly.

He sighed.

"No, baby," Clint said. "I'm not busy."

He shrugged at Ed. She signed the letter 'O.' Clint shook his head. Ed followed with a 'G.' He nodded.

"Where are you?" he asked.

He touched his forehead.

"Okay," he said. "Get back in the car. I'll be there in twenty minutes."

Pause.

"I love you too."

He hung up.

"I'm so sorry," he said to Ed as he planted another kiss on her lips. "Her car broke down. There's an accident on the interstate so AAA can't help her for another two hours. I can't leave her out there…"

"No," Ed agreed. "You can't. They'll be other nights."

"Like this?" he asked.

Ed nodded. He reached into her shirt and caressed her breasts.

"Promise?" he said.

She smiled. He carefully arranged each breast in its cup and closed her bra. He then buttoned her shirt.

"You really need to go," Ed said.

He nodded.

"Will you be my date for Olive's fundraiser?" he asked.

"I thought you'd never ask," she said.

He helped her to her feet and kissed her.

"Would you be willing to pack an overnight bag and spend the night with me?"

His bluntness shocked her, in a good way.

"Oh, God, yes."

THIRTEEN

Ed's jaw hit the porch as she emerged from the house. Celeste and Siobhan pulled up in a splashy red convertible Mercedes. Celeste had said she bought a new car, but this…

Ed hadn't expected a Mercedes, and a convertible! Celeste had a wicked twinkle in her eye as Ed climbed into the car, the black leather gleaming and new.

Celeste insisted they would find a formal dress to suit Ed's 'womanly' body (Celeste's word choice). Ed knew better than to argue with Celeste. Celeste said they would find something, if they knew where to look.

Apparently, a red Mercedes with the top down would transport them to the city of their choice. The iPod piped the soundtrack to *Cats* into the sound system, which Celeste turned down as soon as Ed got into the car.

"A fire engine red Mercedes?" Ed muttered.

"Storm red," Celeste corrected her as she shifted into drive, "metallic."

Ed turned to the backseat where three-year-old Siobhan sat in her booster seat, wide sunglasses and a scarf over her head, and the yellow pages across her lap. Beside her, stacked under a metal Superman lunch box, Siobhan also had a French-English dictionary and a grammar book with a vampire on the cover.

"Do you have your heart set on Philly? I need to visit Bergdorf Goodman," Celeste said as the car crested the hill.

"They have a Bergdorf Goodman in Philly," Ed said.

"It's not my Bergdorf Goodman," Celeste replied.

"You have a Bergdorf Goodman? Did your checkbook spring a leak? Last time I saw you, you drove a Saturn."

"Darren has the Saturn," she said. "I am not putting an infant in the back of this car."

"You can't!" Ed exclaimed. "You're lucky Siobhan fits in there. There's no way you'd get a rear-facing car seat. Not very practical, Celeste."

Ed cringed as she surveyed the wood trim and the leather.

"This is, what… a fifty thousand dollar car?" she asked.

"Base price is sixty-five, but then there's the extras and the gas guzzler tax."

"Sixty-five! Gas guzzler! It's a little convertible!"

"The engine's got close to 400 horsepower."

"That's way more than you need," Ed remarked.

"Ed, if you want to lecture me on my eco-footprint, get it off your chest now."

"This is not a family car, Celeste. And the price of gas… And it just seems like you can get something cute and sporty without paying sixty-five thousand. You paid ninety for your house!"

"Ed, you know I've always been thrifty," Celeste said.

Siobhan broke into the chorus of "Mister Mistoffeles."

"I've been poor. I've been hungry. Let me have my materialistic glory—"

"Did you rob a bank? Start moonlighting in some less than savory job?"

Siobhan giggled.

"No, Ed."

"Because I can tell from the fabric and the cut of that jacket, you didn't buy that at the mall."

"No," Celeste said as she merged onto Main Street. "I was in New York last week."

"And they were handing out cash as some new tourist promotion?"

"I had a meeting with my agent and my publisher," she explained. "The last book in the trilogy hit number one on the *New York Times* bestseller list. Of course, that's caused a flurry of sales for the first two. The publisher loved my pitch for two more books, both supernatural suspense, and asked for the prequel and the sequel to the trilogy. That's four books."

"Oh my God, Celeste."

"There's more," she said. "A producer contacted my agent about a movie deal. Remember how we used to cast the movie in our free time?"

"Please tell me Meryl Streep will take the part."

Celeste laughed. "Don't forget Judi Dench. It's a bit part, but so important."

"That explains the Mercedes."

"The house is paid for, and I put money aside for the kids. I'm no millionaire—"

"The way things are going you could be soon," Ed remarked.

"That's why I'm in discussions with a lawyer about

establishing a foundation. For education and environmental causes."

"Really?"

Celeste nodded.

"I'd like you to serve on the board, Ed."

"I'd love to," Ed replied.

"Good. Now, I need to know. New York or Philly?"

"Doesn't matter," Ed quipped. "Nobody dresses fat girls."

"Excuse me? Somebody dresses Queen Latifah and she is hot."

"I'm not Queen Latifah."

"No," she said, "but you're not ready for a muu-muu either."

"Philly," Ed decided. "Because I'd like to stop in New Hope."

"Will that be productive? They don't sell clothes in New Hope."

Ed flashed her a look.

"New Hope it is," Celeste remarked as she merged onto route 611 South.

While Siobhan finished her rendition of "Mister Mistoffeles," Ed quietly broached the topic of what happened with Clint. She spoke with reserve, aware of the wee one in the back seat, but Celeste encouraged her to speak openly.

"Siobhan is used to these kind of discussions."

"She's three!" Ed exclaimed.

"Really, it's okay. Just don't get graphic, depending how much happened. But if something really happened, I hope I would have heard sooner."

"Well, I listened to your advice and rearranged his hands and gave him my breast."

"Miz Ed?" came a tiny preschool voice from the backseat.

"What, Princess?"

"Did you get a baby?"

"No. Why do you ask?"

"Because you said you gave him your breast. That's where you feed little babies."

Ed glared at Celeste. Celeste smiled and shrugged.

"We are mammals. It's what they're for," she said.

"Is that how Mommy fed you?" Ed asked.

"I guess," Siobhan said, as Ed heard the pages of the phone book rustle. "I don't remember. Joey's mommy had a baby. She eats and eats and eats."

'That's how Mommy fed you, too," Celeste explained.

"Milk comes out of the booby buttons," Siobhan said.

Ed burst into laughter.

"Nipples, darling," Celeste corrected her.

"But you have to have a baby before your booby buttons have milk."

"Siobhan, have you checked what Mommy put in your lunch box?" Celeste suggested.

Siobhan unlatched the box.

"Strawberries!" the little girl screamed. "Are these the ones we picked yesterday?"

She retrieved a round Tupperware container with washed and trimmed strawberries. Siobhan held up a juice box and another container with granola.

"Yep," Celeste said. "And that's the granola we made."

"You drive a sixty-five thousand dollar Mercedes but you make your own granola," Ed remarked.

"Siobhan, don't forget to share," Celeste said.

"I won't Mommy."

"And Ed, you know I don't want preservatives and crap in my child's body."

Discussion of breasts averted with the juicy sweetness of strawberries and the tangy flavor of Celeste's homemade blackstrap molasses granola.

"Miz Ed, do you want a sip of my juice box?"

"No, thanks," Ed replied.

"It's berry," Siobhan pointed out.

As Celeste predicted, they didn't have any worthwhile clothing in New Hope. The three of them did have a wonderful time walking in and out of the boutiques, shopping for gifts and novelty items and passing the time. Soon, Ed could no longer procrastinate the true reason for their journey and so they hopped into the Mercedes and took Route 32 into Philadelphia.

After a lunch of fancy sandwiches in a center city bistro (brie, turkey, and apple on a sundried tomato focaccia), they headed into every major department store and lesser known dress shop within walking distance, Ed found nothing but shapeless, loudly patterned junk.

Celeste, on the other hand, bought Louboutin passmules in royal blue with four-inch heels and two pair of Jean-Michel Cazabat shoes, one black and strappy and the other a croc print pump in gun metal. Celeste dropped nearly two grand on three pairs of shoes. Ed shook her head. On the way back to the car, as Siobhan enjoyed a soft ice cream cone and Celeste wolfed a wet walnut sundae, they passed a final row of shops—a jeweler, a newsstand, a corner grocery, a sushi joint and oddly, a dressmaker.

Celeste froze like a deer in headlights, dropping the spoon and empty dish from the sundae. Siobhan picked it up and scampered to a nearby wastebasket. Celeste strode, shopping bags on her arm plump with shoeboxes, to the window, transfixed by the screaming pink satin dress on a headless mannequin. One-shouldered with a draping sash of silk across the bodice and covered with clear and aquamarine beads, tight against the other contours of the plastic body, the dress had the strangest bushy tail of fabric at the hip, also spattered with beads.

"Ed, do you see that?" Celeste gasped.

"That's a skinny girl dress, Celeste. It's supposed to make a skinny curl look curvy. I don't need help in that department," Ed remarked.

Siobhan ran to the window and pressed her nose against the glass.

"Oh, honey," Celeste said as her hand pulled the girl's shoulder. "Don't do that. Remember what Mommy says: When you touch the glass, someone has to wash it and that's not nice."

"It's pretty, Mommy."

Celeste nodded.

"At least my daughter recognizes potential when she sees it," Celeste said. "Besides, anyone who can design that, certainly understands a woman's body and could make a dress for someone full-figured."

"I wouldn't hold my breath," Ed responded.

Celeste then raised her finger to a banner along the top of the window.

"I can dress anyone, guaranteed."

Before Ed could protest, Celeste dragged her inside. Siobhan barreled ahead, as a robust African-American woman in a lightweight trouser suit intercepted her.

"Hey, there, little one," the woman said with a bright smile. "Would you like to play with my train?"

"I love trains," Siobhan said.

"Me, too," she said.

She directed her attention to Celeste and Ed. She offered her hand to Celeste first. Celeste sneaked a glance at Ed and raised her eyebrows as if saying, "See, full-figured. I told you."

"Hi," the woman said. "I'm Louellen. Would you like to see Kristofer?"

"Kristofer?" Ed repeated.

A tall black man with cropped hair and two gold hoops in his ear popped out from behind a curtain, a pincushion in his hand.

"That would be me," he said.

He set the pincushion on the counter. He stepped toward them, his stiff aubergine pants crackling as he walked. He shook their hands.

"I am the dressmaker. You met my wife, Louellen."

Louellen had disappeared with Siobhan. Kristofer took each of them by the elbow and brought them to an upholstered bench.

"Let me guess," Kristofer said as he motioned for them to sit. He eyeballed Celeste. "Water? Coffee?"

"Nothing," Celeste replied. "Thank you."

"I would be flattered if you came to me," he said to Celeste. "I already have some ideas. But I know a woman in need, and I have a feeling that our friend in Berkinstocks has an invitation to an event that's out of her league."

Celeste chuckled.

"It's not funny," Ed replied, knocking Celeste with her arm.

"It's a black tie fundraiser," Celeste said. "And Ed needs a dress."

"Ed?"

"Edna," Celeste explained.

Kristofer nodded.

"She has a special date, too. So she needs to look hot."

"Celeste," Ed barked.

Kristofer rolled his lips and nodded. He grabbed Ed's hand and pulled her to her feet.

"She has a nice shape," he said as he spun her. "Balanced on top and bottom."

He placed his hand on her waist as she moved.

Tugging at her shirt, he jerked the fabric tight. He checked every each of her body with a scrutinizing glance. It made Ed feel like a horse at auction.

"Wide shoulder straps to support a low-cut bosom. Got to show them off. Be a crime not to, especially since there's a lucky man involved."

Ed massaged her forehead.

"Empire waist, wide… almost to the navel. Shiny, like a ribbon, maybe even a rosette. Did that dress have a rosette?"

Kristofer scratched his chin.

"It did," he said. "And you look the right size."

He nodded.

"The right size?" Ed said.

"I made a dress for Louellen," he said. "She wore it to a charity function when we first got back to the States. I had to show off a bit, since we planned to open this shop and no one knew I existed. I spent ten years in various workshops in Europe: Paris, London, Milan. But a black man can't succeed in fashion over there. You've got enough of a handicap if you're straight."

"So you can make me a dress?" Ed asked.

"What does the sign say?" he said with a wink. "I have it. It's Louellen's. But she can't wear it again, people would talk."

"I'm bigger than Louellen," Ed said.

"No, you're not," Kristofer said. "If I put Louellen in a shirt, baggy slacks and Berkinstocks, she'd be your Black twin. Now, I'll be right back."

Celeste released a hearty sigh as soon as he disappeared behind the curtain.

"You sure don't know when to keep your mouth shut," she said.

As Ed began to rebut, Kristopher returned with a garment bag that he unzipped dramatically in front of them. The navy blue silk dress that appeared matched his description, with a flare to the hips and a thigh high slit.

"No slit," Ed replied, shaking her head vehemently.

"Let me warn you," Kristofer said, as his index finger wiggled, "that a slit allows the drape more movement. It makes it easier to walk, and to dance—"

"I'm not dancing," Ed interrupted.

"You don't know that," Celeste replied.

"Oh, yes I do," Ed responded.

"Irrelevant," he snapped. "If the dress is stiff, it hides less. The movement and the freedom of the fabric will cooperate with the body. Wear dark hose and a nice heel. Very sexy. Try it on."

"It is beautiful, on the hanger," Ed remarked. "Will it look good on me?"

"I guarantee it," Kristofer said.

"Come on, Ed," Celeste said.

Kristofer hung the dress in a fitting room between a mirror and a Queen Anne chair.

"It will show off those curves in a positive way," Celeste said, shoving her into the booth.

"I couldn't have said it better myself," Kristofer said as he drew the curtain closed.

Alone in the little room, Ed scanned the garment for a price tag. She found none. Ed peered into the mirror, then to the dress, and to her reflection. She stripped to her underwear and unfastened her bra. She carefully got into the dress and closed the hidden zipper in the side seam. She swallowed when she turned to the mirror. She pulled her hair off her shoulders and could not believe the sophisticated lady in the glass. As she poked her head from behind the curtain, a crowd had gathered to see her: Celeste, Siobhan, Kristofer and Louellen. They applauded as she tentatively made her way to the three-way mirror.

"My work here is done," Kristofer said.

Louellen nodded. "It's perfect."

Celeste circled Ed, tittering the whole time.

"Mommy, I think Miz Ed needs shoes. They look funny."

Siobhan pointed to Ed's sandals.

"That's okay, baby. We'll get Ed a pair of Pradas or Guccis and she'll look better."

"But how much?" Ed asked.

"On sale, a couple hundred. Nobody's buying summer shoes now," Celeste answered.

"No, the dress," Ed said. "There's no price."

Kristofer smiled. He gazed at Louellen and then to Ed.

"It's a twelve hundred dollar dress, easily," he said.

"Forget it," Ed barked, beelining toward the changing room.

Kristofer stopped her.

"But it's used. The most I could take is six hundred."

"Six hundred?" Ed repeated.

Celeste jumped. "That's a steal, Ed, and it fits like it was made for you. You have to buy it."

"That's still a lot," she said quietly.

"It's the night of a lifetime, splurge," Celeste pleaded.

"Okay," she said, even quieter. "But no fancy shoes! I don't have any money left. We'll go to Payless. Maybe they have prom shoes on clearance."

"Damn it, Ed," Celeste said.

Kristofer bit his knuckles when she said the word 'Payless.'

"You don't buy a dress like that and wear cheap shoes! It's like a man in a tux wearing white sneakers," Celeste continued. "I'll buy the shoes."

"I can't let you do that."

"Why the Hell not?" Celeste replied. "I have the

money and the taste. Someone has to keep you from committing the fashion crime of the season."

The day-to-day grind of the week passed with much less excitement than the thrill of spending every dime of Ed's money on a ridiculously over-fancy dress with the navy blue Prada shoes Celeste insisted on purchasing.

Ed had a trunk full of printed materials: a solicitation letter, brochures, menu cards for the benefit, posters, stationery, business cards, and return envelopes, but she wouldn't head to the Hooper place until the installation of the sign.

Ed reviewed the file one more time on the computer even though she knew she'd see the real sign later today. It had a simple dark green background to blend with the natural landscape, as much as a sign can. Ed chose Tactile for the typeface. It it worked well both large and small and blended well with Clint's logo. She couldn't help it. It was her first sign.

Coming Soon:
Olive Branch Ranch at Hooper Farms
A rescue and rehabilitation
center for wild animals

(Don't worry, farmstand will remain open.)

She left early for her appointment with Olive, figuring she could do some errands along the way and buy some of the aforementioned produce. Clint had been busier than usual with plans for the fundraiser and his traditional busy season and the farm chores, but he called Ed every night about an hour after the sun set. She thought about their conversations and almost missed the vivid purple sign about a store in the strip mall. She slowed. Inside the square was a lime green circle with a squiggle... Then Ed read the name of the store.

"Condom Deluxe Superstore."

Ed laughed. It wasn't a squiggle! That was a sperm! Ed pulled into the parking lot, if only to enjoy the clever graphic design. Bold colors, recognizable shape, easily reproduced branding… Her students could learn a thing or two from this. She whipped out her digital camera and fired a few shots.

Something tugged at her. Maybe she should go inside, check it out. Didn't hurt to be prepared.

Good Lord, Ed, she told herself. Go to the corner pharmacy and buy yourself some Trojans.

She went inside, immediately attracted to a display of condoms with fancy names and beautiful packages. "Her Pleasure," "His Pleasure," "Textured," "Glow-in-the-Dark," "Warming Sensations," mint and even citrus flavors.

Get a grip, Ed, she said to herself. You can forgive yourself for selecting a book by the cover or a wine by the label. But condoms? Really, now.

Her hand closed over the pleasure assortment pack, a half-dozen condoms in the most popular styles: one each of his and her pleasure, warming sensation, twister, mint, and a plain one. The cashier packed everything into a lime green bag. She dropped a business card into it. As long as Ed remembered to remove that card, she could recycle the bag for gifts. Ed tossed the bag to the passenger seat and headed to the ranch.

The girls rushed to greet her. A van with the sign installers arrived directly after her. Mr. Hooper crossed the porch in the midst of the commotion. Two men carted the sign from the rear of the van with Mr. Hooper only a few paces away. Olive brushed her hands together. Ed popped Aretha's trunk, Genny immediately dug in. The sign guys distracted Olive. Ed let her be.

"Your dad around?" she asked

"Nope," Gen answered from behind a carton of posters. "Something about a raccoon, somewhere where a raccoon isn't supposed to be."

She and Ed carried some boxes to the house and Olive still stared at the sign guys as they wrestled with the post. Genny crept behind her.

"Olive," her twin said, "this is all your stuff we're unloading."

"Sorry," Olive said with a chuckle.

Olive seized two cartons of envelopes. With the three of them, it went much faster than it did for Ed to load the car. They finished in time to gather around the signpost, and survey the installers in their final efforts. Of course, Mr. Hooper had supervised the whole project.

"Don't step on the petunias," he chided the workmen.

Finally, the workmen erected the sign, casting a shadow across the farm stand. Mr. Hooper shook his head as he read it.

"Farm stand... remain open," he muttered. "You didn't have to put that on the sign."

"I most certainly did," she replied. "This is the only farm stand left around here."

Mr. Hooper shook his head, again. He headed toward the barn. He stopped after a few strides and turned to the girls.

"Don't suppose anyone would want to help me milk the cows?" he asked.

"I'll help," Genny replied. She looked to her sister and then Ed. "Unless... you guys need me."

"Nope," Olive said. "I was just going to offer Ed some more of that famous Anderson lemonade. Would you like some, Ed?"

"I'd love some," Ed answered as Genny and Mr. Hooper disappeared in the barn. Ed dropped into an old wooden rocker while Olive vanished into the Hooper house to get the beverages. A shiny gold car, long and rounded in all the wrong places to pass for an ordinary car, pulled into the driveway across the street. The car traveled slowly to the loop, and paused before the house. A tall woman, dark-haired, in an impeccably-tailored suit got out of the car. Ed couldn't see much else at this distance. She didn't think anything of it, other than the fact that once the car stopped she could decipher the letters in the car's metal. They read 'Jaguar.'

"Hey, Olive," Ed yelled. "You know any fancy woman in a Jaguar?"

"No," Olive replied. "I've never been within ten feet of a Jaguar."

The woman progressed to the Anderson homestead porch. Before she went to the door, she ran her hand across the railing and surveyed the gardens. She didn't move for quite some time. Olive's footsteps echoed toward the door. The screen door creaked. Across the street, CA burst from the farmhouse waving a shotgun.

"Olive, does your grandfather—"

Olive, who had been handing Ed a glass of lemonade, turned before Ed finished the sentence.

"Almighty!" she screeched. "Gramps has got a gun!"

Olive ran from the porch, into the road, and down the lane like a track star. Ed sprinted, but kept a comfortable pace behind. Despite the summer heat, the newcomer had a single-breasted cropped jacket closed and long pants. If her shopping trip with Celeste had taught Ed nothing else, she recognized the Manolo Blahnik's on Ms. Jaguar's feet.

"Get off my property!" CA screamed.

"Now, CA," the woman said calmly.

He lowered the shot gun.

"We don't need you," he bellowed.

Ed got a good look at the eyes, the brown hair, and the shape of her face. As Olive raced up the stairs, coming alongside the woman, Ed thought someone had flattened her with a piano, just like in the old cartoons. Sure, the woman had a few years on Olive, but other than that, they looked identical... like twins... but Olive had a twin. What Olive didn't have was...

"Emma, get out of here!" CA continued. "Get off my property and never come back."

"Gramps," Olive barked. She reached for the gun. "Give me that."

The old man heeded.

"I'm Olive. Olive Anderson," Olive said, extending the hand without the gun.

The woman shook hands.

"Have we met?" Olive asked.

"My name is Emma Meriwether," the woman stated.

"Oh, for God's sake, Emma," CA said. "Don't act all professional. Look at her, Olive. It's your mama."

"My mother?" Olive said stunned.

She peered into the barrel of the gun.

"I heard about the fundraiser," Emma said.

She pulled a check from the zippered pocket in her patent and patterned leather purse. The silver plate about the pocket glared in the sun.

"I didn't want to cause trouble. I just want to give you something. I thought I could help," Emma said.

Olive didn't touch the check. Behind Ed, Clint's truck rolled into the driveway.

"I'm sorry," Olive said as her hand gripped the shotgun tighter. "Did you say you didn't want to cause trouble?"

Olive raised the shotgun to her shoulder.

"I think my grandfather was right, ma'am," Olive said, her tone deadpan. "You better go and not come back."

Clint cautiously got out of his truck, and upon seeing the commotion, joined everyone on the porch.

"Olive, what are you doing?" Clint scolded her.

"Daddy, I think she ought to leave."

"I reared you better than that, Olive," he continued.

"Daddy, she's been gone twenty years," Olive replied.

Mr. Hooper and Genny crossed the street.

"Please, Olive," Emma said, as her chest heaved. "I'm proud of you and what you've done. That's all, Olive."

"If you cared about me, or what I've done, you wouldn't have left," Olive said.

She lowered the gun.

"I can't ask you to understand," Emma said. "And I certainly can't ask you to forgive me."

"Because what you did," Genny said as she walked up the stairs, "was unforgivable. We were babies, Mama. How could you leave your babies?"

Emma cried now, thin rivulets of tears marring her perfectly made-up face.

"Looking back," she said, choking on the words. "I don't know. I should have mailed this."

She handed the check to Clint and started down the stairs.

"I don't want her money," Olive yelled.

"You haven't even looked at the check," Emma said.

"I don't care if it's for a million dollars," she said. "You can't buy me."

"Us," Gen added, roping her arm around her sister.

"Girls," Clint said. "Can't you at least listen to your mother?"

"This woman isn't my mother," Genny remarked. "You are my mother and my father."

"She was just a uterus," Olive cracked.

"Girls," Clint snapped. "Stop it."

"Clint, I'll go," Emma said as she reached the path at the bottom of the steps.

Clint followed her. Ed went to the porch, lifted the shotgun from Olive, and pulled the girls toward the house.

"Come on, girls," she said. "Your mom and dad have to talk."

Ed pushed them inside the screen door.

"Clint," Ed called. "Let us know when you're done. I'll do my best to keep them corralled."

"Maybe we'll take a walk to the cabin," Clint said.

Emma almost smiled. "The cabin."

Olive had heard the exchange.

"The cabin," she said as she paced the living room. "That's where we lived. The cabin. It's obvious now."

"That's why no one would explain it," Genny replied.

Ed went into the kitchen and grabbed some spoons out of the dish drainer, chocolate ice cream, and a bag of chips. She carried them into the living room.

"I didn't know if you preferred salty or sweet in these situations," Ed said.

"Sweet," the girls replied. "Definitely."

Olive and Genny sat cross-legged on the floor and demolished a quart of chocolate-chocolate chunk-marshmallow ice cream. From the window, Ed kept watching for Clint and Emma to return from the woods. The girls talked until their throats turned raspy. That was when Ed spoke.

"I was barely sixteen when my mom died," Ed said. "And I miss her terribly. You'll never know what it's like to depend on your mom, but this is your chance to find out who she is, who you are. You don't have to like her, but get the answers to your questions. She has them."

"You're right, Ed," Olive said. "I think I'll go sit on the porch and wait for them."

"Me, too," Genny said.

"I wonder how much that check is for," Olive said. "I plan on taking strangers' money. I can take my mother's."

Ed laughed.

"I'm going," she said. "You're okay now."

Genny grabbed her wrist.

"Don't go, Ed," she said. "We need you."

Ed smiled. "You don't need me. You have family."

As Ed crossed the street back to the Hooper place, and opened Aretha's door, Clint and Emma glided across the porch, arm-in-arm. Even with her make-up streaked, Emma was thin and gorgeous. Ed collapsed into the driver's seat. She looked at the green bag on the other seat and tore open the fancy box of condoms. She dumped the colorful foil squares out the window and drove off.

She thought about her daydreams, their dates, the expensive dress in the garment bag in her closet, the restaurant in the woods. And she thought of Emma on Clint's arm.

Forget the party, Ed, she said to herself. The homecoming queen ruined your big dance once again. Nobody wants the fat girl. Nobody.

She'd learned that lesson long ago, but something about this past year made her forget.

She wouldn't let that happen again.

FOURTEEN

The two-liter Coke bottle did not falter from its proud stance in the middle of the dining room table, the condensation bubbling from the side of the plastic as Ed circled the kitchen with the glass clutched so tightly in her hand she feared she might shatter it.

The last thing she needed was a steady shot of caffeine and sugar.

Or maybe it was the thing she needed most.

Or not.

She must have walked six miles in the humidity, stopping only once to duck into the pizza parlor for this ice cold bottle of Coke. In a few more minutes, it would lose its chill, not that Ed cared about the temperature.

She had covered every public inch of the abandoned steel mill. She had trudged up and down the hills in the good neighborhoods and the bad. She had walked so long the callus on her big toe from the leather of her sandal had burst open and bled. Not that she felt it. Not that it stopped her.

Sweat had drenched her. Her back, her pants, the crease in her belly, her arm pits. Even her hair had not escaped, a damp and unruly mess. She had kicked her shoes off at the door and now her feet traipsed the kitchen floor, their flesh white where the sandals had gripped and dingy brown from dirt everywhere else, except for the side of her foot bloodied by her big toe.

In her mind, she twisted open the cap of the two-liter. She could hear the faint hiss and it amplified the craving. She set the glass on the counter, afraid she would give in. No, hoping she would give in. Because if she hadn't planned to sabotage her health, why had she bought the damn thing in the first place?

Could caffeine and sugar block the hurt?

The rejection?

She knew better.

Might as well add a quart of ice cream and a funnel cake to the mix. But Ed knew better. Food never solved problems. Especially for fat girls.

She stared at her phone. She had called Celeste, Hannah, Martha, and even Josie in her frustration. No answer anywhere. No return calls.

She had left a message for Olive sending her apologies. She had then left Clint a message, in the steadiest voice she could muster, stating that she would not be available for the fundraiser.

Earlier this afternoon, she had provided the shoulder to cry on. Now, she needed one. And all she had was a bottle of Coke.

No matter. She and the Coca-Cola bottling company had a longstanding partnership. She could wait to hear everyone else say, "I told you so."

Three strikes, you're out, Ed.

Still clutching the glass, staring at the Coca-Cola bottle and fighting her own tears, Ed listened to the lecture spinning through her head.

You were out before this inning. You should have learned your lesson after Frank.

Sure, college kids are immature. The teacher in her understood this more than she did then. But a man's a man. And a man takes what he wants and goes home, especially when you're fat. But no, after Frank, she fell for Dick… and yes, the name suited him.

She allowed herself to believe the fairy tale and he planned on using her from the start. And the last jackass… Two-timing user bastard… Maybe these things happened to all women, but fat women seemed to attract more than their fair share.

She leaned across the table, her hand closing on the lid of the two-liter. Ed sighed. That expert flick of the wrist and the bottle came to life. She lifted it as she removed the cap. She brought the bottle to the glass and her hand tilted. The initial syrupy dregs hit the glass. The doorbell rang. Ed righted the bottle.

"Shit," she said out loud.

It rang again. Ed could choose to hide in the corner with her two-liter and a straw but the inside door was wide open. Any of her friends would eventually view the open door as an invitation, and her family wouldn't have rung the bell in the first place. The bell rang a third time. Ed started toward it.

"Ed," a voice called.

It was Genny.

"Ed, that you?"

When Ed reached the door she noticed both girls, leaning against the railing on the porch.

"You left abruptly," Olive said as she dropped into

one of the rockers.

"And you stayed in your car a little long," Genny added. "So we thought maybe you had gotten upset."

"Nothing to get upset over. It's your mama, girls," Ed said, forcing a smile. "This is a great opportunity."

"In time," Olive muttered. "She seems nice enough."

"We all went to the cabin," Genny said. "We used to play there. We never understood it. You know there were dishes on the table. And in the cupboards. A fully stocked pantry... I think someone had cleaned out the perishables."

"I think that was Uncle Ricky," Olive said.

"But that's where we were born," Genny said. "Maybe not literally."

"I'd never seen Dad so quiet," Olive said.

"What next?" Ed asked.

"One day at a time," Olive said.

"Your dad?"

"All he said was 'It is nice to see you, Emma,'" Genny replied.

"What about the check?" Ed asked.

"It was a hundred grand," Olive said. "From the Meriwether Foundation."

"So you took it?" Ed said.

"Dad said it would be foolish not to," Olive said.

"He's right," Ed answered.

"Dad told me not to worry about the bills for the fundraiser, that you had to spend money to make money and I'm already in the black," Olive replied.

"Speaking of the party," Genny piped in, sitting on the edge of the rocker. "Ed, can we see your dress?"

"Now would be the time," Ed replied, "I'm sending it back tomorrow."

"What do you mean?" Olive asked.

"I'm sorry, Olive," Ed said, "but under the

circumstances, I think it's best if I lay low. Your dad has enough going on without me complicating it—"

"You complicating what?" Olive interrupted. Her voice rose as she spoke. "No, Ed. You don't complicate anything. It's about her, isn't it? She complicated it."

"It doesn't matter, girls. Your dad has waited for her for a long time—"

"Ed," Genny said calmly. "She's married."

"It doesn't change the way your father feels about her," Ed replied.

"It doesn't change the way he feels about you," Olive remarked. "Ed, we've waited forever to see our father take an interest in a woman. Don't let her ruin it. He can't pine over her forever."

"Girls," Ed said. "It's not about her. It's about her type. You wouldn't understand."

"Her type?" Genny repeated.

"What do you mean we wouldn't understand?" Olive replied. "We're not children, Ed."

"No, but you're young and you're pretty and you're thin," Ed told them. "Men don't waste their time on fat women."

"Do you really think Dad's that shallow?" Genny said.

As if on cue, Clint climbed to the porch.

"I'm shallow?" he said. "Is that why you've decided to dump me, Ed?"

"No, Clint," Ed said, turning red as she realized he held her discarded green gift bag.

"Ed forgot something at our place and I thought I'd return it," Clint said.

"What is that?" Olive asked, pointing.

"Nothing," Ed said.

Clint smiled. "It's private. Girls, I think it's time for you to head home."

"Daddy, you can fix this, right?" Olive said.

He kissed her and tousled her hair.

"I think so," Clint said. "And if not, there's always kidnapping."

The girls chuckled as they departed.

"See you later, Ed," they hollered.

Clint and Ed stood silently on the porch.

"You're not going to make this easy, are you?" Clint said.

"Nobody asked you to come," Ed said.

"No," he replied. "But I'm here anyway. I was on my way when I heard your message—as if I'd let you back out of our date now—and then I noticed the condoms in Mr. Hooper's driveway. Now either he's a busy old man—"

"Clint, please don't make jokes."

"Sorry, but I don't know what else to do. I don't understand why you left, what's going on—"

"Clint, Emma's return made me realize... I'm not right for you."

"Ed, you can't mean that."

"I do," she said. "Your girls are grown. You can't use them for an excuse. You can find someone, someone pretty and charming, like Emma. Thank you, for everything, but I think you should go."

She turned and headed into the house, dreaming of the now tepid Coke in the kitchen. She pulled the screen door open as Clint's hand seized her shoulder.

"Ed, what the Hell are you saying? I know us men can be stupid, raising two girls on my own certainly taught me that. But you're not making sense. I don't know what I feel for you," he said.

His hand nudged her toward him.

"I think that maybe I could love you," Clint said.

Ed's chest tightened and she lost her breath as her hands and face grew hot. Tears drowned her eyes even as she fought them.

"I'm going in the house," she said.

She stepped into the door.

"I'm coming, too," Clint insisted.

He pushed his way in.

"Leave me alone, Clint," she said. "Why do you have to make this so hard?"

"A man deserves to know why he's being dumped," he said.

He set the condoms on the end table. He progressed past her and to the kitchen.

"I'm going to get us a couple beers," Clint said.

Ed collapsed in a nearby armchair as he went to the basement. She set her arms on her knees, wrung her hands and let the tears tumble down her face. Hearing his footfalls on the stairs, Ed drew in a deep breath. Clint proceeded into the kitchen. The beer bottles tapped the counter.

"Oh, Ed," Clint said. "You didn't."

The next sound that carried to the living room was the glug of the soda bottle as its contents spilled into the sink.

"Hey!" she yelled.

She leapt to her feet, striding into the kitchen with her hands on her hips. He smooshed the empty bottle and tossed it into the recycling bucket.

"You can't come prancing in here—"

"And, what, Ed?" Clint interrupted. "You didn't

really want that. You only want that when something's bothering you. Now out with it."

He got two glasses from the cupboard and marched to the freezer for ice.

"You don't want me," Ed blurted.

One ice cube clinked into the glass. Another cascaded to the floor.

"What?" he replied.

"It won't work," she said. "As soon as someone pretty comes along, someone thin—"

Clint set the glasses on the table, and reached for her, but realized he left the freezer door open and slammed it closed.

"You use those words a lot, Ed. Pretty. Thin. Why?"

"Because it's what men want."

"No, Ed."

"Yes, Clint. I'm tired of being used and replaced. So let's just end this now."

"How could I replace you? Why would I? Emma made you feel this way?"

Ed shrugged. "Look at her, Clint. Rich, polished, gorgeous. No wonder she's the love of your life."

"She was," Clint said. "Was. There's nothing there but a really special memory."

"Doesn't matter, Clint," Ed said. "I can't compete with her. I worried about competing with that memory, but now that I've seen her there's no way—"

He popped the beers and poured them into the glasses. He took a hearty swig of the portion still in the bottle.

"Do you even remember what I told you about Emma?" Clint said.

Ed puzzled over his statement. She blinked. Hard. She wished he hadn't dumped the Coke.

"I knew she was gorgeous and rich, as you put it, and when I asked her out, I expected her to say no," Clint explained. "She didn't, Ed. And she shared some of the best, and easiest, years of my life with me. Because she didn't judge me. And now you do. Yeah, she was gorgeous and fun and wonderful, Ed, but as soon as life stopped being easy she left me. With two infant girls."

He handed her the other beer.

"So, now that my life looks a little more complicated,

you plan on leaving, too?" Clint asked. "Because it all looked pretty nice last weekend, before Genny interrupted us."

"It did," Ed admitted. "But that would have changed."

"Why, Ed?"

"Because," she snapped. "Every man who's ever seen me naked has changed their mind. But, of course, they take what they want first, with no care about me, because I'm just a fat cow."

"Goddamit, Ed. Take your clothes off."

"No!"

"I'm serious. You have some serious body issues and I want to prove to you that I don't care."

"No, Clint."

"Then let's at least go sit on the couch and you can at least show me your breasts."

"Clint, every lover I've ever had dumped me once we had sex."

"Every one?" he said as he took her hand, stroking it gently.

She nodded. "Three. Not exactly worldly in that department."

"Do you want to talk about it?" he asked.

"No," she answered.

"We should," he said. "If you really want to trust me. Or as you once said, if we plan on being serious."

Ed wanted to believe him. She also wanted to hide. She needed to think. She grabbed her beer and left the kitchen. He followed. She pivoted.

"I'm going upstairs. I'm smelly and sweaty and generally gross. I'm going to hop in the shower. I'd prefer you were gone by the time I come back."

She kept walking. She paused, overtaken by her mother's ghost. She looked over her shoulder.

"But you can finish your beer," Ed said.

She took a few more steps. She stopped again.

"Don't drink it too fast," Ed instructed him. "You get pulled over and Tootie will see it in the newspaper and I'll never hear the end of what a loser you are."

Once upstairs, she filled the tub and left the beer on the side. She laid under the bubbles forever, waiting to hear the screen door creak. She washed everything she could think of and still no door. Her feet pruned. No door. The water went cold. No door.

She drained the bath in defeat. She tugged her hair into rogue ponytail, slapped on her Pépé le Pew pajama pants and a tank top and paraded downstairs. She no longer had fire under her skin, but she was mildly irritated that he hadn't listened. Only mildly irritated because she liked the fact that he had outlasted her little tantrum.

"I was beginning to think I'd be sleeping on this couch," Clint said.

"Tootie wouldn't like that," she replied.

He took his phone out of his pocket and waved it. "I turned off my phone."

She approached him.

"Nice jammies," he remarked.

"I've born the brunt of many skunk jokes this past year," Ed said.

"Welcome to my life," he said with a smile.

He patted the couch beside him. She took his hand and snuggled against him, his arm around her waist and her head against his chest.

"Is this where I tell you about my troubled past?" she asked.

"Unless you have plans to have your old boyfriends show up, that seems to have worked well for my family."

"What do you want to know?"

"Who hurt you? What happened?" Clint inquired.

"It isn't pretty," she said.

"And it's not thin?" he joked. His face turned very plain and stoic. "Okay."

"Frank and I met in college. He knew I was a virgin, but he didn't care. So, it was horrible and awkward, and he was the only one who enjoyed it. He didn't say much, but he tried again, and I let him, but nothing changed," Ed said without much breath. "He told me to get out before his roommate saw him with the fat pig. His entire fraternity used to prank-call me and spread nasty rumors about me."

"Jerk," Clint muttered.

"And I can't prove this," she said. The tears resumed. "But I really think the whole thing was part of joining the fraternity. What do you call that?"

"Initiation?"

"Yeah," she said.

He passed her the tissues from the table. She accepted one and dabbed her eyes.

"After college, I dated some. The occasional movie or dinner. But never more than once or twice. That's when I started getting fat. I was fifty pounds lighter in college."

"So who broke your heart next?" Clint asked.

"Lane," Ed replied. "I got this awesome design job and he was one of my coworkers. He was perfectly toned, broad shouldered, loved football, and dreamy. I think he used to highlight his hair and he had eyes like an angel..."

"What happened?"

"We worked as a team on a lot of projects, so we'd talk and it seemed like we had everything in common. We had a client, an art gallery, having an opening.

He suggested we meet up beforehand, expense dinner, and attend the exhibition, on the company's tab."

"Did you?"

"Yeah," Ed said. "We went to the same restaurant our boss dined the big clients at, and Lane even ordered French champagne. Maybe the champagne prepped me for what happened later, after the gallery."

Ed paused. Dryness lined her throat.

"I need water," she said as she hoisted herself up.

"No," Clint said, motioning her to the couch. "I'll get it."

He brought her water with a bendable straw. She drank some.

"I went to his place, Clint," Ed said. A deluge of tears made it impossible for her to open her eyes. "He kept using this sweet tone with me, 'Come on, baby.' And after a few of his kisses… I did. I stripped while he was in the bathroom and got into his bed. But then something changed…"

She had to pause again. The memory was choking her and she had to give herself a minute. Her skin pinched as if Lane's hands were on her once again.

"He jumped on top of me, Clint," Ed said. "Very literally. And while Frank may have been a fumbling idiot, Lane hurt. He was jamming himself against my body anyway he could."

"That was rape, Ed."

"I didn't say no, Clint. I didn't say anything."

He pulled her against him and let her sob.

"Date rape then, Ed," Clint suggested.

"That didn't exist back then and you know it."

She wiped her tears. The pile of tissues on the table had certainly grown.

"Anyway. He had groped me so hard, my sides were black and blue. My legs and my… middle… hurt from all the friction and the force. I was lying there shaking, willing myself to get up and get dressed. I finally did… and he knocked me on the floor, onto my stomach, and he punched me in the back… I think he was aiming for my kidneys but he missed."

She inhaled deeply.

"He dropped his entire body weight against me, his chest against my back, and his hands pushed against my butt and before I knew it, he had his dick in my ass," she said. "I started screaming and fighting and I don't even remember what happened exactly except on Monday he had scratches all over his face."

"He deserved them," Clint remarked.

"You haven't heard the best part," Ed said. "I was the one that signed the bill at the restaurant. And Lane told everyone about our date and how I attacked him when he asked me to leave… The boss was pissed because of the one hundred dollar tab I signed on the company's credit and now Lane was talking sexual harassment. I was asked to resign."

"And you did."

"Yes," Ed said. "When I handed the letter to my boss, she told me something that cleared everything up. She said, 'I hired you because we needed another smart woman in this office. Because of your creativity, proficiency and dedication, I had planned to promote you. I told the senior staff last week. But this lapse in judgment shocks me, Edna.'"

"He knew," Clint replied. "He heard about the promotion."

Ed nodded. "He was drinking buddies with the vice president. He wanted me out of the way. The sex was a bonus."

The silence surrounded them to the point where Ed could count the clicks of the clock.

"It's not your fault," Clint said as he brushed her bangs from her face.

"I just know how to pick them," she replied.

His hand continued over her almost dry hair.

"My next job was at the newspaper," Ed said, "and I didn't date for a very long time. When I met Dick, I told him I had bad experiences and alluded to some of the details… and he swore he would be different."

"But it wasn't?"

"I guess it was… I don't know. We dated for a year. Dick invited me on a ski weekend. I didn't want to, but he talked me into it. I even started going to the gym. I didn't know how to ski, but Dick said I'd learn."

She smiled at him. The memories of her on the ski slope made her laugh, despite the eventual humiliation. She might have enjoyed skiing, had the circumstances played out differently.

"After a couple hours on the slopes, we had a nice dinner at the lodge. He was an excellent skier. We went back to our room. One thing led to another. When we ended up in bed, well, when he saw me, naked…"

Her jaw quivered.

"I repulsed him," she said. "I could see it in his eyes. And whatever mood had been set was broken. He was a sweet lover. Tried to coax me along and it was almost nice."

"So he got over it? His reaction?"

"No," she said. "He wouldn't look at me."

Clint pulled her forward and cupped her face. He kissed the tip of her nose.

"Ed, our bodies are shells. They change all the time. They wrinkle. They sag. Mine's incredibly hairy," he said. "As long as two people want to be together, the beauty is there. Shouldn't sex be about a moment, not a body?"

She sighed.

"Do you trust me, Ed?" he asked, releasing her.

"I don't know," she said. "I want to—"

His lips struck hers. He tasted like the microbrew. As he kissed her, his hand wandered across her shirt, supporting one of her breasts. Her body trembled. He broke away.

"God, I wanted to do that all night," he said. "I hope it wasn't insensitive of me."

Ed touched her chin and shook her head.

"Go ahead and finish your story," Clint remarked.

"We left the mountain early and Dick never tried to make love to me again. When we saw each other, it was nice. We went to movies, special events in New York, anything really. But never again did he touch me. Months passed. We were walking to the car one afternoon and he stopped. He said he couldn't see me anymore. That he started seeing someone after the ski trip and she was pregnant."

"And he didn't tell you about her earlier!" Clint interjected.

"That's not the good part," she said. "He said he loved my company, valued my friendship and that originally he wanted it to work between us."

"Why didn't it?" Clint said skeptically.

"He said he tried, but he was not attracted to me."

"Jackass," Clint muttered.

"That he really tried not to let my appearance affect his feelings, but he couldn't... you know."

Clint soared to his feet.

"That's the lamest excuse I ever heard," Clint replied. "Probably was having trouble getting it up in general."

"Clint, don't."

"Sorry."

He took her hand and pulled her to her feet. He kissed her again. Her ankles wobbled and even with her eyes closed Ed could feel the world spin.

"I'm not going to make love to you now," he said. "You're vulnerable. But I will take you to bed and tuck you in."

"That's not necessary," she replied.

"Ed, come with me. I have lots of experience in the tucking in department."

He led her up the stairs.

"Which one's yours?" he asked.

She pointed.

"Go do whatever you do before bed," he instructed her. "I'll wait."

As she brushed her teeth, she heard the fan in her room oscillate. When she finished, she found Clint on her bed, his clothes nicely folded on the chair, her sheet covering him below the waist. He had arranged her quilt at the bottom of the bed.

"No funny business," he said. "I'm going to hold you until you fall asleep. Then I'm going to sleep. Okay?"

"Now is not the time," she answered.

"Ed, you had an emotional day."

"So have you," she countered. "You should be home with your family."

"You need me more," he replied.

She traced the outline of his body with her eyes.

"Are you naked under there?" she asked.

"No," he said. "I'm a gentleman. I kept my boxers on."

He flapped the sheet revealing his dark blue underwear. Dark hair covered his body. It was sparse around his neck but it thickened toward his belly.

"You are hairy," she remarked.

"I know," he said. "Told you."

She lingered.

"Am I on the wrong side of the bed?" he asked. "I can move."

She shook her head.

"This feels weird."

"We're grown-ups," he replied.

She smiled and crawled into bed. As soon as her head hit the pillow, her eyes dropped.

"Good night, Clint."

"Good night, Ed."

She turned out the light. His hand laid against her hip. She fell asleep almost instantly. She woke in the morning to an empty bed and a letter on the nightstand.

"Dear John," Ed said to herself with a grunt.

She read the paper.

"Duty calls. This business requires some work at daybreak. I'll be back with dinner. And pack your clothes for the weekend. I'll bring them to the ranch when I go home. I'm thinking Chinese. Call me if that's not okay."

Ed smiled.

It all sounded fine.

FIFTEEN

Ed did most of her work on the porch that day with the MacBook. Every few hours, she'd realize that tomorrow was the formal fundraiser and her subsequent *rendez-vous* with Clint. It sent chills down her spine, flushed her cheeks and heated other newly revived sections of her anatomy. She finished the annual report that had been scheduled to go to the printer January 10… Ah, the joy of working with non-profits. After a quick flight check and exporting the file as a PDF, she uploaded to the printer and considered the job done.

She put the computer aside and toasted to herself with her home-brewed unsweetened sun tea. Clint's truck pulled up on the other side of the street, the passenger side of the cab stuffed with her garment bag and her luggage.

Somehow, Genny and Olive had convinced her to join them at the salon in the morning and to dress with them at the Hooper place. Ed felt way too old for such girly camaraderie, but they were so earnest in their cajoling that Ed melted with what she called the double-eyelash-bat, two sets of pathetic eyes peering at her. So, Clint had all of her necessities in the truck.

And now he headed toward her with a large brown bag. In the glowing evening light, his hair seemed grey with dust, the left side of his face smudged with dirt and his clothing barely recognizable as fabric.

"What happened to you?" Ed asked.

"Typical day at the office," he replied. "Bats, squirrels and mice in an attic."

He dropped into the rocker beside her and set the bag on the porch.

"Thought I'd freshen up here so I wouldn't be late," he said. "Didn't want you to think I stood you up."

"I'm not that unstable," she said.

She closed the MacBook.

"Okay, maybe," she continued. "But I would recognize I was being irrational. And to the world I remain cool, collected and independent."

"So you spent the day cramming memories into your subconscious in hopes of repressing them forever."

"No," she said, meeting his eyes. "I called my gang of Nosy Nellies… and told them what happened last night, and told them how you listened. Then I told them the parts I'd left out in the past. So I feel better."

"Good, I'm glad."

"They sent you a message. About what happens if you hurt me."

"Oh, no," Clint said with a smile. "Is this like something from the Godfather?"

"You trap skunks, rats, and rescue birds of prey caught on window netting and you're scared of a doctor, a novelist, and an executive?"

"Let's see," he said leaning into the rocker and gazing toward the porch roof. "Martha… a doctor who's a lesbian. I could lose my manhood, quite literally. Hannah doesn't worry me all that much, but she's the rugged outdoors type so she would know where to dispose of the body."

Ed chuckled.

"And that leaves Celeste. She's young, impetuous and has quite the imagination," Clint said. "The girls have read her books."

Ed roared in laughter.

"She has witches, vampires and werewolves on her side," he said with a wink.

Clutching her midriff, Ed choked out words as she cackled.

"That's the funniest thing I heard all week."

"That's my job," Clint replied. "To amuse you."

Ed's laughter slowed.

"I think you do more than that," she said.

"Good," he said.

They sat quietly for a moment, only the passing cars, the creak of the rockers and the subtle noise of insects disturbing them. Ed exhaled as her laughter finally died.

"What's in the bag?" she asked. "I'm starved. If it's Chinese, it's getting cold."

"It is cold," he said, pulling the bag between them. "Running late as I was, and with the big day tomorrow, I opted for salad. It's all anyone will eat in my house these days. But I know I said Chinese so if you're disappointed—"

"No," Ed said. "Salad is perfect. With everything that's happened, I don't know if I could digest Chinese."

"My daughters can ingest lettuce indefinitely if they

think it increases their chances of being hot…"

"Clint, your daughters are gorgeous."

"I know that," he replied, pulling the black plastic containers from the bag. "PETE."

"Really?" Ed said as she accepted the salad. She held it over her head so she could read the bottom. Sure enough, the number inside the arrows was a two. When she brought the salad to her lap, she noticed pinkish-white chunks on top of the greens.

"I can't even think about my daughters as hot," he said.

He handed her a plastic fork.

"Sorry, we could have used your silverware. I wasn't thinking," he said.

She shrugged.

"Any man who wants a girl because she's hot is up to no good," Clint added.

"Clint, they aren't little girls anymore."

"I know," he said. "Salmon."

He pointed to the salad.

"With celery, red pepper and fresh dill. Have you ever stopped at Sherri's? It's out by the dairy store. She has lemon vinaigrette."

He passed her a tiny clear plastic cup.

"Omega-3s," he said cheerfully. "And I have foccaccia."

He placed a loaf of flatbread with sliced tomatoes on the small table.

"And I have a chilled Pinot Blanc."

"I'm impressed," Ed responded. "Let's put it back in the bag. You can clean up and I'll set the table on the patio."

Clint lumbered across the street as Ed reassembled the bag of food. Clint retrieved the wine and fresh clothes from the truck.

"It's your lucky day," Ed said.

He passed her the wine, the chill from the bottle inspiring shivers despite the heat.

"I don't think Toot has soiled the bathroom," she finished. "Feel free to shower."

"Sounds delightful," he admitted.

She wiped the patio table, even laid a tablecloth, lit a citronella candle and arranged their food. She almost transferred the salads from the plastic containers to real plates, but decided that would be wasteful since then she'd have to wash dishes. Ed wandered into the garden while she waited, snipping some roses and adding them to a vase on the table. The blend of roses and citronella felt like summer to Ed, though the combination wasn't exactly the most pleasant. She retrieved a small compact disc player and set some Marvin Gaye on low, the lack of volume not for mood as much as she didn't want to disturb Tootie.

Clint emerged, hair wet from his shower. In the twenty minutes since he went upstairs, the air had cooled. Ed poured them each wine. He dove into his meal without hesitation, and Ed, although very hungry, ate slower, mesmerized by Clint's movements. The candle crackled. The stars appeared in the indigo of the sky. Ed kept smiling.

The salad tasted fabulous. The wine and the music relaxed the nervous, emotional energy that had clung to her since the previous evening. They cut the foccaccia and nibbled it while sharing stories, the meaningless type that evoked laughter or knowing glances or sometimes reminded them of things they had both lost, like family members that had passed. The compact disc must have repeated three times, with the last remnants if the wine in their glasses, as a bold and crotchety voice erupted from the top of the house.

"Who the fuck is in my yard?!?" it screamed.

Ed hung her head.

"Toot," she muttered.

"What motherfucker is milling about in my yard at this hour?" she continued.

"Gertrude!" Ed bellowed back.

"Ed?" she hollered. "What the hell are you doing fucking outside at this hour? You're lucky I didn't call the goddamn cops on you."

"Because I was in the backyard?" she replied.

"Maybe I should go," Clint said. "I don't want to cause trouble."

"Edna! There's someone else fucking down there and it sounds like a motherfucking man!"

"Tootie," Ed said, pleading bursting from her voice. "It's a friend. Have another beer and go back to bed."

Ed turned to Clint. "I'm sorry about this."

"Guess that stint in rehab didn't help," Clint said.

"You don't have any goddamned, motherfucking man friends. No man would want to be seen with a fat bitch like you," Tootie ranted.

The house boomed as Tootie crashed down the stairs.

"Oh, dear God, here she comes," Ed gasped.

Ed didn't know whether she should chase Clint around the house or remain still on the patio and hope Tootie forgot where she was going by the time she hit the first floor.

"Hey, it's okay," Clint said as his hand brushed hers. "Every family has one."

Clint smiled and finished his wine.

Great, Ed thought. He had no idea what they were in for if Tootie came out here.

"Clint, you better go."

"Ed, we're having a nice time. Tootie can't ruin that."

"Oh, yes, she can," Ed replied. "Don't say you weren't warned."

"I can handle your drunk sister."

As if on cue, Tootie exited the house in her threadbare housecoat, transparent with age, and open, sagging breasts exposed in the patio's motion detector beam. Between the dim light and the stretch marks, her breasts seemed gray. Her disheveled and matted hair swirled like overgrown shrubs and her eyes bugged, with cheeks drooping so badly her face could have been mistaken for her ass. She held out her arms like a zombie. Ed swore she saw fangs and talons.

"Christ, oh Lord, Ed!" Tootie screamed as she filled the door. "Your so-called fucking friend is the skunk guy. That is the friggin skunk guy, right? Hiding behind your obese butt… Holy damn, Ed. Did you start banging the fucking skunk guy? Who's next, Ed? The garbage man?"

"Clint," Ed said quietly, the sarcasm about to burst from her like a grenade. "Have you met my charming sister, Gertrude?"

"Can't say that I have, officially."

"Up close and personal with the fucking skunk dude," Tootie went on.

The extra light went off.

"Clint, this is Gertrude. Gertrude, this is Clint."

"Fucking Christ."

"Go back to bed, Tootie," Ed said.

"Not until you tell me," Tootie said, her half-naked, wrinkled body leaning forward, "what I want to know."

"I'm sorry," Ed replied. "In my mortification did I neglect something?"

"If fatso, uglyhead Ed is getting a piece… fucking, banging, riding, boinking… Is he giving our Eddie's titties and cunt some beefy attention—"

Tootie stepped onto the deck, setting off the motion detector again. Tootie reached toward her crotch and grabbed her baggy white briefs with a vulgar squeeze. Ed covered her face with her hands, but also praised God that Tootie had underpants. Even with her face hidden, Tootie's pounding feet and the shaking of the patio told Ed exactly what her sister was doing. Tootie danced.

"Gertrude," Clint said forcefully.

Ed lowered her hands. Tootie swung her hips and pulled her elbows into her body with a thrusting motion.

"Ed's got a man. Ed's getting some," she paused, then resumed. "Ed's got a man. Ed's getting some... Not that she'd know what to do with a man."

Clint stepped toward her.

"Gertrude, I think you should go in the house," he said.

Tootie flashed her middle finger at him. Her breasts and her chest fat jiggled with the motion.

"Look at you," Clint said. "No wonder your husband doesn't want you, and your sisters threw you out."

Tootie froze. Ed grew wide-eyed.

"Just proves how good-hearted Ed is," Clint said.

Clint retreated to Ed's side, slipped his arm around her waist and kissed her forehead.

"To put up with a beast like you," he added.

Tootie's eyes reduced to tiny slits as she stared. No one usually talked back to her. So, she stood, stared, and, in Ed's opinion, formulated her attack. But she did nothing.

Tootie turned, stomped toward the house, and stopped in the doorway to shoot a loud, wet fart toward them. The sound overpowered the music and the smell, well, even Clint recoiled.

"That's almost as bad as a skunk," he said. He waved his hand in front of his grimacing face. "Wait, the skunk is better."

Tootie disappeared.

"That was a little toot," Ed said. "Maybe one day she'll treat you to the real thing."

"Can't wait," Clint replied.

He tapped his lips against her nose and then her mouth.

"With that performance," he said. "Maybe I should go. It's late and we have a big day tomorrow."

Their lips toyed with each other, causing ripples of anticipation in Ed's body and soul.

"I wish you didn't have to go," she whispered.

He tucked the hair behind her ear and planted light kisses along her jaw.

"Tomorrow," he said.

By the time she collapsed into bed, a layer of sweat covered her body, from the heat boiling inside her, and the longing between her legs seemed just as wet. Ed refused to satiate herself, preferring to save the energy for the following day. As difficult as it might be.

She slept well, though her dreams betrayed her no longer secret wishes of spending the night in Clint's arms, his body clutching hers, the two of them lost together. When the morning came, it punctured the realm where everything flowed perfectly and returned her to the stale reality that was life with Tootie.

Judging from the pungent and greasy odor in the house, Tootie had mysteriously dragged herself from bed before noon and managed to burn something... scrapple? Bacon? Definitely blackened bacon, Ed decided, as the smoke alarm pierced the air.

Ed sighed. At least her dress and items for tonight were at the Hooper place, which meant even if Tootie burned the house down, she couldn't ruin tonight. Ed slapped her walking clothes on and ran down the stairs. She arrived in the kitchen just in time to dump some baking soda on a grease fire in the frying pan and tear the nine-volt battery from the alarm. She fanned her arms like crazy as she opened the window. With the noise stopped, she heard moaning from the adjacent bathroom.

"Fucker," Tootie growled.

Ed lifted the frying pan of smoldering grease and now yellow baking soda and tossed it outside. Then, she went for a walk. Dawn had scarcely broken the horizon, the hills outside of Millville flush with red, pink and purple.

Ed had a few hours before she needed to meet the twins at the salon. Gen and Olive had talked about massages, facials, haircuts and nails as if they faced a wedding, not a fundraiser. Whatever, Ed thought.

Clint had seen her at her worst: sweaty from walks, dirty from skunk-proofing, emotionally unstable with the details from her past. Did she really need expensive preening? She'd rather donate the money to Olive. But Olive insisted.

Ed slammed her feet against the sidewalk harder. Olive and Gen meant well, wanting to include Ed. This whole event had blown Ed's budget for the next several months, and she still didn't have a donation to submit.

How could she attend the function without a re-spectable gift? She planned to give Olive the pickle jar. Ed had filled it with loose change, the kind she found in her walks and in the couch cushions.

Ed logged five miles while contemplating her

quandary. She returned to the house, which still stank of burnt meat, and headed upstairs to the shower. Ed slapped on jeans and a tee-shirt. She gathered her purse from the coffee table and a slice of cantaloupe from the kitchen, happy, but a tad concerned, that she had not seen Tootie.

She drove to Salon Beverly, a cute stone Tudor a mile outside Millville, edging toward the trendy suburbs. She parked Aretha, fed the meter, and climbed the stairs.

As Ed opened the door, opulence sang in her face. She found herself surrounded by marble columns. She stood on a hardwood floor that seemed like exotic African something or other. The stairwell spiraled up with wide planks of stone. Between the stairs and the massive fireplace, Genny and Olive snuggled against each other in thick Turkish cotton robes. Genny sipped pomegranate juice and Olive a liter bottle of Evian, brought by a slender brunette that manned a tiny juice bar. The girls reclined on an antique mahogany loveseat.

Another woman, at a small writing desk, sat beside a price list and an appointment book. The schedule had a leather case. Ed peeked toward the prices and had to stifle a gasp.

"Ed!" Olive hollered.

"You made it!" Genny added.

Ed bypassed the woman at the desk and inched toward the girls.

"Hi," she said quietly. "Guys, I think I'm going to the farm. Really, this is out of my league."

Genny giggled. "Don't worry, Ed. We got it."

"What do you mean? I couldn't let you pay—"

"We don't have the money," Olive whispered. "Dad's a sweetheart and would cave on just about any request but this isn't one of them."

"Ed, don't worry about it," Genny insisted. "Whatever you want, it's on the house."

Olive motioned Ed closer. Ed leaned in.

"Imagine rats all over the floor. Wouldn't be good for business, would it?" Olive said so softly Ed could barely hear her.

"Here?" Ed replied.

Olive nodded. Genny piped in.

"Remember when Millville required neighboring communities to tie-in to the central sewer, last fall," Genny said.

Ed nodded.

"They did this place right before Thanksgiving," Olive said. "Gen and I were home for the holiday and the city managed to disturb a rat colony."

Ed giggled. It was a tiny noise, but for the first time all day her tension dissipated. She settled into a nearby chair to listen. The server from the juice bar handed Ed her own bottle of Evian.

"Rats infected this whole block, and because of the sewer network needed for the salon, you can imagine how many rats came in here," Genny said.

"Beverly freaked," Olive continued. "Dad and Gramps spent the weekend in the sewers. Gen and I eradicated them from the shop. She was so grateful, she gave us gift certificates in addition to payment. Dad won't use his, neither will Gramps, so we'd like you to have it."

"No," Ed insisted. "If there's four, that's two visits for each of you."

"Afraid not, Ed," Genny added. "Dad made his instructions clear. We weren't to bring you home until you had the full treatment."

"You're not putting me in one of those robes," Ed said.

"Why not?" Genny said with a smile. "They're cozy."

"No," Ed replied. "That's all there is to that."

The girls shrugged. The woman behind the desk rose and sashayed her way to them in stilettos.

"Anderson party," she said as she pressed her hands together.

"Yes," the girls responded.

"I have three for a manicure," the woman went on.

"That's us," Geneva said, as she leapt from the loveseat.

The girls gathered behind the woman with Ed tailing them. Her shoulders dipped as she gazed around the building, the flow of water coming not only from shampoo sinks but also from fountains augmented with bronze sculptures. As they turned toward the manicure room, Ed froze before a painting with lots of blue squares and part of a face.

"That's a painting," Ed said.

The woman from behind the desk paused and pivoted.

"Yes," she said. "Beverly has an extensive art collection."

"Is it… a… Picasso?" Ed asked, her stammering not helping the fact that she already felt like an idiot.

"Yes," the woman confirmed. "But most of her good art is at her hotel, on the mountain. Here we are."

Good art? Ed's eyes had to be the size of coasters. Who considered Picasso lesser art?

Three tall, thin women in lab coats swirled around them. Each woman, equipped in matching six-inch platform stilettos, slacks and cashmere tanks—all black, grabbed one of them. Ed ended up with a freckled redhead. She grabbed Ed's hand and surveyed her nails while smiling. Every dollop of her make-up was perfect. The manicurist seemed like a sophisticated doctor, not the torn jeans and slinky sweater type at Sexy Nails in Ed's neighborhood.

"I'm Bethy," the redhead said.

The women came over and introduced themselves. Then Olive went with Stephanie, Geneva with Kayla, and Ed with Bethy. Olive and Genny start jabbering immediately, mostly about the party later in the day. Ed followed silently. Since there were footbaths ready, Ed assumed pedicures were first. It had been a long time since she had a pedi, and was actually looking forward to it. The room smelled incredible from the orchids which filled the room and the lavender scent emitted from the warm soapy water.

"So what are you wearing to the big shin-dig?" Bethy asked.

"Oh, um, a long very dark blue dress. It's almost black." Ed replied. "My friend bought me some Prada shoes, they're a lot higher than I usually wear."

"Prada makes a nice shoe. I prefer Louboutins myself."

"The ones with the red soles?"

"Yes."

"My friend bought a pair of Louboutins for herself that day. It's the only reason I knew."

"Ah. What style Pradas did you get?"

"I have no idea. They're navy matte silk satin, with a rounded open toe, curved strap, and they buckle at the ankle.

"So no hosiery, and toes exposed. Have you given any thought to toe polish?"

"RED," Olive shouted from the other side of the room. "Live a little Ed."

"Red would look really nice. A nice Chanel red."

"I don't know. Wouldn't that be a little garish. I usually put red on my toes, if I do them, but I don't want my toes to draw attention from the dress or the shoes. I was thinking French, making them look as natural as possible. My fingers would match."

"Come on, Ed. They've got a hundred colors to pick from and you pick natural. There's some great blues over there. I can see a nice dark on that looks like sapphires," Genny said.

"Ms Anderson" Bethy said, "I think your talking about 'Light My Sapphire' and it would look stunning with the dress. So would the almost black blue called 'Fantasy.' If you want something a little more we have one called 'Give me the moon.' It's a baby blue."

"Blue nail polish? I don't think so."

"Come on, Ed, think outside the box. It would sure surprise Dad."

"Shock your Dad, you mean."

"Mine's going to be almost black. Charcoal with a hint of maroon glimmer. It should look hot with my dress," Olive said.

"You can wear that, you're young. I need to go with something more age appropriate."

"I think I'm going for the rich bronze," Genny concluded.

"Ms. Gardner…"

"Ed, please."

"Ed, I wouldn't never let you walk out of here with something not age appropriate. Beverly would fire me on the spot."

"Alright. Light or dark?"

"Dark," everyone, but Ed, said in unison.

That was just the first battle that Ed lost that day. Gen and Olive also convinced her to get a different haircut and red highlights. It looked great, the best her hair had looked in a long time. Clint wasn't going to recognize her when he saw her.

Ed was getting hungry. "Girls, are we done? I'm

getting hungry and I'd like to eat now. I probably won't eat tonight."

"Rebekkah's cooking, you better eat tonight. Besides you'll need your strength for later."

"Olive!"

"Ed, stop being such a prude. You don't get invited to stay over without a little something-something happening. Especially when we've been given direct orders from Dad not to bother you this weekend."

"I'm not going there with you. Sorry. Now back to lunch. Are you two hungry?"

"I am," said Gen, "but we have one more stop to make, waxing. I'm getting my money's worth out of this gift certificate."

"Me, too," said Olive, "and so are you, Ed."

"Me, waxing. You have to be kidding?"

"Nope," said Genny. "you, my dear friend Ed, are signed up for brows, pits and a bikini wax. The same as us."

"Bikini wax? Arm pit wax?"

"It will hurt a little but Dad will appreciate it. I know my boyfriends have."

"Ms. Gardner, Ms. Andersons," an effeminate voice said. "We're ready for you now."

Standing before them was the most beautiful woman Ed had ever seen with long flowing red hair. Except she was a man. An Adam's apple protruded from her neck.

"I'm Ginger and I'll be taking care of your waxing needs today. Who's first?"

"Ed!" the girls said in unison.

"'Ginger, Ed's never been waxed. She's a tad bit apprehensive." Olive added.

"I'd say more than a tad. She actually quivering. How cute," Ginger smiled. "Come with me, my little virgin, I will take very good care of you. We'll be back in about 15 minutes, ladies. You won't recognize you mom when we get back."

"I'm not their mom," Ed protested. Ginger took Ed by the hand and led her toward a small room.

"But after tonight," Olive called out after them with a smile in her voice, "it will be within the realm of possibility."

Ed was thinking about what Olive said. Do they really like her that much? That they want her to be their mom? She didn't even hear the door close.

"Ms. Gardner, could you please—"

"Ed. Please call me Ed."

"Ed, could you please sit on the table? We'll start at the top and work out way down."

This looks like a gynecologist's table. I have to get out of here before it's too late, Ed thought. She wondered if Ginger locked the door.

"Really, the brows are plenty," Ed told the aesthetician. "The girls will never know, I chickened out of the rest."

"Yes they will, when we come back in two minutes. So relax, it will be fine. Trust me."

Ed thought to herself. Whenever a man, even one who identified as a woman, asks her to trust him, something bad always seems to happen.

"So do you tweeze?"

"Occasionally. I have a uni-brow if I don't."

"I can see that. Let's put a beautiful arch in the brow, get rid of the unibrow, and open up your eyes. You'll be a new woman. Now this will be warm, then a slight pinch. It's nothing really."

She applied the wax with what looked like a Popsicle stick, and covered it with cloth.

"One, two... three," Ginger counted.

Ginger ripped off the wax.

"Ouch!"

"That wasn't so bad," Ginger said as she applied cooling gel.

Ginger held a mirror in front of her.

"Look."

"Wow," Ed said. "What a difference!"

Ginger repeated the process under her arms. That hurt a little more, but all in all, it was not horrible.

"Okay, Ed," Ginger said. "Now the moment you've been waiting for: the bikini line. Do you normally shave?"

"Rarely," Ed said. "I don't go to the beach, and there wasn't anybody else in my life interested in looking."

Ed's thoughts wandered to what might be about to happen.

"You know what," Ed said. "I think I'll stick to shaving."

She slipped off the table.

"Drop your jeans and get back on the table," Ginger commanded. "Open your legs. I'm going to do a basic, American bikini wax. You leave your panties on and I remove the hair exposed at the top of the thighs and just under the navel. I'll just groom you a little."

"You called it basic. There's other types?"

"Yes, there's a French wax which leaves a vertical strip in front, two to three fingers in width just above the vaginal area. The Brazilian wax removes everything, front to back. You'd be as bare as they day you were born."

"Ouch!"

"Someone should have told you ahead of time you were going to have a wax. Then you could have worn panties that expose what you wanted removed. But then you wouldn't have come."

"Truer words have never been spoken."

"Now, all that I am going to do is trim a little with the scissors, and then apply a little talcum power to make sure the wax doesn't stick to your tender skin," Ginger explained. "Then I will apply the wax and do it just like I do for your brows and arm pits. I will be as gentle as possible."

Ginger paused.

"Trust me," she said.

"Okay," Ed muttered as she removed her jeans. Ed was glad her shirt was long, covering her hips and thighs, not that that would matter in a minute. "I'm ready."

Her heart was beating a thousand times a minute. The pain was more substantial than the previous procedures, but remarkably, she didn't scream.

Ginger handed her the mirror.

"Here, take a look at how great you look. He's going to love it. After you shower, take a small comb and small scissors and tidy up the rest of the area. Quite easy. There is nothing like a well-groomed vagina to make a man, or a woman for that matter, want to go down on a girl."

Ed blushed, but was immediately excited at the thought.

"I'm going to clean up and sterilize my work area." Ginger said. "You can put on your jeans and join your family. I'll be out in a couple of minutes."

Ed went out to meet Gen and Olive. She still felt flushed.

"Oh my goodness. Look at you. You look totally different." They said together. "Look how big your eyes got."

Ed lifted her arm to expose her cleanly waxed arm pit. They applauded.

Olive said, "Ed, stop keeping us in suspense. Did you do 'it' or did you just hide in there for fifteen minutes."

"How much was the bet?" Ed asked.

"How did you know that we made a bet?" replied Olive.

"I would have," Ed responded.

"Mucking out the stable tomorrow morning after a long night of partying," admitted Gen.

"Who ever had yes goes next."

Ginger came out of the waxing room. "So who's next?"

"I guess that's me," Genny said as headed toward Ginger, "but hey, I get to sleep in tomorrow."

SIXTEEN

"Noah's ark."

Ed coined the term in high school to refer to how everyone did everything in pairs. Pairs went to football games, movies, parties, and the prom. As Ed took another glance in the full-length mirror, she imagined this is what it felt like to get ready for the prom. Hair swept up, make-up highlighting her skin tone and her glittering eyes, sapphires at her ears and throat (borrowed from Celeste, Darren's birthstone and one of her favorite gems), the details transformed Ed from the ugly duckling into the regal swan.

Using the old cliché was hardly original, but as she looked at herself, she couldn't believe it. The neckline and structure of the gown kept her breasts tall and pert, the high waistline drew attention to her narrowest points and the drape of the satin gave her a fluidity, a smoothness, that she would never match in everyday clothes.

She stepped forward, her leg peeking from the slit, showing off her fancy Prada heels. She shivered, unaccustomed to how feminine, maybe even pretty, she felt.

Ed had never gone to the prom. Now, she quivered with the prospect of a second chance. Every girl needed a night to shine, would this be hers?

On the nightstand, a discarded plastic fork and a picked-over salad kept her cell phone company. She checked the phone for the time. She peered out the farmhouse window. The tent spread across the field, opposite the relative stillness of the Anderson Farm. The band plucked at their guitars, tuning. Dishes clattered faintly.

Ed should eat some more of that garden salad. She didn't plan to eat tonight. Nerves would stop her, plus with her sloppy luck she didn't want to embarrass herself in front of Clint.

If she kept the dress clean and didn't sweat too much, she could sell it at the consignment shop next week. But she'd keep the shoes. It was rude to hock a gift.

A light rap on the door interrupted her thoughts. She strode over to answer it surprised at how much easier she was now walking in these shoes. Beyond the door, Olive and Genny appeared, two visions of vivid color.

Olive wore a vintage 1950s red chiffon evening gown with ruched cummerbund waist and a beaded tulle caplet. Genny, in her attempt to attract less attention than her twin, had selected a single-shoulder satin sheath in shimmering bronze, with crystal beads along the neckline and the side.

Yet, the two of them stood gaping at Ed.

"You look… fabulous," Olive said.

"Not compared to you two," she muttered.

"Ed, don't even say that," Genny chastised her.

Ed nodded.

"You're right," she said. "I feel really pretty right now and I don't need my lack of self-esteem ruining it. Do you think your dad will like it?"

Olive smiled. "He'd be a fool not to."

"We just stopped to tell you we're heading down," Genny said.

Olive had a beaded bag on her wrist. It was big enough to hold the checks she would collect over the course of the night. As their beads caught the light in the hall, Ed slapped her forehead.

"Girls, wait!" Ed exclaimed.

Ed rushed to her overnight bag, her skirt rustling as she did. She unzipped the front pouch and grabbed the envelopes. She shuffled through them, counting. One, two, three, four, good. She zoomed to the door and handed them to Olive.

"From my family. And friends," Ed said. "Celeste and Hannah. Martha and Josie."

"Did you solicit on my behalf?" Olive remarked.

"Yes," Ed said, her lips slipping into an embarrassed half-smile. "They all earn more than I do, and they know how much it means to me… but…"

Olive looked at her with big eyes and eyelashes thick with mascara.

"Well…" Ed stammered.

Olive waited. Ed's hands fidgeted.

"None of them are from me," Ed admitted.

Olive cast her twin an odd glance.

"Other than being your dad's date," she continued, "I don't have anything to offer. I'm sorry."

"Ed," Olive sputtered. "I so couldn't have done this without you. The design. The guidance. Your attention to detail. Just finding a reasonable printer. That's worth thousands, right?"

"And don't underestimate the value of Dad having a date," Genny added. "That's amazing. And if it goes further, well, that might be worth a million."

Ed blushed. The girls hugged her. The embrace surrounded her with love, the kind that made her feel welcome, needed. Her family didn't hug. To have these girls offer a gesture like this… Ed remembered her jar.

Clint had given her one of his "what the?" looks when she put it in his truck.

"I do have something," Ed said, tugging reluctantly away from them.

She pointed to the jar.

"It's full of change," Ed said. "I throw some in it from time to time, but mostly it's money I found on my walks. I'd like you to have it. I'll even come over and help roll it. Maybe a hundred bucks."

"Thank you for everything," Olive said. "Everything you have done. For me. For Genny. For Dad."

Ed's face grew hot again. Thank goodness for make-up.

"Now," Olive said. "I'm taking my jar of coins and I'm heading to Dad's before the guests get here. Gen, complete our mission. Nab her bag."

"My bag?" Ed repeated.

Genny went to the bed and took Ed's overnight bag.

"Dad wants it," Genny explained.

"Though you better not need clothes," Olive remarked as she disappeared into the hall.

Genny followed her sister. Their shoes echoed like cannon-fire on the steps and then Ed watched them enter their father's house.

Ed checked her reflection and got herself a glass of

water from the bathroom. Alone in the guest bathroom, Ed set the glass against the edge of the sink when she noticed how badly her hands shook.

She had to believe in the magic. She had to believe tonight would be different. She had to believe in Clint.

She sat on the corner of the bed and listened to her own breath, trying to slow it and calm the knot in her stomach. After all, if she got too nervous she might get the dress nasty sweaty.

She wanted to trust Clint. She wanted to, but the odds did not favor her. If she didn't have this dress on, she'd put her head between her knees. She thought of the wrap-dress and the flip-flops she'd packed on the top of her bag. Easy to wear, easy to take off, even easier to put on in a hurry. Nothing in her bag held any real significance. She had left her car keys in the ashtray with her driver's license. Again, hardly original, but would help facilitate a quick escape if needed. Even her purse was a 'dummy.'

She tilted her head toward the window, the sun dipping into the glass and reflecting off the mirror. *Please, let my fears be unreasonable,* Ed prayed silently. Like a soundtrack to the desperate plea, "At Seventeen" played in her head and opened every hurt from Ed's past. She could hear Janice Ian as if the folk singer sat beside her, cooing in her ear.

> " I learned the truth at seventeen
> That love was meant for beauty queens…"

"EDNA," an elderly voice bellowed.

"What are you deaf, girl?" Mr. Hooper called up the stairs. "There's someone here for you."

Showtime, Ed thought.

"It's Little Clint," Mr. Hooper added.

"Call me when Brad Pitt shows up," Ed returned as she emerged from the guest room.

At the landing, she gripped the chestnut banister as if she would crash down the stairs if she didn't. The sun lit the stained glass over the door. She carefully descended, remembering all of her mother's chiding. Stand straight. Walk slowly, deliberately. Her hand slid with her steps. She had to remind herself to breathe. Mr. Hooper and Clint, both in black tuxes, gasped. Ed froze in the middle of the stairwell as the tornado of panic swirled in her stomach.

"Damn," Clint said.

Turn around, she begged herself, unable to move. Turn around. She closed her eyes. God, what's wrong? she thought. Was her dress tucked into her pantyhose? Did she ruin her eye makeup and now resemble some rabid raccoon? Or worse—did she look like one of the cows dressed in satin?

Her feet finally lifted off the step and she began to turn and head back to the room.

"Have you ever seen a woman so beautiful?" Clint said lightly.

"Not since my Sarah died," Mr. Hooper answered.

Clint proceeded to the bottom of the stairs. Ed squinted at him. Was he wearing a black Stetson? She exhaled and her entire body felt a hundred pounds lighter.

She continued down the stairs. His tails had a square cut, with notched lapels, simple, three-button style but breathtaking, especially with the dark silver vest and black bow tie. The next step closer revealed how clean cut and shaven he was.

He reached for her as she finished the stairs. His hand took hers, revealing his antique cuff links on

French cuffs and a four-button jacket cuff. As he pulled her closer, his cologne teased her and set her hormones on fire.

"Dear God," she whispered as heat filled her.

Recovering, she looked into his eyes.

"You're not really wearing that hat, are you?" she said.

"Yes," he said.

She must have grimaced, because he laughed.

"In this neck of the woods, a Stetson works for formal, trust me," he said.

He spun her into him and brushed his lips against hers.

"My lipstick," she protested.

Yet her lips fell against his as he pulled away. When she opened her eyes, Mr. Hooper had set his brown leather Stetson on his head. Ed studied the blackened patina.

"I don't understand," she said. "Is there some kind of cowboy-farmer-rancher formal dress code that I'm not aware of?"

"Apparently," Clint replied, smirking.

He leaned against her lips again. Mr. Hooper started toward the front door.

"I guess I'll head over," Mr. Hooper said with a chuckle. "I think there's some car trouble brewing in this house."

Clint paused.

"We're walking a thousand feet," he said.

Mr. Hooper winked and tipped his hat.

"Do what you gotta do," he said as he closed the door behind him.

Clint returned his attention toward her lips, while his fingers danced along the edge of her plunging neckline. Something about the moment reminded Ed…

"I forgot my camera!" she exclaimed.

Her flesh tingled as she removed herself from his grasp. She returned to her room, Clint on her heels, and she seized her camera from the little table. Clint placed his hands on her waist and walked toward the bed. Ed stepped backward.

"Clint," she said.

His hands meandered up and down her sides, rocking through her in ways she couldn't hide. She groaned softly.

"No," she said. "Not like this. I don't want to disappoint Olive."

"So, this wasn't a ruse?"

She shook her head. He smiled.

"You really needed your camera?"

She nodded.

"You're not working."

"Clint, it's for Olive. Publicity, featuring the who's who of the Valley."

"Ed, this is a special night. No work."

"I'll remind you of that when you start buttering up clients," she said.

"That's different."

"How?"

He didn't answer. She reapplied her lipstick while he stared. She hung her camera from wrist. Then, Clint took her elbow and guided her downstairs. As they stepped onto the veranda, the warmth washed over them. The humidity stayed low, thank goodness. The tent spanned the field, the dark colors of the mountain the backdrop along the horizon. Corn infused some green into the picture with the tenant's farmhouse in the middle of it. The catering vans made a small row near the back of the small food preparation tent and the driver of bio-diesel shuttle bus sat on the step of his vehicle with a plate of food. He would start his first run to the local mall where the guests would park.

The menu included locally raised meat and fowl, in addition to as many vegetables as the neighboring farms could provide. The winery, located on the border of the next county, donated the wine and the services of a bartender. Olive had found composting porta-potties. Rebekkah also promised to compost any food waste from the kitchen. Ed made sure the printed materials used soy ink on 100 percent post consumer waste recycled paper.

Ed and Clint slowly walked toward the tent, hands clasped. With each step, they came closer to the safari campsite. Ed noticed fabric lining the poles of the tent, muslin that invoked the lightness and rustic nature of the African landscape.

It covered the tablecloths and chairs, with strips of tiger print tying it in place. Black dishes, tiger cloth napkins and caramel-colored glass vases holding branches twisted with vines decorated the tables. Mr. Hooper lingered at the edge of the tent, stroking a preserved deer.

"Wow," he said. "Are we still on my property? Sarah would have loved this."

Someone had scattered animals strategically throughout the tent and environs. A beaver by the dance floor. A bear on his hind legs by the kitchen entrance. Several birds that Ed didn't recognize and a breathtaking bobcat by the head table.

"Clint," Ed said. "Those animals are amazing. Where did they come from? Did Olive find somewhere to rent them?"

Clint chuckled. "No. I have a friend who does incredible taxidermy. Maybe I'll introduce you. Maybe I should have had her preserve your skunk."

"No, thank you," Ed replied.

To round out the atmosphere, large clay pots with groomed shrubbery and small trees dotted between the tables. The mountain goat near the coffee station seemed a tad out of place, but he was cute.

The ground below her feet gave with the bounce of sisal rugs. Most of the men, at least those who had arrived thus far, sported Stetsons. Ed grimaced. In her distraction, she nearly tripped over a ram. Clint caught her.

"Can I get you a glass of wine?" he asked.

"Yes. White would be lovely," she said, thinking of her resolution to keep the dress clean.

The shuttle returned from the mall with guests spilling forth more tuxes, satin and fancy hairdos. Olive navigated among them, her body movements flustered at first, but her arms and her posture and eventually her smile eased. She found her footing as hostess, and from time to time her sister would join her.

Clint returned with the wine. Eventually, Genny joined her father, Ed, and Mr. Hooper on the sidelines.

"Dad, you look great," Genny said, playfully pulling her father's arm.

"Thanks, Pumpkin," he replied.

"And Mr. Hooper," she said as she kissed the old man's cheek, "I had no idea you cleaned up so nicely."

"Thanks, darling," Mr. Hooper said. "I wish my Sarah could be here to see this, and you."

"She would have loved you in that tux," Genny said.

"I know," Mr. Hooper said. "And we'd probably still be in my house, conjuring some excuse to be late. That woman never could keep her hands off me."

"Even after all those years?" Genny said.

"We were married for fifty-seven years," he told her. "And I don't think the candle ever went out. It changed, sure. But we always loved each other."

"I'd love to feel that way," Genny said.

Me, too, and I wish someone would feel that way about me, Ed thought. She peered at Clint.

Ed sipped her wine slowly and wondered what the night would hold…

"Remember, missy," Mr. Hooper told her. "It's hard work. You put in the work, and the love grows brighter. No fire burns without steady care."

"Ed, shall we go try Rebekkah's *hors d'oeuvres*?" Clint asked, hooking her arm with his elbow.

"I don't know," Ed replied.

"I'll keep Mr. Hooper company until Olive comes down," Genny said.

"I'm her official escort," Mr. Hooper told Ed.

Ed didn't think she could swallow any food with her nerves such a disaster. But as soon as she caught the fragrant aroma of the meatballs with garden herbs, she decided to try. She nibbled that meatball, shaving bits of it with her teeth, amazed at how rich yet lean it tasted.

"Buffalo," Clint said, as he dipped his meatballs in whatever orange-colored, tomato-based sauce had ended up on his plate. "It's buffalo meatballs."

"Incredible," Ed replied.

Ed wandered to one of the tables and read the menu card for what had to be the millionth time. After all, she designed it.

She also discovered Rebekkah liked to change her mind based on what produce arrived from her supporting farms. In the end, they kept the card simple: "A multi-course meal featuring the best of the Lehigh Valley's locally grown produce, free-range and organic-fed cattle, and the bounty of the hills, thanks to the hunters in our midst" followed by Rebekkah's logo and contact info.

It took about an hour for the bulk of the guests to filter into the tent. Clint greeted as many people as Olive did, making sure the necessary connections cemented between his daughter and the community. He introduced Ed to every arriving face, which Ed took to be a very good sign. Servers, with tiger print cummerbunds, swirled among the guests with their trays. Ed sampled the spinach mini-quiches and wondered how Rebekkah kept her crust so... so... succulent. It maintained the required crispness without tasting dry or overcooked.

With her white wine in one hand, still three-quarters full, and a plate with a quiche and crustini with roasted garlic spread, slow-cooked until the taste was more like butter than pungent herb, Clint pointed out Suzanne, the taxidermist. They meandered toward her and had a lovely conversation about disposing of leftover animal guts.

The servers placed their trays of *hors d'oeuvres* on tables and arranged themselves in a crescent, each holding a triangle which they clanged gently.

The lead singer of the band lifted his microphone and welcomed everyone. He explained the schedule for the evening and introduced Olive and Mr. Hooper.

The two of them, Mr. Hooper now with a red rose on his lapel, floated into the tent, the old man beaming ear-to-ear. Olive walked confidently to the microphone, while Mr. Hooper and the rest of the guests went to their seats. Clint even held Ed's chair. After everyone sat, Olive spoke. Ed almost forgot about her camera, but managed a few shots while the guests settled.

"Good evening, everyone," Olive said. "I am so happy you could join me tonight. I don't need to tell you that this ranch is a dream of mine, that with your help has manifested sooner than I could imagine. Our region is faced with a dilemma. The loss of farmland and forested area has greatly diminished habitat and put our native wildlife in danger. As men, we are the greatest threat to nature, and therefore we must do what we can to cohabitate and protect the environment and the creatures in it. That said, let's eat."

Applause thundered through the tent. Ed snapped a photo of Clint, as the pride lit his face and he clapped perhaps the loudest. Ed put her camera down and placed her napkin in her lap. The servers arrived and passed bowls of chilled cherry soup from the right.

Two of the musicians in the band entered the table area and entertained the group with violins. Of course, the one played classical and the other used more of a fiddle style but it worked for this crowd. Ed reminded herself to spoon away from herself and enjoyed the music and the sweetness of the first course.

As soon as Nigel, the last person at her table to rest his spoon against his plate, finished, the servers cleared. Nigel had spent too much time explaining his role as head of the county's animal response team to a middle-aged woman, Joan, who accompanied a veterinarian, Dr. Humphrey. Dr. Humphrey came from the neighboring county, which didn't have a CART, as Nigel abbreviated it.

"I'm hoping Olive's work will alleviate some of the stress on both counties," Dr. Humphrey said. "These small towns aren't equipped to deal with animal problems, and they don't have the money for professionals. I hate to say no, but I don't have the time and I'm not young enough to have the energy."

Ed wanted to listen, but the second course had arrived: catfish bake with paprika and parsley. She pulled it apart with her fish knife, impressed at the texture and the flavor of the fish. The food kept coming for ages, each course more scrumptious than the last. The strawberry sorbet washed away the fish flavor and provided a brief respite before the entrée. Servers refilled wine glasses with whatever beverage best suited the dinner selection. The band reunited and played a quiet version of "The Lion Sleeps Tonight," in English and then in French.

Ed had chosen the roasted pheasant for her meal, embracing the adventurous aspects of the evening. She could eat chicken any time. Clint ordered the brandy-marinated grilled steak and ever since he selected it, Ed swore she could smell the meat on the barbecue. Clint leaned closer to her, sipping his burgundy. She hadn't touched hers, afraid she would spill it.

"I'd love to taste yours," Clint said. "I know it's not proper but I'll share my steak."

"Deal," she replied.

"It was a tough choice," he said.

"It was," she agreed. "You played it safe."

"Do you see beef cattle in my yard?" he remarked. "This is a special occasion. And beef is a rarity in my house."

CA slipped between them.

"I'm taking some of the gifts to the house," he said. "Not comfortable with it here."

"Okay, Dad," Clint said.

He tipped his Stetson toward Ed and disappeared. More conversation, an accordion (what didn't these guys play?), and finally the main course. As promised, Clint carved off a piece of steak, so tender he used the knife only out of propriety. She pulled aside a portion of pheasant. And they swapped.

"Dress us up, but can't really take us out," Clint joked.

The others at their table laughed. Ed surveyed the meat. It seemed a little pink in the middle. To her, meat always looked a little pink in the middle. She dropped a piece into her mouth. It tasted fabulous, but the color freaked her out.

She turned to her pheasant. A few bites of that, a nibble of her baby carrots, and a slice of twice-baked new potato and she stopped. She hated to waste, but really, she couldn't keep going or she'd most definitely soil the dress somehow. But the pheasant was so… so… rich.

She reluctantly settled her fork and knife against the plate, in the lower right hand portion. The server leapt to attention and removed the dinner.

Ed struggled with the guilt. Next came spring blend with sunflower seeds and honey dressing, followed by beer bread and goat cheeses infused with herbs. Luckily, dessert turned out to an angel food cake, perhaps far from elegant, but certainly welcome in its lightness after the culinary delights.

The pace of the music quickened as the servers cleared the table and offered refills of coffee and full pitchers of farm-fresh cream. The younger guests clamored to their feet and overtook the dance floor. The older crowd lingered at their tables, some shifting to other places to talk with guests they hadn't visited yet. Ed excused herself to pursue some photos. Dance floor shots were always crowd pleasers. When she returned to the table, Clint rose.

"Since you scoped out the dance floor, Ed," Clint began as a smile crossed his face. "Shall we?"

"Dance? No," Ed said with a nervous titter. "I don't. Dance. Too clumsy."

"I'll take my chances," Clint replied.

"No," she repeated. "I really don't. I can't. Besides, someone needs to hold the fort down with Nigel."

"Do I have to go get my daughters?" Clint asked. "Because they'll hound you into it."

"I can't, don't, won't dance," Ed said strongly.

She folded her arms across her chest.

Clint turned and surveyed the room. He started in the direction of Olive who had joined a string of women country line dancing.

"Oli—" he called.

Ed seized his arm.

"Don't you dare," she spat.

Clint peered at her from over his shoulder.

"Will you dance?" he asked again.

Her jaw tensed. She knew Olive would be dragged into this if she refused. She gazed back to Clint. Nigel burst into laughter.

"Clint, you met your match," he sputtered between breaths.

"Fine," Ed snapped. "I'll dance. But no laughing when you see what happens."

Other couples approached the dance floor and the band dropped the tempo in response. The band launched into Poison's most popular slow song, which might be their only slow song, and Ed nearly laughed as the young people filtered to their seats and the people closer to her age took over.

With so many people milling around, it took until half way through the song to reach the dance floor. Clint circled her waist with his arm and grabbed her hand with his other. They swayed together, but Ed kept watching her feet and making sure she didn't step on the dress.

"What are you doing?" Clint asked.

"I don't want to fall," she said.

"Look in my eyes," he directed her.

"Why?" she said, as she fought her own will to listen to his instruction.

"Look in my eyes," he repeated, releasing her hand and tilting her chin up with his fingers.

He replaced his grip on her.

"If you look in my eyes," he said.

"I turn into a pile of goo," she finished.

His eyes sparkled. His face seemed so smooth. She wanted to stroke his cheek.

"Maybe," he replied.

His body closed the gap between them. His hip brushed hers. His head came nearer. Her chest rubbed against his. His body nudged hers, hip tapping as his hand interlaced with hers guided, and his shoulder, the one of the arm around her waist, also directed her. She moved, subtly, and he smiled.

"That's why," he said. "If your not worried about everything else—"

"I can follow your body language," she interrupted.

"Exactly," he said.

"Oh my God," she said as his hip pushed her a few degrees to his left. They danced a few steps and he moved her further. "That's why people think dancing's so sexy."

"Having fun?" he asked.

"Yeah," she said.

The proximity of his body against hers made her heartbeat accelerate. His warmth washed over her and increased her own body temperature as other parts of her reacted to his movements. Each gentle nudge trickled along her skin and made her wonder what else would happen. The song ended and Ed parted from Clint.

"Where do you think you're going?" he asked.

"Back to the table," she said.

"Oh no you don't," he said.

He pulled her toward him and kissed her. The pressure of his lips rocked her from head to toe and back again. As their mouths found each other and their tongues met with gentle yet fervent need, the band started the next song. Clint wrapped her arms around her and danced again, without separating from her lips. Ed thought she recognized the music, but the pheromones buzzing through her head kept her from thinking.

"Close your eyes, make a wish," the lead singer of the band sang in a voice that sounded too close to Luther Vandross.

Ed's body collapsed further into Clint's. He stopped kissing her and their cheeks grazed each other as she nestled against his shoulder. His hand pulled hers tighter into them, torsos met Clint's legs guided hers, thigh against thigh, at least as much as the dress would allow. Ed quivered. The passion, the ambiance, the warmth, it was killing her.

"You like this song?" Clint whispered into her ear.

"Yes," she replied faintly. "How did you guess?"

Her breasts ached with longing. His fingers dipped across her chest and sneaked into the bodice of her gown.

"Clint," she whispered sharply as pulled away.

His hand on her waist kept her close. His fingertip flicked across an erect nipple. As he touched her, she thought she noticed something firm against her hip where his body rested against hers during his exploration.

"Thought so," he said as he removed his hand.

"Clint, stop," she said feebly.

"There's a lot of nooks and crannies on a farm, Ed. Let me touch you."

"Clint, there's a hundred people here."

"Ed, you're gorgeous. And I've been fighting it all night," he said. "I can't fight it anymore. I will make love to you, Ed. Right now. Please."

"Do you mean it?"

Clint's face didn't twitch.

"You know I do," he said.

He stepped closer. The bulge under his pants pressed tighter against her.

"I know it's not what I promised, Ed, but I want you right now, in this moment," Clint said. "Under the influence of this song."

"Then we better hurry," she said. "This is the last chorus."

He squeezed her hand. Clint walked very calmly from the dance floor, tugging her. She followed. They stepped into the open air, the breeze cooling their bodies. He paused. He spun her body toward him and position her in front of him, criss-crossing his arms under her breasts, almost brushing against them from the bottom as his groin pressed against her. She trembled. Her body practically split in half with its own readiness.

"Look at the stars," he commented.

The sky glowed dark blue and the horizon appeared dark purple.

"I don't care about the stars and neither do you," she said.

His hand massaged the side of her breast.

"Ed, I told you to look at the stars. I'm creating a mood here."

Her eyes fluttered closed as he grabbed her flesh, so close but yet so far, his thumb almost teasing her nipple.

"I got the mood already," she said.

"True," he responded.

He unwound her, kissed her again and jogged into the field.

"Clint," she called. "I can't run in these shoes."

He returned to her. He took her hand and they walked toward a shed. A woman panted from inside and something guttural and masculine followed.

"Guess we're too late," Clint remarked. "Hope no one took my barn."

"I am not sharing a stall with Claude," she joked.

They slipped into the barn and within seconds, Clint had his hands raking her thighs. His nails against her pantyhose ricocheted into her, causing her legs to wobble and her groin to drip. He pawed along them frantically.

"Ed, how do we get these off without ruining them?"

She teetered with the taunting pressure of his confused fingers, body arching into him reflexively.

"I don't care," she said. "Destroy them."

His fingers darted up her legs, his nails scraping now, trying to puncture her nylons.

"I don't think I can stand," she said breathlessly.

"We'll be there soon," Clint told her.

"No," she said. "I mean literally. I'm going to fall over."

"Oh," he said.

He deftly removed his jacket and laid it over a nearby rail. He grabbed the horse blankets and covered the hay with them. His arms circled her body as he lowered her onto the wool.

"My dress, Clint," she exclaimed. "It will be filthy."

"I'll brush you off," he replied.

Then his lips fell against hers and his body forced hers further against the hay. His hand reached into her skirt, sinking between her thighs and against her. Her folds tingled in anticipation. His hand caressed her bottom.

"You're not wearing panties, Ed."

"No," she muttered.

He tore the hose as he yanked it to her ankles. He tore some extra on purpose.

"So you're not restricted," Clint said.

He got to his feet and undid his belt. His own pants and boxers fell to his ankles and he tumbled against her in the hay. His hands carefully arranged the dress out of the way as best he could, gathering the fabric at her hips as he kissed her thighs. His tongue tickled her flesh. His lips pressed against her. Her bodice against her breasts teased her as thoroughly as his mouth against her legs.

"I'm sorry, Ed," Clint said.

"Why?" she asked.

"I want to see you, all of you, and prove that I love you, not take you in some barn..."

"Like an animal?" she finished.

"Like an animal," he confirmed.

"It's okay, Clint," she said. "I don't mind."

He shifted his weight and his legs parted hers, his pants covering her feet and probably getting filled with hay. His hand reached across her and into the depth of her moisture. Her flesh threatened to explode with that preliminary touch as his fingers coated with her desire fondled her secret folds.

"Please, Clint, please," she begged.

Her body rocked into him and her spine arched until her breasts threatened to spill from the gown. Clint buried his face in them. As he kissed and sucked on her generous flesh, Ed felt something. It caused nervousness in her soul and overwhelming lust from her body. Clint's groin settled against her, the tip of his erection sliding across her. His pulsing nearness made long-forgotten nerves revive and threatened ripples of release within her. His thickness pushed her thigh.

"Hurry," she whimpered.

His face emerged from her chest.

"But—"

"Now, Clint," Ed said.

His body dipped. He merged with her, girth sunk into her, gliding along her wetness. He groaned. It was like... It was like latching onto a missing piece.

"Oh, Ed," Clint said as his body continued meeting hers.

His legs tensed as he prodded further. Ed held her breath. From there, it felt like the dancing: body against body, a nudge and a motion to guide as the two of them swayed, rocked and pushed with the urges.

"It's been so long," Clint said as he paused.

He brushed the hair from her face.

"Why did you stop?" she asked.

"I realized I hadn't got a good look at you."

"But," she protested. "I feel it, so close."

"I know," he replied. "And I want to see you when it happens."

He readjusted his weight, and suddenly his body against her spread her delicate feminine petals. Her arousal spilled across her as his friction electrified her. With a deep thrust into her, he bellowed. As he slowly withered, he continued to roll across Ed. Sensation flickered across her groin, into her abdomen and crawled throughout her organs as she slammed her body against his for a final burst. Something trembled against the top of Ed's foot. Ed laughed.

"What is it?" Clint asked.

"Is your phone on vibrate?" she replied.

"Yeah," he answered. "Oh no!"

He scampered off her.

"It's ringing on my foot," Ed revealed.

Clint tugged his boxer shorts into position.

"That was the best sex I ever had," Ed admitted.

"You ain't seen nothing yet."

He kissed her. He jerked his pants up, retrieving his iPhone from his pocket. He tapped the phone icon. He read the number and rolled his eyes.

"Hey, Dad."

He perched the phone on his shoulder and zipped his fly. Ed climbed to her feet. She smoothed her dress as best she could. She slipped out of her shoes, pulled the hose free and discarded them in the garbage can.

"We just took a walk, Dad. Yeah, I'm on my way. I'm composing a toast now."

Ed tucked her feet into her shoes.

"Ricky's missing?" Clint chuckled. "I think I know

where he is. Yes, I think Judy is with him."

Ed peered into the metal of the horse's bit to check her reflection. That proved impossible.

"Five minutes, Dad. I'll get Ricky and be there in five."

He hung up and put the phone in his pocket. Clint grabbed his jacket.

"Olive's ready for the champagne toasts," he explained. "Of course…"

He flashed her a suspicious look.

"What?" she gasped, wondering if she had an embarrassing tuft of hay somewhere.

"Well, now that you've got no panties and no hose…"

"Clint!" she snapped.

He scratched his head.

"Speaking of which, I have to find my little brother," he muttered.

He caressed her hand as they left the barn.

"Thank you, Clint," she said.

"For what? A quickie in the barn?"

She shrugged.

"You know my past," Ed said.

"That's not your future," he said. "Not with me."

As they approached the shed, giggles carried into the night, followed by a strange clatter that sounded like brooms and rakes falling. More giggling ensued. Clint banged on the shed door.

"Hey, bro, put the little man back in your pants and get Judy back to the party," Clint yelled.

"What the Hell?" Ricky exclaimed.

Judy screeched. Ed could almost distinguish words but then the reverberation of more tumbling tools interrupted them.

"Nobody will come looking…" Judy muttered.

"Then how come Clint found us?"

"You've got to learn to be quieter," Clint said. "We heard you from the tent."

Clint winked at Ed. Ed suppressed a snicker.

"Oh, God, Rick, I can't go back there," Judy said. "We should have gone home."

"Dad wants you in the tent in five," Clint said. "Don't make me tell him where you've been and what you're doing."

"That threat stopped working when I hit my twenties, Clint," Ricky returned.

Clint seized Ed's hand and they playfully jogged to the tent, as fast as her Pradas would allow. Ed smiled, the glow of the moon welcoming against her skin. Olive paced the narrow aisle between the open flap of the tent and the now empty tables. She had her arms crossed and she spent too much time staring at her feet. When Clint and Ed arrived, Olive exhaled and dropped her arms.

"Dad," she said. "I've been looking all over."

Clint squeezed Ed's hands. Ed peered to it.

"We wanted some fresh air," he answered. "Sorry, sweetheart."

He kissed her cheek. Olive looked at Ed. Ed's cheeks grew red.

"Dad," Olive said. "Why is Ed blushing?"

"We ready for those champagne toasts?" Clint asked. "I don't want to miss it."

The waitstaff delivered the sparkling wine to everyone as Olive, with her father at her side, approached the dance floor. Ed missed every word of Olive's toast, because Ed's eyes and attention focused on her beaming father. Genny slipped beside Clint, taking his hand. Ed raised her camera and photographed the two of them as they listened to Olive. The crowd of guests gathered, rapt. They cheered as Olive finished. Glasses clinked. That burst Ed's reverie as Clint returned to her.

"That's my baby," he said quietly, pointing a thumb over his shoulder. "One of them anyway."

Rick and Judy stumbled into the tent, intercepted by C.A. who glared at them. He had one arm on his him and the other thrashing a finger at them. Clint pulled Ed toward them, though Ed resisted, wishing to avoid an awkward family moment.

"Where the Hell were you?" C.A. asked.

"We went for a walk," Ricky said, shuffling his weight from one side to the other and avoiding his father's gaze, Suddenly Judy's shoes distracted him. "Stuffy."

"You bored?" C.A. snapped. "It's not hot. You're surrounded by friends, family and more importantly clients."

"Dad, this isn't my shindig. We went for a walk. I don't need your permission."

"Boy," C.A. said. "This is a family business. And in this family, we support each other. Olive needs you working the crowd. You had your job handed to you, now you help Olive build her dream."

Clint lingered on the fray, collecting empty flutes and arranging them on a table.

"So you sent Clint after me," Ricky said.

Clint grabbed Ed's hand and headed in the opposite direction.

"Not what you expected," Ed whispered.

"Maybe," Clint said. "I think Dad's being hard on him."

"Because you did the same thing," she continued.

Clint shrugged. His mouth sagged. Guilt lined his face. Ed patted his cheek.

"Clint!" C.A. called.

"What does Clint have to do with this?" Ricky asked.

"I'm going to the restroom," Judy said.

C.A. said nothing as she left. Clint swallowed and joined his father and brother.

"What do you need, Dad?"

"Where did you find him?" C.A. replied.

"Over there, Dad," Clint responded, tilting his head toward the Anderson farm.

C.A. rolled his hand in an encouraging motion.

"Where, Clint?" C.A. repeated.

"Dad, really. This isn't necessary. Don't ruin a wonderful evening," Clint protested.

"I'm not ruining anything!" C.A. yelled. His voice calmed. "Neither one of you boys is fooling me. Keep it in your pants and mate when you get home."

Clint blanched. Ricky snickered.

"It's not funny," C.A. said. "This is business!"

The guests had assembled in the field beyond the tent, facing the direction of the sunset, ribbons of pink, red, purple and blue flickering in the sky as if the breeze had laid them there.

"Gentlemen," Ed said. "Look."

She pointed in the direction of the crowd.

"I think we won't want to miss that," she said.

Clint wrapped his arm around her shoulder. Judy returned from the bathroom and Ricky laced his fingers in hers. C.A. sighed. They all proceeded to the group. In front of it, a chorus gathered. Ed caught a few more photos, adding more notes to the tiny notebook in her purse full of email addresses. Each address belonged to someone who wanted to see the photographs.

About twenty women comprised the chorus, two rows of them blending into the horizon. They sang in

Gaelic, the words unfamiliar but ethereal as the light dissipated leaving them amid the twinkling white icicle lights along the tent.

Dancing continued as the band commenced a new set. Some guests filtered to the shuttle bus. Nigel, the CART head, tried to coerce his son Jasper home, but Jasper just smiled in Olive's direction while coddling a cup of coffee. Olive and Genny danced in that playful way that only sisters can share. Somehow, Jasper's gaze never wavered from the twin in red.

By midnight, Jasper had danced a few songs with Olive. C.A. had retired to his house by the pond. Ricky and Judy had crept away. Olive's eyes lost their sparkle as the adrenaline faded and fatigue replaced it. Genny had removed her shoes.

Clint surrounded Ed's body with his arms as they enjoyed a slow dance. Lips brushed sensuously as they did. As Clint's mouth moved away from hers, the ground shook. Clint peered at her, wide-eyed and trembling as an orange glow washed from the behind her across his face.

"Ed," he murmured.

She turned. The remaining guests also froze. Clint reached into his pocket, retrieving his phone. He stared at it, while Ed registered the strange pulsing orange color of the horizon. Popping and crackling drowned out the song of the crickets.

"Dad!" Genny yelled. "What is it?"

She ran toward them, hanging on her dad's shoulder and reading over his shoulder. Other men had whipped out cell phone and seemed to have the same message to greet them.

"Shit," Clint muttered.

"What?" Ed asked.

"Explosion," Genny said. "A ranch about fifteen miles away."

"Genny, get our horses ready. See if Gramps called in," Clint ordered.

The other men who received the message gravitated toward them.

"Clint, what does this mean?" Ed asked, her voice cracking in confusion and fear.

"I don't have the details," he answered, slipping the phone into his pocket. "Dad will get them. But judging from the location that explosion could have affected a turkey farm, a dairy farm and a bison ranch. They need help. The animals... Don't want bison running free and scared."

"So, you're going?" she said.

He nodded. "Badly timed, I know. Please stay."

She nodded. Olive and Jasper skirted the other guests.

"Dad, I'm going to change. Can Jasper use the spare clothes in the shed?"

"Yes," he said. "Be careful. Uncle Ricky has been known to—"

"Dad, don't even go there."

"I'm right behind you," he said. He then directed the other volunteers to the shuttle. "Ed, I have to get changed. I will make this up to you."

In her heart, Ed wanted to believe him.

SEVENTEEN

Ed would have preferred silence to Hannah's cackling on the other end of the phone. Suddenly, she regretted her decision to call Hannah instead of Martha or Celeste. Here she stood, on the porch as not to attract Tootie's attention, on the morning after what had been both the best and most disappointing night of her life.

And her best, oldest friend couldn't stop laughing long enough to comfort her.

This did not qualify as her happily-ever-after ending.

Oddly, it seemed the appropriate interpretation of how happily-ever-after would apply to her.

"That's a first," Hannah stammered. A pause and further guffaws accosted Ed. "A herd of buffalo. The man dumped you for buffalo. Hey, Charlie… Listen to this—"

"Bison, not buffalo," Ed corrected her. "He didn't dump me. It was an emergency."

"Ed, getting you laid is an emergency."

"Well, technically," Ed began.

Hannah's laughter continued. "A quickie in the barn doesn't count."

"You're supposed to be making me feel better."

"I'm sorry," Hannah said. Another long pause as she got a hold of herself. "But, sweetie, it's funny. Since when does a man pick buffalo over a woman?"

"Bison," Ed said.

"Bison," Hannah dutifully repeated.

Ed peered across the street, then up the hill and down it. She sighed. Hannah was right. The situation was absurd. The realization made her heart sink. She cast her eyes to the porch floor, but the glimmer of her nail polish shining from her Berks intensified the empty feeling. Really, was she any better than a bison? Overgrown, ugly mammals…

Lifting her head, she caught a glimpse of the mailbox. That reminded her of something. Something less painful.

"Did Gene look at his Bar Mitzvah invitation?" Ed asked. "I emailed the PDF and haven't heard anything. I need to get those to the printer this week."

Hannah exhaled. "Slick, Ed. Nothing says you want to change the topic as much as a reference to design."

"Sorry," Ed said.

"He loved it," Hannah said, "but I said you were busy and I forbid him from emailing before Monday."

"So he liked it?"

"He showed every person we ran into at Temple," Hannah said. "His friends, the rabbi, everyone. His friends were disappointed he didn't have a big, crazy party planned. Charlie, on the other hand, is thrilled. As a Catholic, he never did understand the fuss."

"Doesn't the luncheon thing count?"

"What? As fuss? The Kiddish?"

"That's fun, right?"

"Sure," Hannah said, "But his friends have all had the big party—the folk dancing, getting hosted into the air on the chair, the disk jockey, the whole nine yards. Some have themes and bands and paid dancers. He went to one with a circus. With elephant rides. Those are the ones that cost more than wedding receptions."

"But that not Gene's style."

"He is his father's son," Hannah said with a drop in her voice. Ed knew how much Hannah wanted a big party. Hannah never shied away from a party. She might not have elephants, but she would indulge some frivolity.

"Thank goodness the Rabbi could convince him that it wasn't an all-or-nothing event. That you could celebrate in a personal, modest way."

It was Ed's turn to chuckle. Hannah did not like to do anything modestly.

"Really, Hannah. You should be proud," Ed said. "What other 13-year-old would charge a can of food as admission to his Bar Mitzvah."

"None," she quickly replied.

"And the invitations stipulate no gifts—"

"Not that anyone will listen," she interrupted.

"He'll end up with a stack of checks for the food bank."

"A Jewish food bank, at that! I didn't even know we had a food bank out here, let alone the Jewish connection. Who would have thought…"

"Be proud, Hannah," Ed said. "He's a great kid."

"Thanks to Charlie, and you—"

"You had something to do with that," Ed told her.

"But you always encouraged his environmental interests. The social issues, that's all Charlie."

"Yeah, because we know all about my success with social issues."

"Speaking of…"

Oh no, Ed thought. "Maybe Gene will be celibate like me, too. One less thing for you to worry about."

Hannah ignored the comment. "Are you bringing Clint to Gene's party?"

"I haven't asked," Ed admitted. "I mean, don't you think it's early in the relationship to suggest a family function?"

"We're not related," Hannah pointed out.

"Close enough."

"You're not even Jewish," Hannah went on.

"Hannah," Ed said drolly.

"My house is your house," Hannah said. "By September, if we're over the bison, you may need a change of scenery. A little variety. A little danger, with me right next door. Trying not to let us hear you, if you get my drift."

"Got it," Ed replied. "You were very subtle with that. So, can I send the invite to the printer or not?"

"Yes," Hannah responded, "but I do have a question. I don't understand how the paper can be so cheap if it's recycled. It just seems—"

"Did Gene tell you it was recycled?" Ed interjected, aghast.

"I guess not," Hannah said. "I think he kept saying it was not virgin. That's why I'm confused. It's not cotton, because I know cotton paper costs more than this estimate."

"It's a multi-fiber paper," Ed explained. "Primarily hemp, with some flax and cotton mixed in to improve the printing surface."

"Hemp?!" Hannah exclaimed. "Dear God, Ed, you can't use hemp in a religious ceremony."

"And this is why he didn't want to tell you."

"Kids will be smoking the invitation."

"Because you'd freak out," Ed said. "You can't smoke hemp. What you smoked was not hemp."

"It's the same damn—"

"It was not hemp, Hannah," Ed replied. "Besides, how will anyone know? It doesn't come with a watermark that reads 'x percent hemp.' Hemp is a very environmentally responsible fiber."

"That's what we thought in high school. We were just ahead of our time."

"It's just paper," Ed insisted. "For an intelligent woman, you sure can be dumb."

"We're two-of-a-kind, Ms. Dating-the-man-who-prefers-bison."

"We'll talk soon," Ed said. "Especially if anything changes. Or happens."

"Don't give in until he's ready to make a firm commitment," Hannah said. "Legs clamped until he's got the proper time on his hands. And hide the damn iPhone."

"I couldn't do that," Ed replied. "What if there's an emergency?"

"Like the bison?" Hannah asked. "Ed, this conversation is about to start all over again."

"Well then, goodbye Hannah."

"Goodbye, Ed."

Ed sneaked into her own house and up the stairs to her office. She downloaded the photos from her camera, fiddling with each one to accent the best characteristics in the shot.

By the time she got through them, there wasn't a red eye or pimple in the house. Everyone looked gorgeous. She organized them into categories (like group shots, candids, dancing, and food). Then, she uploaded the jpgs to Snapfish. That took another two hours, as she flitted between small computer projects and some dusting.

Despite the Andersons lack of availability, she forwarded the link to them. That was the nice thing about email. It waited until you were ready for it.

Next, she selected some for her editor and laid up a photo page for the newspaper. She retrieved the list of guests who requested photos and sent the appropriate shots to each.

Finally, she opened the one shot of her in her dress, taking in the Hooper place before the event. Ed stared at the photo and lost her breath. She looked radiant. She looked gorgeous. The dress looked even better.

She emailed Kristopher, thanking him profusely and gushing about how everyone complimented her. She also said that she ran out of business cards and was scrawling his name and address on napkins by the end of the night. Daydreaming about Kristopher's potential success as an *haute couturier* for real women lifted her spirits.

That left one more duty, she thought as she hit 'send' and watched the pale blue bar slide back and forth.

Ed had taken photographs for her editor of the animal rescue during the explosion the prior night. Flipping through them proved a drama, lots of flame and soot, people and animals bathed in that strange orange glow.

If it hadn't happened when it did, the adrenaline of it could have heightened her desire for Clint. Who wouldn't go for the hero on his horse lassoing wild beasts?

Okay, maybe the wild beasts were an exaggeration. Ed focused on her work. No one accomplishes anything obsessing over a knight in shining armor.

The emergency. Focus on the emergency and caption these photos.

Do your job, Ed chastised herself. Picture one featured at least twenty fire trucks. Ed recognized most of the area departments by the color and the partial letters on the trucks.

"At least eighteen fire departments responded to the situation," Ed typed, "including Millville, East Millville, Millville Township, Miedinger, Lower Franklin, Vellburg, and Bodoni Township."

She should have put them in alphabetical order. She deleted them and reordered the list. She moved to the next. It showed six women corralling turkeys. Ed liked the fact that the volunteers were all women (one was Olive) with their faces dirty and their hands in heavy garden gloves. One of the women had a turkey pecking at her pants. Ed looked over her glasses at the photo. That was Dr. Ryan!

"Dr. Eleanor Ryan," Ed typed, "a local veterinarian, helped capture turkeys…"

The next photo on Ed's electronic pile came from a neighboring farm. The chaos had spread farther than the initial disaster as animals panicked from the noise, the flames, the smells, and the shaking ground. A man, unidentifiable thanks to the darkness and the plumes of smoke, lead a horse back into the barn, with a grateful farmer standing nearby. The horse's eyes conveyed its fear.

"John R. Nicholas, a farmer who lives on the Millville side of the Meleagris Farm," Ed typed, "thanks A. Frutiger for his help retrieving Misty."

The next photo sickened Ed. In it, a man piled dead animals, primarily turkeys, into a truck. He had a turkey hanging in one hand as he reached for a rooster from another man whose body hung heavy with fatigue. His blank face sung of grief.

She checked her notes.

"Brothers Claude and Gary Mond dispose of dead animals. Claude Mond oversees fowl operations at the Meleagris farm," Ed wrote.

Ed paused at the next photo. Clint and Rick directed a crowd of about a dozen people, all mounted on horseback with wireless radios and miner's hats. They were charged with rounding up stray cattle, primarily Jerseys and the bison.

The daily newspaper had covered the explosion and its aftermath. Lifting the front section from her desk, Ed reread their coverage with one fiery photograph of a barn encompassed by orange and smoke. The *Millville Daily Chronicle* listed the cause of the explosion as teenagers illegally joyriding all-terrain vehicles around the property and leaving a trail of cigarette butts. One landed on an exposed propane line.

Since her paper wouldn't come out until Friday, Ed had focused on the animal rescue for its human interest value. She hoped the CART might gain some new recruits from the coverage.

Ed had left the scene at three a.m. She had no idea how late Clint and his family had stayed. She hadn't heard from anyone yet. She glanced at the clock on the computer's menu bar. It was noon. She hoped they were all home in bed. Clint probably wouldn't call until tomorrow.

If anything, Olive might send along a grand total for the fundraiser to meet Ed's newspaper deadline.

Even though she had told her online students that she would be unavailable until Monday, she logged into her classroom. Only two posts in a class of twenty. They obviously had taken advantage of her announcement.

With her busywork done, Ed headed to the garden. The sunshine and fresh scents refreshed her spirits. With that done, she poured herself some iced tea and took her laptop to the porch. In her porch rocker, she finished one of her pro bono projects and indulged in the first draft of Celeste's latest novel. She couldn't put it down, though she had to when the Macbook's battery died.

Ed didn't hear anything from the Anderson family until a brief email from Olive arrived Tuesday morning.

"We're exhausted," the email read. "It's been a long three days. Dad finally came home really early this morning. Genny, Gramps and I have been covering at Wranglers. Details in person. Saw the photo links… will check later. Thanks for the media coverage. The fundraiser had brought in $1.5 million, more than I ever dreamed. I hope that I'm not too late for your deadline. I look forward to seeing the paper when it comes out."

By nightfall, Ed had this twitching in her chest that warned her that maybe she'd been dumped. She rationalized with herself: The man was tired, in bed, and had not tended to anything yet. But the fears would not subside. She concentrated on her class and she responded to every partygoer who thanked her for the photographs. Many people kept 'ordering' eight-by-tens, no matter how many times Ed explained they could order directly from Snapfish.

"It's $3!" one person argued. "You can't get a decent picture for $3!"

Oh, yes, you can, Ed thought. She had used Snapfish for years, but you couldn't explain to the average person how internet commerce worked, let alone the cost savings from internet photo developing. Another person wanted to know how photo studios could charge $25 for an eight-by-ten if Snapfish was so cheap.

Ed wasn't about to explain the idea of paying for the artist as well as the art…

While convincing herself that she did not need a Coke, she received an email from Kristopher.

"My phone has been ringing for two days now," he wrote. "They all ask for 'the guy who makes plus-sized women sexy' and immediately book appointments. Everyone has occasions. I might be booked through Christmas!"

She also heard from Nigel "Ed, can I use your photos on the website?"

"Nigel, I would say yes in a New York minute. Technically, they aren't mine to give. I shot them for the paper. Email my editor. I'm certain they will give you permission.

He called back later that he "received permission, but he had to wait until Friday when the paper hit the streets. However, he could only use a maximum of ten, and they needed to have the credit line ©2008 |

Ed Gardiner, *The Millville News* | Used with permission. If he ever wanted to use them in print, he had to get a new permission.

Over all, he seemed pleased. He had never gotten that kind of cooperation from big dailies.

"Nigel, pick out the one's you'd like to use and tell me about how big. I'll size them so the quality looks good on the screen, but will be dreadful if they try to print it. I'll also add digital watermarks?"

"Why?"

"So it makes it harder for people to steal them. The link I sent you was private. I theoretically have control over who gets to see the pictures. Once they are on you site, every Tom, Dick and Harry with an animal rescue site will be using them without permission."

"Does that work?"

"Not all the time. There are ways to get around it, but it stops the amateurs."

"How about if I call you, and we'll go over them together. You can help me pick. I want to use them all."

He called back as he promised. They talked about an hour and picked the strongest shots. For a minute a Pulitzer Prize in news photography danced in Ed's head.

She was getting into bed when the phone rang.

"Who the hell is calling at this hour," she said as she picked up the old fashioned yellow princess phone in her bedroom. "Somebody better be dead or having a baby. And it's way too soon for Celeste's baby."

Annoyed she answered, "hello?"

"Ouch, I guess I deserve that calling so late."

"Clint, is that you?"

"You we're expecting someone else at this hour?"

"No. I just figured you were mad at me or

something."

"Why would I be angry with you?"

"I don't know. I haven't heard from you in days, and my imagination was playing tricks on me."

"Were those tricks being fed by the Nosey Nellies?"

"Maybe."

"I thought so. Do you have plans for the Fourth? It falls on a Friday. We could make a weekend out of it."

"I don't have plans, but my body does."

"Crap. So are you one of the women whose hormones are raging the week before?"

"They rage right out of control."

"Hmmm. Will they be raging on Friday night?"

"Most certainly."

"Why don't you come over for dinner, and then I'll see what I can do about that hormone problem."

"What are you going to do, play doctor?"

"Among other things."

"Sounds like fun."

"100% money-back guarantee."

"Why don't you come over now?"

"I might fall asleep half way through. I'm exhausted."

"Too exhausted to tell me about the last couple of days?"

"No, but it will have to be the abridged version for now. Okay."

"Okay."

He fell asleep about half-way thru his story. She could hear the snoring in the background. He must have dropped the telephone. She put her phone next to her pillow and went to sleep.

EIGHTEEN

Ed arrived at Clint's house Friday night wearing what the Lane Bryant online catalog called a "fun, flirty dot dress with crossover V-neckline and flattering empire waist" in red, matching espadrilles, a red lace bra, and low-rise panties.

She tried the thong that Celeste bought, but she hated it. It was either going to be the low-rise or none at all. Therefore, she chose the low-rise. She didn't want Clint thinking she never wore panties.

As she got out of the car, she saw him leaning against the doorframe. The screen door opened wide and he came out as she approached the house. He was wearing tan cotton trousers and a red 1950s style bowling shirt. "I see you got the dress code memo."

"Apparently."

She stopped. Clint came to her.

"Hello stranger," he said as he reached for her. He put his arms around her waist and drew her close for a kiss—a deep, probing, and long kiss. At that point, Ed did not think she would make it through dinner.

"House rules, no making out in the front yard!"

Clint spun around. Olive crossed the field.

"You made the rules, Dad. You really need to follow them," she said. "Hi, Ed."

"Hi, Olive. Didn't you know that rules were made to be broken?" Ed replied.

"Not on his watch they weren't," she retorted.

He offered her a knowing smile.

"Clint, you didn't give them an inch did you?" Ed asked.

"No way! Look, they turned out okay. Didn't they? So, Olive…What are you doing here? If I remember correctly you moved to the farm next door."

"Indeed I did. I brought Ed a present."

"Present? I like presents."

"Here." She handed her an envelope. "Many people took pictures the night of the fundraiser, but nobody seemed to get a picture of you and dad."

"I'm good at avoiding pictures. As far as I know only one was taken of me by Gen. It was the one I had to send to Kristopher as part of our deal."

"Well, my friend Caleb is kind of weird. First, he never RSVPs. It ruins the surprise."

"One time he knock on our door at 3 a.m. carrying a pizza," Clint said. "So he was in the neighborhood and thought he drop by."

You could see Olive processing the memory. "He also hates technology. He has this old 35-millimeter film camera from his granddad, with interchangeable lenses. He loves that thing."

"I saw the camera. I didn't realize it was that old."

"His big ambition is to be a photographer for *National Geographic*. I keep telling him to go digital, but he loves playing in his emulsions rather than in Photoshop."

"Ed," Clint said, "are you going to open the envelope?"

"Sorry."

She tore open the envelope.

"Oh, my goodness. It's beautiful. Clint, look."

She handed him the 5x7 black and white photo in a simple black wood frame. It was of the two of them as they arrived on the dance floor, hand in hand. Ed though she looked like she was floating across the floor. She looked shapely rather than fat, tall and gorgeous.

"Wow," he said. "I may not give this back."

"Daddy, your copy is already framed in your bedroom."

Olive kissed him.

"Gen slipped it in earlier today. It was supposed to be a surprise. She says it looks like you haven't started packing yet."

"Packing?" Ed said with more than a little shock in her voice.

"No, I haven't. I have no time to breath yet alone pack. I'm having some labor issues."

"Labor issues. You don't have laborers. You have family."

Ed was trying to keep up with the conversation. Her head was spinning.

"Exactly. One daughter quits to open a wildlife sanctuary. Then another daughter informs me earlier she's working at Hemlock Hills for the next three weeks because the wildlife expert had an accident."

"Well, don't forget Gramps, Daddy. And Jaspers is 'interning' this summer."

"I know. With urban sprawl and overdevelopment of the Valley, we can barely keep up as it is."

Clint was exasperated. "Your grandfather reminds me he's retired—daily."

"Daddy, I can help a little. It's just that the getting the ranch up and running is taking more time than I anticipated."

"Olive, stop. I'm confused," Ed said. "So, Clint are you leaving?"

"Ed, I'm not leaving. I'm trading places."

"With who? Why?" Ed asked.

"With Uncle Dickey and Nancy. It all happened yesterday. I have to go."

She started to walk away, but she paused and looked over her shoulder at them.

"Bye. Daddy. Ed, behave yourselves tonight."

"What fun is that?" Ed shouted back.

"Ed, come. Let's sit on the porch and I'll give you the nickel update."

"Okay."

They walked toward the porch. Sitting there was a small child, definitely under five, crying.

"I think you have company," Ed said quietly.

"She's part of the story."

He went to the child and picked her up, sat down, and arranged her on his lap. She immediately buried herself in his chest.

"What's wrong, Patty?"

"I went to visit the kitties in the stable. My favorite ran into visit the horsey. So, I followed him."

Things were becoming clear to Ed. Dick and Nancy inherited an instant family. They live in a one-bedroom apartment attached to the barn. It was cute for a couple, horrible for a family. Clint lives in a huge Victorian house, alone. It didn't take a rocket scientist to figure this one out.

"Uncle Dick yelled at me. He told me not to go near

the horses alone, and not to play with the barn cats. I don't like it here."

Patty was sobbing into his shirt.

"I want to go home," the frightened child whined.

"He yelled at you because he was trying to protect you. You're very little and the horse could hurt you by accident," Clint said softly. "He doesn't know how to be a daddy yet, so that's why he yells."

He looked over at Ed. With his free hand, he motioned one more minute.

"Why can't I play with the kitties? I was going to ask Aunt Nancy if I could bring one to the house. We had dozens of kitties at our old house."

"Yes, you certainly did." Clint shook at the thought. "Barn cats can't live in the house. They would be very sad."

"Why?"

"It's a long story. I'll tell you another time."

She was no longer sobbing. She looked to him.

"How about this, I'll talk to your aunt and uncle and see if we can get you a house kitten. If they say it's okay, we will find you one we can socialize."

She offered him a smile of agreement. Then, the child noticed Ed.

"Who are you?" Patty asked.

"I'm Ed. I'm Uncle Clint's friend."

"Do you live here too?"

"No, but it is a pretty place to live," thought Ed. "I come to visit."

"My sisters and I came to live with Aunt Nancy. We're all camping in the barn until we move into Uncle Clint's house." Her whole demeanor changed. "Sissy says it's like summer camp."

Clint set her on the ground and gave her a hug.

"Do you still want to leave?" he asked her.

"No."

"Then I think it's time we got you back to your Aunt Nancy."

"Ed, are you coming too?"

"Sure. Maybe we'll see Patty's favorite kitty."

They walked Patty to the barn. Sissy turned out to be eight-year-old Rachel. Rounding out the trio was six-year-old, Claire. On the way back to the house, Clint explained the whole situation.

When the National Guard sent Nancy's sister, Sandy, to Afghanistan two years ago, she left the children with their father, her ex-husband, Bob. What she didn't know was that in addition to using, her ex was also dealing drugs. Six months into her tour, Sandy was killed in the line of duty. After the funeral, Bob left with the kids.

Nancy didn't hear from them again until about two months ago. Rachel found her aunt on the internet. Within days, they were embroiled in a custody battle. Nancy insisted that social services visit the family unannounced.

They found the children living in a crackhouse full of addicts and cats. Nancy flew to California Tuesday, gained custody of the children Wednesday, and returned Thursday with the three kids in tow.

They were going to look for a house in-town. However, Clint insisted them move into his place, fully furnished.

"Ed, you can't farm for a living and commute."

The family planned to spend a week or two "camping" while everyone paints and decorates. Nancy and Dick are taking his room, because there's a nursery attached.

"Do they need a nursery?"

"Before Olive's party, Nancy announced she was pregnant."

"They will go from childless to four kids in less than a year…. wow."

"No more family talk. It's starting to sound like a bad soap opera."

He took her hand and led her to the back porch. There was a beautifully set table waiting for them. Instead of taking her to the table, he led her to the porch rocker facing the grill. She watched as he filled the coal chimney with briquettes and the light it.

"Where are my manners? Let me get you a drink. Then you can watch me cook."

"Hot damn."

"On television they said women can't resist a man who cooks."

"Is it supposed to make a woman sizzle?"

"Among other things."

He leaned over and kissed her. Hard."

Ed was getting warm.

"Is it hot out here?"

"Not yet. But the temperature is rising."

He kissed her again and brushed his hand across her chest. Ed wanted to pull him into the chair.

Don't rush him, Ed, she scolded herself. He went inside and came back with a tall frosted glass filled with what looked like lemonade. He leaned over, took the glass and set it against her chest. He followed the "V" of her dress. Ed quivered.

"This may look like lemonade, but it's not. Drink very slowly. I don't want it going to your head."

"What kind of mystery meat are you making?" she asked.

"Just plain old filet mignon. Didn't want to risk giving you game and making you unhappy."

"That's expensive."

"No, it wasn't. I got it from the butcher who

processes our game. I traded him a portion of the game for beef."

He put a tray of vegetables on the grill, and then added a steak next to it.

"How do you like your steak?"

Ed really wanted to say "super well done" but he would freak.

"Medium well if possible."

"I thought so. That is why I only put one steak on the grill. I like mine warm."

"I would have guessed that."

Ed looked at her nearly empty glass.

"This is good. What is it?"

"A little of this, a little of that," Clint answered.

"You're not going to tell me," she said. "May I have more?"

"Are you planning on taking advantage of me tonight?"

"Yes" she replied coyly.

"I hope so. Then the answer will have to be no. If you had two, you'd be sleeping on the porch."

He took the class from her and gave he another deep probing kiss.

"Hmm. You are so right. It is good and so are you."

He kissed her gently.

"I have to go put the other steak on. Dinner in five minutes."

Who needs dinner, Ed thought.

NINETEEN

Somehow they made it through dinner. She said "somehow" because the alcohol had turned her knees to jelly and her arousal had distracted her from every flavor in the premium cut of meat.

Clint had invited her to his bedroom — and Ed knew that this would be not only her first visit to his private chamber but his last, due to the upcoming move.

Ed trembled with the odd sensation of exposure, despite the fact that she hadn't removed a stitch of clothing. They stood, quiet and facing each other, the only sound between them the repetitive heft of their breathing. Clint stepped into her, his foot slipping between hers, one hand resting on her side, almost brushing her breast casually. She didn't move. She didn't dare. She couldn't. Her lips tightened as she pulled them into her mouth.

Clint chose that precise moment to smile. His

mouth opened with a soft grin that highlighted the sudden sparkle in his eyes. That unexpected glimmer of pleasure, an emotional connection that had nothing to do with any potential physical response, caused a shift in Ed. Then, without any chance to stop herself, Ed smiled, too.

And when Ed thought the moment could get no more perfect, Clint kissed her. His body fell against hers as his arms circled her. His lips greeted hers gently.

It made her quiver, but unlike her shaking earlier, this did not stem from her nerves. This came from her core, a spot that had remained empty for so long. His kiss tasted like something slow-cooked, a passion brewing, just tempting enough to interest her, but not a flavor that could be rushed.

He lifted his head and held her in his arms.

"I told you I could be patient," he said.

She had no words. She wanted to answer, "Take me," as she had almost told him a hundred times before, but she didn't need to feel or sound like some desperate, loveless fool.

Who was she kidding?

"Take me," she whispered, except it didn't come out a whisper. It came out more like a croak.

"I'm sorry, Ed," he replied. "What did you say?"

The temperature of the room soared.

"Ed, you okay? You look a little red," Clint said.

"Nothing," she muttered.

He chuckled.

"Maybe I should go," she said.

Her feet instinctively side-stepped Clint in a race for the door. He blocked her path.

"Whoa, there," he said. "Did I do something wrong?"

Ed peered at him. She shook her head. He brushed her hair back, his hands resting near her ears.

"Nothing bad is going to happen," he said, "but if you don't believe that, then you can go."

She swallowed. She stared into those eyes.

"I won't stop you," he said. "You should know me by now. You should trust me."

His head tilted slightly toward the bed. She sat. Her hand brushed across the antique quilt.

"That's pretty," she said.

"My grandmother made it."

She spotted a glimmer from the bedside table, an ice bucket with pale green glass. Two flutes, each with strawberry slices in the bottom. His gaze followed hers. He reached into the bucket and retrieved the bottle.

"The girls," he explained.

The neck had been peeled clean and the cork removed. He poured them each a glass. He handed Ed hers. Ed took it, and sipped, the champagne sweet and tickling. Clint sat beside her, one hand on the flute, the other against her skirt.

"Your dress," Clint said. "It's very nice."

Ed fought a smile. "Your shirt…"

Clint gazed to his chest. His eyebrows wrinkled.

"… is hideous," Ed finished.

Clint laughed, a hearty laugh that made the whole bed shake. His champagne swirled and splashed inside the glass. He leaned toward the table and set it down.

"I better take it off then."

Ed merely nodded.

"It's bad utilitarian design, wrong on multiple levels," she said as he unbuttoned it.

His traveling fingers revealed a black tee under the

bowling shirt. The offending shirt got tossed aside, and Clint kicked off his shoes, sliding them under the bed. Ed continued drinking her champagne, the tips of her fingers and the ridge of her ears growing warm. Clint swept his hand along the edge of her face as his body came closer to hers, twisting at the waist so his face could approach hers. He brushed the hair away her face and neck, the pressure of his palm meeting her skull as his thumb grazed her earlobe.

His lips pressed against her neck and the unexpected kiss spurred a gasp from her. Gripping the flute intensely, Ed feared she might crack the stem. She finished the champagne as his lips moved across her neck to her ears and to her bare shoulder. She giggled from the tactile sensations tickling her, the heat of his lips and the bubbles from the wine. S

he scanned the area for a place to put the glass, but saw none. She contemplated leaving it beside her on the bed, but imagined a re-enactment of the Audrey Hepburn classic, <u>Sabrina</u>.

As if sensing her dilemma, his hand left her body and took the glass. He placed it beside his.

She used the moment to remove her shoes. She tilted her posture so one leg pulled higher onto the bed, and her body faced his. He shifted so one arm landed beside her hip and the other slipped the straps of her halter in attempt to unfasten it. It loosened and tumbled down her front.

His fingers did not stop there but continued by unzipping the dress, and unsnapping her bra, in such a clean motion, she didn't quite realize what had happened as her breasts came free.

Before she responded, before she made a sound or a move, Clint leaned against her, a breast in each hand, his lips against hers. The flavor of the champagne dissipated as his mouth greeted hers, their lips parting as she entered his mouth. His hands stroked her breasts, his skin offering a different texture than hers, and its slight leathery presence providing an unneeded reminder that someone was touching her body and she could neither control nor anticipate what he would do.

And that made a spot under her belly flutter, just as a fingertip grazed one of her nipples. She moaned. His lips left hers. Somehow, their bodies twisted together, craned toward each other as Ed fell back against the bed and Clint buried his mouth against her cleavage, his hands still supporting her breasts as his mouth devoured her flesh, kissing, licking, sucking, as his hands groped anxiously, but gently. Then, he suddenly inhaled, and sat up. His face was red, his hair tousled.

"God, I'm sorry, Ed," he said. "I was acting like an animal."

Underneath her red panties, she throbbed. It was pain, this burning between her legs and the dampness pooling there did nothing to cool it.

"No," she said in a voice that could barely escape her. "It's fine."

"I don't want to use you like that."

"Use me?" she said, recovering to her normal state and trying to ignore the pulsing heat in her groin. "Clint, I want to be loved. I want to be touched. I want someone to see the beauty of me."

"We've been through this, Ed," he replied. "I do. I want you so badly, I might have to change my clothes, just from having touched you as much as I have. You do things to me, Ed. And it's been so long since I really loved someone, since it meant more than something physical—"

"Stop," Ed said. "You love me?"

"Yeah," he responded. "I do, Ed."

And then he kissed her, softly.

"And I don't want you to get hurt."

Clint seized a pillow from the head of the bed and swiftly planted it behind her. He followed it with another. Ed leaned against them and swung her feet unto the bed.

Clint loomed over her on his knees as he planted a kiss on her cheek. He removed his t-shirt, tossed it to the floor and slid toward her, one of his thighs splitting hers, one arm sinking against her side as the other reached for her breast again.

He grabbed unapologetically, his hand squeezing her as his fingers traveled back and forth across her nipple. He kissed her forehead, then her nose, and as he went for her lips, she hooked her fingers into his waistband. She unfastened the button and the fly, and he finished removing them, while kissing her. She wondered whether or not she should wiggle free from her dress, the top now pushed to her waist and the skirt creeping up her thighs.

Before she had the chance to answer, Clint, now only in his navy blue boxers, tugged the dress over her hips and down her legs. His mouth trailed her stomach and her abdomen as he did. She sucked in her breath as the disappearing dress revealed the volume of flesh underneath, but as he dropped the dress to the floor, he did not stop kissing her flesh and tracing it with his hands, gripping her hips.

As he moved above her, the fabric of his shorts jutted at odd angles. His fingers slipped under her red panties and pulled them away from her, his fingers caressing her curls as he did.

Her panties joined the other discarded clothing on

the floor. His lips dipped against her groin, in the delicate spot under her navel but above her pubic hair. One hand massaged her thigh lightly while the other resumed its play with her breast. Ed placed her fingers in his hair. Each of his touches sent a quiver through her, and each time his mouth struck her flesh, heat would flash across her body.

His head rose from her torso and kissed its way back to her lips. His hands fell away from her body, but under the affections of his mouth against hers, she had forgotten, until the warmth from his nude body leaned against her. She froze.

His hands clasped her breasts as he took one nipple between his lips. His head began to roll as his tongue stroked her teased flesh. Her stiff nipple ached with its own reaction, but the heat and the moisture from his mouth soothed it in a way she could not label.

She relaxed as his own stiffness navigated the folds between her legs. He didn't enter her, but as he toyed with her breasts with his hands and his mouth, he would bump against her, sliding in her moisture, taunting her by nudging the underside of her clitoris.

He gazed at her face. She peered back.

"We don't have to do this," he said. "We can stop at any time."

"I'm not protesting," she said.

From somewhere, he lifted a small foil package. Ed smiled. It was one of the condoms from her infamous trip to the adult store. The ones she had sprinkled on his driveway. He ripped the paper, leaned back to his knees, and rolled it on.

Ed's legs fell apart. He returned to his place on top of her and smoothly popped into her, tight yet easy, slippery yet full, as his movements began to rock both of them against the bed. With each stroke, Ed had to remind herself not to hold her breath. He tipped into her neck and kissed the skin there as her hands stroked his back.

His body pushed against her upwards and into her, opening her and filling her. The maneuver graced her clitoris in a way similar to his motion before he entered her, but with his bulk inside her and riding against her walls… She had not choice but to arch and buck in an attempt to apply more stimulation to what was beginning to feel like an itch. The wonderful frustration of it escaped her lips in a minuscule moan, and he nibbled her lips as the sound left them.

And then he sputtered. And he squeaked. And that fullness, that stiffness she had just started to plunge herself against, seemed looser. But before she could think too much about it he rolled off her. She wanted to scream. She wanted to plead. But the realization came over her that while she didn't have an orgasm, he did.

And while she didn't reach ecstasy, she hadn't been humiliated. Then she realized that Clint hadn't completely removed himself from her, but had leaned against her, sideways against her, a mouth again on her breast as his hand reached between her legs and fingers massaged the folds wet and gorged from desire.

He started lightly, pulling the folds apart as he moved back and forth, across her lips and to her aching clitoris. His touch remained light when he reached her bud, circled around it and then back toward her vagina. Her body curved toward him. With each buck of her hips, his touch grew firmer, but always precise, and she gasped. Her sounds, that she didn't recognize as her own, reminded her of a tiger, and as they intensified so did his touch and the pressure of his mouth, teeth leaning against her nipple.

She closed her eyes as spots overwhelmed her vision. Her thighs couldn't decide whether to open farther or close. The warmth flooded her whole body as her muscles rippled. She stifled a scream and looked to Clint. He was grinning. He was hard again and he mounted her.

As soon as his body merged with hers, she moaned. Each of his thrusts amplified the rippling and the exploding and she tensed her walls against him trying to slow the sensation. And that made him freeze. And kiss her. They swayed together.

Ed quivered from that place where her worries and her self-consciousness knotted under her stomach, right through all her abdominal organs into her groin. And Clint collapsed against her again.

"Ed…"

"Yes?" she answered, panting.

"You're fantastic."

TWENTY

Ed spent the bulk of the Fourth of July in Clint's bedroom packing boxes for the move to the barn apartment. Patty and Claire found her and came to "help." Patty clutched the oddest-looking kitten. This cat looked part calico and part red mackerel tabby. It also had tiny ears and a big bushy tail… a cat mutt?

"What are you doing?" they asked.

"Helping Uncle Clint pack for the big move today."

"He's not home."

"I know. He went to work a long time ago."

"Did you sleep here?"

"No, I met him for breakfast," she said. "I volunteered to help him pack so you could move into the house today."

The child didn't need to know about the huge make-out session in-between. Her period stopped the actual fireworks.

"Is that your new kitten?"

"Yes. Uncle Dick said it was okay."

"I heard."

Actually, Uncle Dick wasn't a bit thrilled about it, but it was Clint's house, so if Clint said yes, what could he do? He was stuck.

"What's her name?"

"I want it to be Mabel," Claire said. "One of the cats at Daddy's house was named Mabel. Looked just like this."

"No," Patty said stamping her foot. "It's my kitty. I asked Uncle Clint for it."

"Girls. Stop," Ed said loudly. "If your any of your uncles hear you, they might send the kitten to the barn."

She took a deep breath. Control, Ed reminded herself. These children have been through a lot.

"Claire, we left Mabel. We should start fresh," Patty said.

Suddenly, the cat was thrust toward Ed.

"I've never seen a calico like that," she said.

Ed feigned interest, but she really didn't care what they named the cat.

"Coco!" Claire shouted. "We could name her Coco, 'cause she is a calico."

"Coco," Patty looked at the cat. "Perfect. Coco, you're going to like it here."

"So that's settled. Her name is Coco, right?" Ed asked.

"Right," they said in unison.

"I'm sure Coco loves being held and petted, but don't you think she should run around a little?"

"Maybe. Uncle Dick said I have to keep her in the crate until all the moving is finished. She doesn't like the crate."

"I have an idea. Why don't we close the door, and she can run free in here for a little while."

Ed closed the door. There wasn't much to pack. The bulk of the furnishings were staying. Clint was pretty much just moving his bedroom items. Other things would stay in the attic. There was no room in the barn apartment.

"Then we can finish packing."

Patty released the cat and Coco dashed around the room as they worked. Ed gave Coco some tissue paper to play with. It took twice as long to finish with the children's help, but they seemed to like doing it. Soon they heard Nancy calling.

"Nancy, we're in here, in Clint's room."

They heard footsteps in the hall and saw the door handle turn.

"Wait! We have to grab the kitty."

Patty scooted under the bed to get the kitten.

"I got her, Aunt Nancy."

The door opened.

"Hi, Ed. You about done? We need to get Clint's boxes and clothes out of here."

"Yep, we just finished."

The boxes were stacked and labeled quite precisely. She emptied the drawers, packed one box per drawer and labeled it. She labeled the books by subject matter. She even made a box labeled Olive and Geneva and filled them with the drawings and craft items gifts they had given him over the years.

"I actually came looking for you two. You are supposed to be working on your school work."

"It's a holiday!" they cried.

"I know. If you want to be ready for school in September, you have to get to work. There isn't much time. I'll join you in a minute. Now go."

Patty stormed out the door with Coco.

"Bye, Aunt Nancy," Claire said.

Claire closed the door. The two women were alone in the bedroom.

"You're quite the task master, Nancy," Ed said.

"I have to be. Patty can't do the alphabet song, doesn't know numbers past twenty and even has trouble with colors and shapes."

Ed could sense Nancy's frustration. She was, after all, a teacher.

"Rachel and Claire are behind, but Patty is starting at square one."

"She never went to preschool or day care?"

"I don't think so. Claire and Rachel told me they rarely went to school. I'm not trying to ruin their summer. I'm only asking for an hour every day."

"You have your hands full."

"Yeah, but it will be worth it."

She went to leave.

"Ed, how did you get stuck doing Clint's packing?"

"The business is shorthanded. He couldn't let his father and Jasper work on a holiday, so he's checking traps."

"The girl's don't know it yet, but Clint bought them a swing set. Dick told me Clint had one out there when the girls were little, but it was falling apart, so they took it down. Besides, the girls had outgrown it."

"Are they putting it up today?"

"As soon as we're done moving."

"Let's get busy."

For the next hour, boxes and beds came and went. The children's toys and school work were the last things to go into the house. By the time they finished moving Clint's belongings to the barn, he had arrived at the house.

"Hi, honey, I'm home."

"Yeah, now that the work is done," Ed said, as she leaned in for a kiss.

"Hey, I'm going to supervise putting the play set together. That's work!"

"Sorry, baby, but your dad and Mr. Hooper already secured that job. You're too late."

"Damn. They always get to supervise."

"The benefits of age."

"Clint," Nancy said, "you can help Dick and the others dig holes."

"And hang the swings. Nancy and I are waiting for you to push us on the swings."

"You can't do it yourself?"

"Well of course I can. But what fun would that be?"

"Okay, I'll push you. Nancy's on her own. She's got her own man to push her."

"That will be the day," she said with a laugh and she walked away.

"Daddy, will you push me too?" Olive said as she ran over to hug him.

"No. I stopped doing that 15 years ago."

"Please, Daaadddyyyy," Olive whined.

Feigning exasperation, Clint said, "What am I going to do with the two of you?"

"I can think of a couple things," Ed said, surprised that Clint had lumped her in the same category as his daughter.

Clint blushed.

"Uncle Clint, Uncle Clint, Uncle Clint!"

The children yelled as they ran across the yard. They grabbed his legs and squeezed him. He had a fence of little girls.

"Should I be jealous?"

"Perhaps. As you see I have a way with girls."

Giggles ensued.

"Uncle Clint," Patty said.

"What, baby?" he replied.

"Thank you for the swing set. Can we put it together now?"

"Yes, I think construction has started. I can't walk until you all let me go."

The children grabbed his arms and pulled him across the lawn. It took about two hours to put the swing set together. It was a heavy duty wooden set, with a "treehouse" and a slide.

Ed and Patty were the first ones on the swings.

"Patty, do you need help?" Clint asked.

"No, Uncle Clint. I'm a big girl! I can do it myself."

"I'm not. I need help," Ed said with a wink.

"Be careful what you ask for."

He grabbed the swing.

"Daddy, you're not," Olive remarked.

"Oh, yes, I am."

He grabbed the seat and pulled it as far back as he could, and raised it high in the air.

"Ed, hold on tight."

He left go and stepped to the side. Ed soared through the air, reaching almost a 90-degree angle, before the swing reversed course. Olive and the children cheered. Clint smiled mischievously.

"Clinton Anderson, that is not pushing a swing!" Ed yelled.

"Yeah, but it's fun. We have to wait for you to stop so we can get someone else airborne. Now that's a problem."

When Ed returned to earth, Clint pulled her aside.

"Did you have fun?" he asked.

She made a pouty face. "Yes, but that's irrelevant. I wanted you to push me. Nicely. Not launch me into space."

"I'll make it better," he teased.

He kissed her.

"Better?" he asked.

"Almost," she said.

He kissed her again. The children had gathered around the empty swing. Patty hopped on, while the others took turns planting their hands firmly against her back to shove her.

"Not high enough!" Patty screamed.

"It looks like the swing line is getting impatient," Clint remarked.

"Go ahead. I should go home anyway."

"Why? Tired of me?"

"No," she said, wondering if that were even possible. "I have to check my online class. Then, I have some pro-bono work to do. The nonprofits never meet deadlines, but I still have to."

"That's a lame excuse," he said. "I know we are a

backwoods farm but we have computers, and I bet you have your laptop in the car."

"I do," Ed replied, "but Clint I came to meet you for breakfast. It's way past lunch and I'm still here. I'm not prepared to stay all day."

"Prepared?"

She raised her eyebrows at him.

"Oh, prepared," he repeated. "Woman stuff prepared. Ask Olive, Nancy, or Judy. Seven women live on this property. One of them has to have what you need."

"If I stay here you won't get any work done. Too many distractions."

"Me included?"

"Especially you."

"Well, you're staying. So you are going to have to learn to work through distractions," Clint declared. "You haven't experienced the Fourth, until you've experienced it at the Andersons."

"Do you have a parade?" she asked, hoping her intended-as-playful tone didn't come out as sarcasm.

"No. Better," he said. "We haul out sawhorses and boards and make this huge communal table for friends and family. Everybody has to bring their own plates, flatware and chairs. The corn and tomatoes come straight from the field, and Dad roasts a pig behind his place. It kind of turns into stone soup because people start arriving with the most wonderful food."

"It sounds wonderful."

"That's not the best part." He seemed lost in a memory. "After dinner, we walk over the ridge and spread out blankets. You can see fireworks from three or four towns."

"I love fireworks."

"By the time it's all over, it gets pretty late. So, we

have to carry the children back to the farm and to their cars, and everybody goes home."

"Okay, you sold me," Ed said. "I'll go find Olive. I'm sure she has supplies."

"While you're at it, call Celeste and Martha. Have them come and bring the kids. It's a night they'll never forget."

He started to walk toward the swings.

'Clint, you realize if they come, they're going to grill you about our relationship."

"I can handle the Nosey Nellies," he said. "Ed, if I'm serious about you, I have to do it."

So, Ed thought, Clint was serious?

He reached the swings and waved to the children.

"Okay, who's first?"

Ed called her sisters and Celeste. They jumped at the chance to spend some quality time with Clint. They had never met him and had tons of questions.

Clint was right it was a surreal experience. At about 5 p.m. the sawhorses and plywood came out of the barn. The longest table she had ever seen appeared organically like some sort of salad dressing commercial on television. Olive took the kids into the field to pick corn. When they returned they pulled off the silk and put it in water to soak. The corn would go on the coals with the pig. Nancy led the tomato picking team of daughter-in-laws.

By 5:30 p.m., people started to arrive, carrying baskets and totes with plates and flatware, folding chairs and usually a container of food.

Stone soup indeed, Ed thought.

Of her guests, Martha, Bea and Jarrod showed up first. "Terri had to work. She was quite disappointed when I told her where we were going for dinner."

"Why? Because she can't quiz Clint?"

"Perhaps," she said. "Kids, why don't you go introduce yourselves to the other children. Stay where you can see me."

They dashed toward a game of dodge ball.

"Martha, be good tonight," Ed requested.

"Heck, if I wanted to do that, I would have stayed home. Where is he?"

"Over there," she pointed toward the work shed.

Celeste came next. Siobhan was excited to be on a farm.

"Come on, Mommy! They have horses and cows and chickens."

She nearly pulled Celeste's arm from the socket.

"Siobhan, Daddy will take you. Mommy needs to talk to Ed for a minute."

"No she doesn't," Ed said quickly. "You go ahead, Celeste. I'll talk to you later."

Darren said, "Slick Ed."

He smiled.

"You know she only wanted to come to interrogate Clint, don't you?"

"Yes. Her and everyone else."

"On her way out the door, she grabbed some wine. Where should I put it?" Darren asked.

"Rick is right over there in the Grateful Dead t-shirt. Ask him," Ed suggested.

Darren headed into the crowd. It didn't take long before the table was filled with food and dishes. As people arrived they set down their contribution and set up their chairs. Ed went to grab her camera. Clint strode up out of the group. She wasn't quite sure where he had gone.

"You never leave home without that, do you?" Clint said when he saw the camera.

Bur, before she said anything, he kissed her.

"This is extraordinary," she said. " I know it's not your house anymore, but do you think Dick and Nancy would mind if I went up to the sleeping porch to take overhead pictures?"

"Well technically it is still my house," Clint said.

"You know what I mean."

"I think it will be fine," he said. "But make sure you get to dinner on time."

"I'll be there," she said. "I think I see Josie and Geoff. Isn't that their car?"

"I'll get them," Clint headed toward the Prius. "You go get your photos."

From the sleeping porch, Ed could frame the entire scene — the massive table, the people, and all that food. C.A., with the help of Ed's family, brought platters of roasted pig and set them along the table, while the other Andersons brought corn and tomatoes. The husks and the cobs could be tossed into galvanized buckets on the ground. By the time Ed got to her seat every one was well into eating.

"Glad you saved me some food guys," she joked.

"Well, if you'd arrive on time young lady," Mr. Hooper scolded in a joking manner, "you'd have more to choose from."

He made a sly smile.

"Dang, Geoff, that cheese is good."

"What cheese?" Ed asked.

Everybody laughed.

"Sorry baby, it's all gone." Clint said.

"I can have Geoff's cheese anytime." Ed said. "Roasted pig, that's a different story."

Celeste passed her the pork platter, and other foods quickly followed. Everyone was still at the tables talking when a bell rang. It reminded Ed of camp.

It was C.A.

"May I have your attention please. As much fun as were having here, we need to clean this up and head to the ridge before dark for the fireworks."

With Siobhan, Bea and Patty leading the cheers "Hurray!" the other children bellowed, and even the adults started to get riled.

"Now, you can scrape your plate into the corn cob buckets. On a farm we call them slop buckets. Make sure it's all food. No paper, plastic or foil. The animals don't like that," C.A. directed. "Guests can put their plates and things in their cars. Family members, I guess you have dishes to wash."

Everyone laughed. Ed liked this jovial side of C.A.

"If we could have some help breaking down the tables, that would be great," C.A. asked.

The farm suddenly became a beehive of activity. Car doors slamming, tables being taken apart and children playing. Cleanup took less than fifteen minutes.

"Ed, are you ready?" Clint asked.

"Yeah, I need to find my family and Celeste."

"And your camera," he added.

Yes, my camera, too."

"Your family and Celeste just left with Olive for the ridge. I thought you'd like some alone time."

He turned to face her, and put his hands around her waist.

"We don't get much of that," Ed admitted.

"No, and I don't think we will for the rest of the summer. Is that okay with you?"

"Yes. It will be fun, stealing nights and little moments with each other."

"You're a hopeless romantic, Ed."

He kissed her.

"I know," Ed said.

"Do you want to skip the fireworks?"

"No," Ed said.

"Didn't think so."

He took her by the hand and they headed toward the ridge.

"How much time do we have?"

"About a half hour, maybe a little more."

"How long does it take to walk there?"

"Ten minutes."

"Let's walk slow."

Skunk Odor Shampoo

**Mix before using. You cannot pre-mix
this solution. It is not stable and will
lose it's effectiveness.**

Ingredients
1 qt. 3% Hydrogen Peroxide
¼ cup Baking Soda
2 tsp. Dawn liquid dish soap.

*This makes enough for a small to medium pet.
Double or triple the amount for large pets.*
Discard unused portion.

- Pet should be dry when you begin.
  Do not wet dog/cat.
- Solution also works on people.
- Mix the above ingredients together. The solution
  will fizz. Use a pitcher or a clean bottle so it can be
  poured a little at a time.
- **Keep the mix out of your pet's eyes, mouth and
  nose.** Clean their face with a cloth or sponge.
- Work the solution into the fur, being careful to
  wash the entire pet with the mixture. Let it sit five
  minutes (if the animal cooperates!).
- Thoroughly rinse with water.
- You may have to repeat.

*Note: Solution will discolor clothes. If your clothes
are sprayed you might want to throw them away.
If that isn't an option, try adding some ammonia
to your wash cycle. Do not add bleach.*

AVAILABLE NOW

From Parisian Phoenix Publishing!

at your independent bookseller or online at Barnes and Nobles and Amazon.com.

MANIPULATIONS

Weirdness surrounds Adelaide Pitney, former house model at Parisian fashion house Chez d'Amille. It always has. When she meets Galen Sorbach, an aspiring photographer, she hopes she's found a normal boyfriend, for once.

She doesn't realize that Galen has been stalking her for latent healing powers, water magick she's used accidentally in large quantities. A fire mage, Galen never mastered water magick. Adelaide's gifts could be the power he needs to depose the Spirit Guardian and become a god.

Galen's sister, Kait, has spent 400 years as the elemental water guardian. Assigned to subdue Adelaide's magick, Kait delays. Her reluctance allows Galen to manipulate Adelaide and threatens the safety of the person Adelaide loves most, couturier Étienne d'Amille, and his lover, Basilie.

These five people — a 400-year-old Irish witch, her adopted psychopathic brother, an American supermodel, a French fashion designer, and his rich ex-wife — find their lives intertwined as they explore how far they will go for love and how much they can forgive.

COURTING APPARITIONS

World famous fashion designer Étienne d'Amille knows he should be grateful. He's survived several personal tragedies and almost died. He and his ex-wife, Zélie, will welcome their first born child into the world after 20 years of infertility. But grief has crippled Étienne. And his depression has threatened his relationships. So many questions linger about recent events: Did he take advantage of his protégé/supermodel Adelaide Pitney? Did he miss warning signs that could have prevented everything? And when Étienne's just about to crack — he discovers his house is haunted and the ghost stuck there begs him to free it before familiar supernatural creatures kill them all. Did Étienne receive the second chance he wanted? Or will he plunge into a magickal universe he's not equipped to understand?

TWISTS:
GATHERED EPHEMERA

Webster's dictionary defines Ephemera as, "something with no lasting significance."

The poems in this collection have been swept together from decades of open mics and feature performances, and pressed between these pages like fallen leaves as fleeting things, now preserved.

This book, complete with nifty drawings and sage bits of wisdom scattered throughout, offers a glimpse into a world of social anxiety and awkwardness with the experience and wisdom to accept an epic unknowing of everything.